TRIBAL

By R.G. Moore

PART ONE.

Thursday 15th July 1982.

George smelled the fortune teller before he saw her. A cloying perfume filled the darkness of the caravan. Then, too close in the gloom,

❧Come in, boy. Have a seat. Rosie, wait outside.

The interior of the caravan was cluttered with battered modern furniture. Its walls were lined with rows of shelves holding jars and bottles, their contents indistinct in the half-light.

An attractive woman about his dad's age was sitting at a card table in the middle of the room. She stared at George for a moment and he felt ashamed, as if caught out lying, then,

- Relax - she breathed.

And he did. More than he would have thought possible, alone with a woman in the dark. At fourteen.

- My niece gave you a drink, didn't she?

The woman didn't quite smile. Except from the eyes somehow.

He nodded. An hour ago, he had taken his first gulps of alcohol, sharing with Rosie a half-full soft drink bottle, its contents golden in the early-summer, late-evening sun. Scrumpy, she called it.

- One of my concoctions. It helps the process.

She did smile that time.

Now in the cool darkness of the caravan, as the first rush of the drink wore off, and Rosie was no longer close, he felt relaxed, even sleepy. More than that, he felt an urge to please.

- We'll do without the cards - said the woman across the table –

That's just a trick really, a charade that some people need. We're going to do the real thing.

She paused and looked at him again, directly in the eyes and, whether because of the potion he had drunk or something about the eyes themselves, George felt unable to look away or resist.

- Some things are troubling you. Some people have been very bad, and one person has been good to you, am I right?'

- Yes.

- And you would like the bad ones to be punished. To see justice done.

He hesitated,

- I...

- Never mind. Tell me. Start with this morning, at school.

And the words began to flow.

***

George took his normal place in the class, next to Clive Brown in the second row of desks. There was the usual clatter and chatter as kids banged desktops and the well-prepared searched in school bags for pens, rulers or books while others borrowed, or demanded, what they needed. As he searched in his own school bag under his desk, George thought he heard something else in the chatter too, an unusual undercurrent of curiosity, interest, even. He sat up and saw a tall girl, a new girl, standing in the doorway beside Mr Benson, the deputy head.

Benson left the girl where she was, came over and spoke briefly to Mr Wenton, the history teacher and this class's form master, then left. By now there was near silence, just some whispering. The girl stood alone in the doorway now. George thought she looked somehow special, but it was at first difficult to decide why. She did not have the dusky appeal of Lisa Stanley or the curves of the redhead, Debbie James. Nor did she have the aggressively sensual look of the skinhead girls with their cropped hair and fringes. She was tall and wide-framed in an athletic rather than bulky way, with a broad, heart-shaped face and warm, dark eyes. Her wavy blond hair gave her a summery, carefree look, like a surfer in an American film. But more than her appearance, it was her physical presence that had silenced the class. Just by looking at her, George knew that no-one would bother her.

Mr. Wenton explained that Rosie Betts would be living in Coseley for a while, with her aunt, and would be in their class while she was here. He turned to address the new girl.

- So Rosie. Let's hear something from you. Are you a... - he reddened and hesitated - from a... Romany family?

- No. We travel with the fair in the summer. *But we're not gypsies and we're not tinkers.*

There was then some giggling as she had said her last sentence in a country 'Oirish' accent. But along with the laughter, there was also a murmur of excitement. The fair had arrived! There were still two weeks of school left until the end of term but the arrival of the fair, with its pulsating music and illicit glamour, was always a herald of the hot summer holidays to come.

Frowning, Wenton told the new girl to sit and join in. A set of tatty history textbooks was given out, one between two, and he asked the class to begin reading page forty-two while he wrote some comprehension questions on the board.

George watched with distaste as the teacher scraped white letters onto the hard, black surface, sweating in his corduroy jacket, his balding head starting to gleam already, only five minutes into the class. Was this, or something like it, to be his own future? To get caught in an unsuitable job like this cajoler of reluctant children? And now old Wenton seemed bothered by the arrival of the new girl. Perhaps he would soon be stealing glances or sneakily watching her from behind as he did with the likes of Lisa and Debbie. Or maybe it was just the disruption of being landed with a newcomer, cheeky and from the fair, only two weeks from the end of term.

As the rest of the class quietened down, George began to read questions and look for answers in the book. Sometimes he quite liked boring classroom tasks. They could fill a dull day and you knew where you were. No-one could bother you.

After minutes of relative quiet, punctuated by the odd whisper or giggle, Wenton told them to stop writing and began to take them through the answers, picking on kids who were sure to have answered correctly. Some had read little and others nothing at all so now there were murmurs of surprise, or at least amusement, when it emerged that the Black Country, their own region, was mentioned in the textbook. It was the answer to question five: in the Black Country, near Dudley. Wenton's mood seemed to lighten at this unexpected interest, to the point of improvising,

- ...and did you know that Whites Lane, just up the road from here, was an important trade route during the first part of the industrial revolution?

For the second time that day, the bored and excluded were surprised into paying attention,

Whites Lane! Slap-headed old Wenton, thirty-odd years old, is going on about Whites Lane!

George knew the place but not much. He had been there three times, on self-conscious trips with friends, never for very long and always ready to run if challenged. The lane, and the fields and woods around it, was an enclave of countryside embedded amongst the suburbs and council estates of Hurst Hill and Sedgley, a place where grown-up rules did not apply. And although the area was also a kind of wildlife haven, and it was said that foxes and even badgers could be found there at dusk and dawn, George had seen that the lane itself was corrupted, littered with the remnants of forbidden fun: crushed beer cans and plastic cider bottles, fag ends, rain-damaged porn magazines, used condoms and glue bags and now and then a burnt-out and abandoned car or motorbike.

George also knew that the class might have been arranged in a continuum from very good boys and girls to very bad boys and girls just by asking how often they had been up Whites Lane. The more daring the kid, the better he or she knew the place. He looked around at his classmates. In the penultimate row, Debbie James' face flushed red.

She's been there!

Lisa Stanley, more composed and darker of skin than Debbie, did not blush, just narrowed her eyes, allowing herself a slight smile, looking at no-one.

Some of the bolder boys, the smokers, the snoggers and the boozers, looked down and around, grinning, snickering. George had heard their unwhispered breaktime tales of the woods: pissing stolen cider and beer into the nettles, lit fag ends bobbing in the dark, snogging and groping against crumbling, ivy-draped walls or behind honeysuckle-scented bushes.

Wenton was explaining that in the early industrial revolution Whites Lane had been a path for donkeys and horses to carry rods of iron up from the foundries of Coseley to the nail-making workshops of Sedgley and Gornal and then to carry lime back down from the deep quarries between Hurst Hill and Sedgley.

- ...in fact, even now you can still find the odd nail or horseshoe from those times if you dig just a little bit underground in Whites Lane.

Rosie Betts, the new girl, had raised her hand but Wenton was ignoring her. Round-headed Andrew Stroud was gazing placidly out of the window, a faint smile on his lips, and the teacher seemed inclined to pick on him, the easier victim. But the new girl's hand stayed up. Then she raised it higher and made slight straining noises, indicating urgency. Her eyes sought his.

Wenton had no choice. He sighed,

- Yes Rosie?

- Why are they underground? The old nails and horseshoes?

George saw the teacher begin to roll his eyes at the stupidity of the question, then pause. It was not stupid. Only one kid snickered, gap-toothed rockabilly Wayne Golder, and he soon stopped. The others were looking expectantly at Wenton for an answer. Even Andrew Stroud turned his gaze back inside the classroom, his curiosity roused by the silence of his classmates.

Wenton was frowning, trying to think of an answer to the question. A fresh layer of sweat glazed his skin.

 - What do you mean Rosie?

- Well, these old things. From hundreds of years ago, or whatever. Why are they always underground? I mean, when people drop them, why don't they just stay where they are on the surface?

The teacher's eyes had widened, and his gaze began to flit around the classroom as if looking for help, or perhaps checking who was paying attention in this moment of humiliation. George looked on fascinated, first at Wenton and then at the new girl, tranquil in her power.

Just say you don't know. None of them care. Not even her.

Now Wenton was looking intently at Rosie, scanning her face for traces of cheek - an excuse to get angry and end things that way. But her expression was that of a student expecting an answer from a teacher, without malice.

Then came the damning punchline,

- Or are ye not knowing yerself, Sor?

The Irish accent again. The class dissolved in laughter and poured out to lunch break at the sound of the bell. As he put his exercise book back in his bag, George glanced at Rosie Betts for just long enough to see her direct a quick smile across the room towards Lisa Stanley and her group. Lisa smiled back.

***

Just outside the grounds of the school, between the playground, the canal and the dual-carriageway, was a patch of overgrown wasteland that, with its wildflowers, long grass and bushes, could have passed for a country meadow. Near the playground the grass had been trampled flat by countless break-time football matches.

George couldn't have explained why he had wanted to join in the game that day. He had tried to play several times soon after starting secondary school but had always been muscled out of the match by older or harder kids. Still, he tried again, uninvited and unwanted, to chase the ball that was never passed to him until the familiar wheezing of his lungs began to slow him down and a wiry kid from Tipton bundled him to the ground for no reason and sprinted away with a shriek and a laugh.

He needed to rest a while before trying to get up. He looked up at the blue sky then closed his eyes and felt the early-summer sun warm his face and body as he concentrated on controlling his breathing. Slow and deep, give your lungs time to fill. The noises of the scrapping footballers sounded distant now as the action moved to a far corner of the rough field.

Then a voice startled him,

- This is good for asthma, you know.

She was kneeling close, smiling and holding a sprig of a plant toward him.

- It grows all around. I could hear you breathing hard from over there, so I got you some.

It was Rosie, the new girl. This was the worst kind of help from the worst source. He already knew that this girl was going to be popular and that her new friends would soon put her right about spending any time with George Merriman. Then all that would be left would be his weakness and her pity. He couldn't accept.

- I'm OK.

- No, take it. Really. You were doing well until you couldn't breathe.

And it was true, it had been different this time. For the first time in his life, and just for a few minutes, he had not been far off the pace. The other kids had not been able to effortlessly barge him out of the way. It had taken a deliberate effort for someone to floor him and even then, he could have got straight back up had it not been for the asthma.

She held the plant close to his nose and mouth, crushing leaves and stem between her fingers,

- Just smell it. Breathe it in.

He inhaled tentatively at first and then with more confidence as he began to feel the effects and breathing became easier.

He moved to get up.

- No. Wait a little more. It's not magic, you know.

For a while he was very conscious of a firm hand on his shoulder, a smiling, fresh face very close to his and a lot of unruly hair identical in colour to the tall, sun-bleached grass around them. He looked down as he focused on breathing properly. It was coming back. The shorter grass between the taller yellow growth was still green and fresh. There was a dead beetle, legs up, shrivelled by the sun. What would her breath be like? Her mouth? The hand on his shoulder gave him a slight push,

- Ok. Now you can try to play again if you want.

Try. Was there a hint of challenge in her tone? He felt a bloom of blood on the surface of his cheeks as he looked up from the grass and scanned her face for evidence. She was smiling, her eyes narrowed, her head tilted slightly to one side. He knew then that she was not mocking him but asking a question that he had to answer.

- Ok. Thanks - was all he said.

Still shaking but now breathing normally, he stood up. The kid who had floored him smirked as he jogged back into the game.

A miskicked ball fell at his feet and he tried to control and dribble as he had seen others do but a smaller kid, bandy-legged and fast, swooped in and easily took the ball away before himself being body-checked to the ground, leaving the ball rolling loose again. Now breathing freely, George felt tireless and was again first to the bobbling ball, managing to get in a desperate kick in the right direction before being clattered to the ground. This time he got up straight away, unconsciously brushing past his challenger, Michael Hickman, who, caught off balance, then fell to the ground himself. Hickman did not get right up, but looked around for onlookers, possible witnesses.

Little Dean Wilson, red-haired and fiery, was bending down nearby, hands on knees as he got his breath back.

- You gettin' up then? Or did he break yer legs?

Hickman's eyes narrowed. He got up grim-faced and jogged back into the game.

Once more a loose ball came rolling out of a crunching challenge and George got to it. He was near the goals and all he had to do now was...

He sensed a hard body next to his own, then, unseen and unexpected, a jabbing elbow to the side of the head sent him downward. Before he hit the ground, the first kick to the face landed and sent him sideways. More kicks from Hickman and Dean Wilson followed, before Hickman mounted his prostrate body to follow up with a flurry of punches to the face.

George felt no pain and, for the few seconds the beating lasted, lived only through flashing lights and exploding fireworks in a black void. A cool numbness swelled his lips. Two formulaic phrases, distantly heard, signalled the end,

- Leave 'im. E's not worth it.

- Fuckin' wanker.

Boys wandered off, not wanting to be involved.

- Lucky you've got a thick skull.

Rosie was at his side again,

Despite his headache, made worse by opening his eyes to the bright sun again, he took a good look at her face. She looked more amused than concerned.

She brushed the hair from his brow to look at the cuts and grazes, then drew her face close to his and spoke quickly,

- It took two of them to do it. They're just cowards. But you don't have to suffer like this. Not any more. Meet me at the top of Whites Lane at seven tonight if you want to do something about it.

She stood up and walked off quickly. Through urgent whispers her breath had been fresh and hot in his ear, close against his face. Earthy and sweet like dew in the morning sun. They had double maths next.

***

- So that was it, was it? A few kicks and punches that you asked for anyway, crashing into the boy like that?

The sharp edge to the voice brought him back to her. Had he been dreaming and talking as he dreamt? He had felt that he was experiencing the day all over again, but it also seemed that this abrupt question was the last of many much gentler queries, and that the witch had guided his story from beginning to end.

- I didn't do anything! And he's Michael Hickman, third cock of the fourth year... and Dean Wilson joined in...

- Did it hurt you? Did you feel pain?

Her voice was still harsh and there was something of Irish in it. Not the country Irish that Rosie had mimicked in school but a harsher accent that brought to mind place names from the grim TV news his dad watched: 'Londonderry', 'South Armagh', 'the Bogside'. The question itself reminded him of Rosie's baffling comment that he had a thick skull. What was that about? Anyway, physical pain wasn't the point,

- It didn't hurt so much. It was just...

He could not bring himself to say 'humiliating',

- ...embarrassing.

But 'embarrassing' was for when you tripped and stumbled crossing the playground, or the time his dad had absent-mindedly tried to hold his hand at the parents' evening before the first day at secondary school. Today he had been humiliated, *mounted*, by another boy and punched in the face repeatedly, unable to defend himself. At fourteen, such a primeval show of dominance could not be forgotten.

The woman was watching him intently,

- But it can't be just that little scrap that's bothering you. There have been other times, haven't there? Tell me.

The voice sounded kinder again now, an invitation to self-pity. The drink was still strong in him and his will was weak and so the stories poured out between sobs and snuffles.

He had been walking to school one frosty morning with his neighbour and timid ally, Jeremy, in front of a group of other kids. It was near the beginning of the first year at secondary school. It was important to walk to school with somebody, the more popular the better. That day he had had to settle for Jeremy. The kids behind were quite close now. Four or five of the more laddish boys of his age had fallen in with a couple of older kids. A sudden pain near his anus caused him to jump and spin around to see Ian Dernell, two years older and already tall and bulky, laughing and holding a stick in his hand.

- Ooh, that one went deep, I could tell.

More laughter. Had the group of girls across the street laughed, too? He couldn't know. He hadn't looked but he felt sure that they had. He and Jeremy put their heads down and walked on.

There were more such stories and they flowed faster and faster now, the humiliations of taunts and name calling, the pushes, the shoves, the jostling. In some cases, like today, the casual kicks and punches from those who know they can, and so do. All of it a constant downward pressure, a putting-in-your-place so that you'll never rise high enough to become a threat to your tormentors.

He stopped talking. Her face framed in shadow across the table, the fortune teller was watching him steadily, her expression serious now, all warmth gone from her eyes as if the real business of the evening were about to be settled,

- So what do you want?

- I...

She then spoke for him,

- I know what you think you want. And it's true that you have... friends. Friends that you don't know about, who can make it happen. But only say it if you really want it.

- I want... it to stop.

She tutted impatiently,

- It won't stop unless we do something to make it stop. What should be done?

- Do something to them. All of them, to make them stop.

- All of them?

She was impatient now,

- Everybody who ever laid a finger on you or made you look small? You think you can ask for that? Choose someone. One.

He knew he was being asked to single out one enemy for punishment but was still reeling from the flow of shameful memories that the voice in the darkness and the doctored drink had evoked. Then the generalised feeling of shame and helplessness began to manifest themselves as a series of words and their associated memories: *deep, humiliate, mounted*. He wavered between Ian Dernell and his stick and that day's beating in the sun, straddled by Michael Hickman. He remembered the sun on his body as he had lain on the grass after the pounding and then Rosie's hair, also like the sun, and her warm smile. She had seen his shame and would not forget it. The memory would always be there, a barrier between them.

- Michael Hickman - he said softly - Do it to him.

She seemed less irritated now. Still serious but not as impatient as before.

- Do what? What would you like to happen? If you really want it to happen, you have to say it. It's yours to order.

He had been carried along by the emotion of it all until then, had believed for a while but now the phrase 'it's yours to order' was so ridiculous to him, a powerless and bullied fourteen-year-old, that the spell was broken. Nothing would happen, whatever he said. He was the victim of a cruel fairground trick of some kind and, once he was out in the fading light of the fair, it would seem all the more ridiculous and Rosie would have gone. But he did hate the boy right now. And it would feel good to say it. So,

- Kill him. Kill Michael Hickman.

***

George stepped out into the still-warm night air. It was nearly dark now, one star glittered in the blue-black evening sky. The air smelled of the fair: hotdogs with fried onions, diesel fumes, dry ice and wet look hair gel, but also of summer nights and promise. He could hear the distorted music of the waltzers: 'Uptown Top Rankin' by Althea and Donna.

Rosie emerged from the shadows, smiling.

- What d'ya think of me auntie, then? She put you right?

George thrilled to see her. She had waited and she was smiling at him, for him. They were apart from the crowds, between the fair people's caravans, and there was no-one else around. George scanned his memory for something to say in response but the best he could manage was a re-tread of a line from some half-remembered American film,

- Well, it was an experience.

She narrowed her eyes more, still smiling, then linked arms with him and they began to walk the edge of the fair together.

George felt that everything was going to be alright.

***

Inside the fortune-teller's caravan, a sinewy figure, thick-boned and heavy-browed, emerged from the curtained-off rear.

- You heard it all? Do you know the boy, Hickman? - asked the witch.

- Michael Hickman. I know him. E's a right 'un. Always up the woods or down by the cut.

- So you know what to do, then. Remember our ways, that's all.

***

The Listener and the Teller

In the dark of the cave, the listener lay drugged and dying on the damp limestone floor.

The teller began his story:

It was a land of hills and valleys where short rivers run down to the sea. The summers were cool and it often rained but was never cold. The sea and the rivers were full of fish, mussels and oysters but the land was poor for farming. Bear, wolf and boar roamed the dense forests of oak and beech, pine in the mountains. The men hunted and fished but were also farmers and workers of wood, clay and stone. They spoke a rich language but did not write it. Some knew how to work wood, bronze and iron to make tools and weapons but others, many, used those weapons to fight their neighbours and pillage so they built their homes close by with mounds and stockades around them. Warlords led their clans. Each village had a stone keep or war tower for the families to hide in when enemies came. Their sports were tests of strength and courage: they tossed stones, wrestled or fought with cudgels. Their gods were of nature and the seasons, fictions to soothe and explain the rhythms of life and death.

One family lived outside the stockades. The smith, Aitor, had built a house on the edge of the forest, looking down on the village, and he worked his metal there, helped by his young wife, Maider. Proud and surly, no-one bothered him, and he lived well from his work, his independence tolerated by the lord because of his rare skills. Whenever marauders came, he rode to meet them on his black and white carthorse and thinking him an outcast from the village they asked no more tribute than that he mend their weapons or shoe their horses.

In time a son was born, Gaizka, and Aitor's black hair peppered with grey but his voice stayed a gruff bark and his arms kept their strength. Maider's face grew lined and her hair lost its lustre but she stayed healthy and loved the boy, shielding him from Aitor's worst moods.

One night, when Gaizka was ten, the boy went to his parents' bed and woke them. He had heard the baying and squabbling of wolves and the low crooning the pack makes before it attacks but he had also heard human cries or something like them.

- Can you go Daddy? It's a mother and child caught in the forest by the wolves.

Aitor knew better,

- I'll not be going out. It might be a mother boar or deer but they won't last long against the wolves and neither would I.

Aitor turned back into his bed and Maider the wife and mother took Gaizka to his.

The next day the breakfast was goose eggs, sardines and acorn bread with water from their spring.

Gaizka asked his father if he could go into the high forest to look for traces of the fight he had heard in the night. Aitor did not answer at first. Then he turned to Gaizka as he was about to leave for his workshop,

- You'll go to the shore, check the eel traps and bring back some oysters, first. Come to my forge and show me enough and then you can play your games.

Maider stopped her work and watched as her small, frail son made his way down through their fields to the tidewaters of the estuary. She did not want him to go into the high forest.

Friday 16th July 1982.

Driven by a compulsion he could never have explained and could no longer resist, a man lurched drunkenly out into the dimly lit street of terraced houses, upsetting empty milk bottles near the doorstep then closing the door behind him harder than intended.

He looked up to the front upstairs window of the narrow house, his mother's bedroom. If the light came on, he would have to make some excuse and go back in. He never went out on Friday night. Not that she knew of.

No light came on. No curtain twitched.

The surprise of the clashing bottles and the fresh night air had sobered him up a little and so he moved more steadily now as he began his walk to nowhere.

Find some in a group.

Bad girls.

Cheeky young ones. Shouldn't be out but they are, somewhere.

These directives rose up to some blearily conscious level together with images, old favourites retrieved once more from a carefully tended memory bank: the uniform tan on that girl's smooth legs; the band of visible flesh just above that other one's thigh-high white socks; rolling hips and rounded buttocks in short grey skirts... Soon these once-seen, long-treasured images gave way, as they always did, to extrapolated fantasies featuring the same actors, imagined scenarios of his own creation, thrashed out countless times in the forty-watt glare of his narrow bedroom.

But he felt no urge to masturbate again. He had already done that in the house, some time after the first few glasses of his mother's sherry. He did not plan to rape or grope, would never have tried to. The urge was to display, to be seen. To be acknowledged, reacted to, by the girls he idolised. Not the exact same girls, of course, but similar. That type of girl.

Where will they be this time? Outside some pub or club? On the fringes?

He was approaching Hurst Hill Working Men's Club, could hear the jovial singsong of bingo numbers being called. There would be girls of the right type in there to be sure, fresh, cheeky and pretty, the type he had never kissed and never would now. But they would leave with their friends and families; protective mothers and rough, boasting dads, keen for a scrap after a few pints. And what would they make of a night-time flasher?

He moved on. At the end of the road there was a pub, the Hurst Hill Tavern.

Won't be any there. An old man's place.

But the couple that spilled from the doorway, nearly banging into him, were in their twenties.

- Sorry mate.

A young man in a denim jacket flashed him a warm, apologetic smile. He had shoulder-length hair and a clipped moustache and smelt of beer and aftershave. Strong, relaxed, happy, the kind they like. A young woman leaned heavily on him, giggling, voluptuous in a tight black t-shirt. Through loose ringlets of brown hair, he caught a glimpse of a dimpled smile, white teeth, but she did not look at him and soon they were stumbling into an old Triumph Herald to shrieks of laughter that became muffled as the doors clunked shut. A starter motor whirred and ground before the cold engine finally caught its stroke and roared.

Going to shag her. Give her one. A good seeing to.

He knew the basic terminology from his own childhood and he was kept up to date on the latest additions by overheard classroom conversations and graffiti on school exercise books; a forbidden jargon of excited boys that as he grew up had slowly become, for him, the tainted language of disappointment and unfulfilled promise.

He had been with a woman once, on a mattress in a small room over a pub in Wolverhampton. For five pounds. But it had been a joyless and humiliating experience, a failed experiment, and that was not what he looked for now.

He turned right into Turl's Hill Road, the posher end of Whites Lane: well-lit and paved and lined with neat houses on one side, Driscoll's fields on the other. Some of the old houses were pretty, white-painted and decorated in a vaguely gypsy style with gates made from old cart wheels and brass lamps on the walls and doors. His thoughts moved from the crude vocabulary of comprehensive school sex lore back to the girls again, then to one girl. The favourite. Not her legs or hips, this time, but her face. He remembered, would always remember, a frank look she had once directed at him in class, her lips slightly parted, her brown eyes deer-like. She had happened to make eye contact with him in a rare unguarded moment, nothing more. But for an instant he had felt that he was face-to-face with the untouchable and that it had not rejected him.

A familiar sadness began to settle upon him, threatening even to dampen the strange and irresistible urge that had driven him out onto the street that night. She was a special one; not only did her tawny beauty outshine all the rest, but something about those dark eyes seemed to promise the possibility of compassion, friendship even, with a man like him.

He knew that for some, youthful beauty like hers was attainable and commonplace. On the bus to Dudley last weekend some teenagers had sat a few rows in front of him on the top deck. Sat, except for one tall, slim youth who remained standing, languidly half-wrapped around the vertical pole of the handrail, chatting and joking with three girls. The boy was good-looking and golden-skinned, wearing stretch jeans, a silky green pilot jacket and a too-small trilby tilted back on his head. The girls laughed and tried to defend themselves as the rude boy mocked them, their clothes and their Dudley accents, twisting his body around the chromed bar. His taunts were cruel but it didn't seem to matter, they were in his power; he could take his pick if he wanted to. So easy and normal to some, yet, when had he ever come close to something like that? As a studious and un-adventurous teenager, he had felt that he was invisible to girls, that they seemed to look past and through him. At university, they seemed to at least see him, but without any interest, as if they instinctively knew of some hidden flaw of his, some curse that would make further contact pointless. As self-pity took hold, his walk slowed to an unsteady shuffle. He was feeling hungry now and depressed enough to cry but he didn't think he was capable of that anymore. Or rather, should not start to cry because he would never be able to stop. He should go back. He had not yet committed a crime, had not endangered his job or broken his mother's heart.

Go back.

He was further down the lane now, halfway to the woods. Here the houses on the right-hand side of the road were scruffier. There were solid shadows of stables in the fallow fields on the left. He heard a harsh yelping that he recognised as the calls of foxes, searching for mates or mating already. He steadied him-self against the stone wall and looked out over the patchwork of fields and saw them far away, only faintly visible in the fading light, clamped together tail-to-tail near a line of poplar trees.

Someone was coming. Was already very close. He turned too quickly and nearly overbalanced but the rough wall at his side prevented him from falling. A tall, broad man in black clothes, something like a donkey jacket, was walking on the other side of the narrow road. He should have looked away to hide his own identity but in his surprise, he glanced at the man's face and the man grunted,

- Alright.

He managed to mumble a response through thick lips and held on to the wall for support.

Groggily, he realised that the big man's face and build were familiar to him but from so long ago that it seemed like another lifetime. He had known him as a youth, envied him. Those memories of happier times, or at least more innocent ones, brought on another wave of sadness and weariness. It was time to go home.

But then he heard shrieks of laughter deeper down the lane, near the allotments´ car park. He had found some.

Bad girls.

Cheeky, young ones.

Shouldn't be out but are.

He looked up toward the more brightly lit end of the lane. The big man, striding fast, was already nearly out of sight.

His heart thumping in his chest, he made his way towards the voices.

***

The High Forest

Gaizka got to the bottom of his father's field and left the bright morning sun behind as he ducked into the tunnel-like path through the wood of small oak trees that would take him down to the rocky shore of the estuary. When he got there, he was supposed to use his father's long knife to prise oysters and mussels from the rocks and to collect the catch from their willow fish traps. It went without saying that the knife was also to be used against any village boy who he might catch stealing their fish, but he had never done so yet and dreaded the day when he would have to. Gaizka was not a big boy and the thieves always came in gangs or with big brothers. There was no need for anyone who lived near that river to steal other people's fish. Every boy learnt in his infancy to make fish traps and the traps never failed to fill if left overnight, even without bait. Rather, the thieves were sent by their fathers or biggest brothers, trusted men of the clan lord, to harass and test the will of Aitor and his family, the family who chose to live aloof from the village.

But Gaizka would not go down to his work yet. He knew what he had heard the night before and wanted to see the aftermath of the struggle for himself. And if he were to go to the top woods alone, when wolves had been abroad, he had better prepare.

He had the long knife in its sheath of hide yet he wanted more protection. From his hiding place in a fig bush he took his heavy polished cudgel, a boy's one, not full-sized, but still dense and hard at the head. There he also found his slingshot and tucked it into his wide cloth belt. Then he picked up a bag of weighty pebbles whose cord he tied around the belt before tucking the bag itself inside. He did not expect to find wolves still at the kill in the daytime, but the carcasses might attract boars, big males heavier than any man, or even brown bears. It would be a long hike uphill, so he plucked some figs from the glossy-leafed bush and dropped them inside his shirt.

He skirted around his father's fields and their fenced-off vegetable patch and began the steep climb up the path through the forest. At this height in the valley he felt most at ease. The familiar woods here were far from the bullies of the village, not high or remote enough for wolf or bear and, on this clear summer morning, too airy and well-lit for him to fear the goat-man Akerbeltz or the mountain creature Basajaun.

Something rustled in the undergrowth of fern and baby oak. They were fast, fussy movements that indicated some small creature: a bird, squirrel, marten or genet-cat. He saw the familiar black and white of an old enemy and heard the harsh cawing. A magpie, robber of eggs and eater of chicks, was rooting for something on the floor. Without taking his eyes from the bird he took the sling from his belt and felt for the bag of stones. Growing up without brothers and not too strong he had had to earn the respect of the village boys somehow and he never missed a chance to practise the special skill that he had acquired through years of practice. He only whirled the sling three times but on the third revolution he snapped his wrist and released one of the cords at the perfect instant to send the river-smooth pebble streaking too fast to be seen. The bird was knocked dead. He would re-trieve the corpse for his collection on the way back.

The path now ran parallel to the brook but separated from it by a rocky ridge so that he could hear its cool flowing water but not see it as he bounced and jogged uphill tireless in his youth but hot and sweaty despite the shade of the trees. While his body was occupied with the labour of climbing, his mind began to wander.

Why was he thin like his mother and not powerful like Aitor? Could he ever grow enough to wield the hammer and tongs in the workshop and carry on their livelihood? He looked more like his blond mother than dark-browed Aitor, he knew, and worried that he would stay like her beardless and thin-armed even as a grown man. How could he ever face down the clan warriors like his father did? Aitor would ig-nore their arrogance and, attending to their horses or weapons, win their respect with some gruff word or gesture that showed his lack of fear. More than that, some warriors seemed to admire him for his skill and independence and laughed loud at his brusque comments and paid him well for a sword or war axe. And even if he could become a man like that, could he do it in the next few years before his father got too old and weak? Or would there be a gap, a period when their small family was defenceless? Probably Aitor had the same doubts. Gaizka knew that his father wanted a dog, one of the big mastiffs used for battle or for defending mountain flocks against wolves; on their trips to the village to buy flour and salt he had more than once heard him bargain with some shepherds for a pup then baulk at the price at the last moment.

The beaten earth track began to change as Gaizka got higher up the side of the valley. There were more rocks poking through the soil now as the covering of earth got thinner. Here the ground was more clay than dirt and soon all but rock and clay was carpeted in a brown covering of old pine needles and squirrel-bitten pine cones as the path entered the high forest. Gaizka became more alert as he entered this darker, less familiar territory. He rarely came this high. There were big beasts here, real and supernatural, and the lower deciduous forest was better for birdsnesting or hunting fat wood pigeon with the sling. Up here in the shade of the pines, hunting was more serious: men with spears and dogs hunted prey that sometimes fought back, like deer or boar or stumbled upon the anti-prey of wolf, bear or Basajaun and returned home with terrible injuries or sometimes did not return at all. In some of the caves there were paintings of giant cats too, bigger than any wolf, but none had been seen in living memory. Sometimes the path forked as he climbed but he always took the steeper of the two routes.

Gaizka glanced up for no reason and saw a sleek, heavy predator, a goshawk, perched on the horizontally jutting branch of a yew tree. It looked down on him impassively. At least he was too big to be prey for a bird, he knew, although it was said that on the bare rock of the highest peaks the lammergeyers would pull unwary climbers off a ridge to later feed on the shattered corpse they found at the valley bottom.

Gaizka was now climbing more slowly, scanning the forest around *him for signs of disturbance. Even if the struggle he heard had been the killing of a deer or young boar rather than a human, it had still probably taken place on or near one of these tracks as the animals used them too rather than pick their way over the fallen trees and rocks of the deep forest. But he heard a sign before he saw one. There was a clearing some way off the track, where an island of ancient beech trees and giant rocks disrupted the uniformity of the pine forest, and high in the branches of one of the beeches a trio of crows flapped and cawed. Gaizka approached cautiously taking care not to crack a twig or kick a loose rock with a careless step, but also keeping his eyes on the beech copse. If there were still wolves, or bear, at the scene of the kill, he would have to retreat as quietly as he could and live with his curiosity, and if he were seen he would not live at all. A wolf could drag him down in an instant and every village boy knew that a brown bear could knock off your head with one swipe of its paw. Or lie on top of you to hold you down while it slowly ate you alive.*

The vegetation between the dark trunks of the pine trees was sparse, thwarted by the lack of sunlight. Only a few bramble and holly bushes grew there so Gaizka used these as cover when he could, crouching low behind them or standing tall behind the trees themselves. He knew he had the right place when he saw three wild boar rooting in some ferns at the base of the giant rocks. It was a huge sow and her young, the small ones still bearing infant spots and stripes on their coats. They were eating something on the floor. He saw bone and gore. But there was something else. In the tree.

The trunk of the old beech tree, immense in girth at its base, forked into two just a little way above ground and from those two trunks sprouted many smaller branches. There was a creature, no, a small red-haired boy in those branches. He had been watching the feeding boar. Tear tracks streaked the dust on his face but now he looked down at Gaizka, unafraid and fierce.

Saturday 17th July 1982

The naked bulb in Cooper's council flat kitchen shed its pale light some way into the bedroom so that he could see the young woman's face and brown wavy hair. She was lying on a double-bed mattress on the floor wearing a t-shirt and knickers. Although asleep, she seemed to sense the light as she then moaned and pulled a pillow over her face, turned and drew her legs up until she was in a foetal position with her back to him. It was a shapely body, the hips wider than the waist, the back lean and trim, he noted as he tried to remember who she was.

There was an unlit lamp on the floor near the mattress and the only other furniture in the room was a dusty cabinet containing a hi-fi and some LPs: Led Zeppelin, Black Sabbath, 'Tommy', a couple of Stones albums. There were comedy albums by Jasper Carrot and Max Boyce. In a corner lay a pile of clothes and some muddy Gola football boots, size 11. The smell of stale beer emanated from a twice-punctured party can between the stereo cabinet and some camping gear.

Cooper sat in his kitchen chair, sometimes sipping bitter instant coffee from a delicate teacup with no handle, sometimes holding his head in both hands. He was dressed in a vest and y-fronts. He was struggling with a throbbing headache but had already established the main facts of last night's events.

Haley. Got an arsehole of a hippie boyfriend. Lanky bastard. Snake tattoo down one arm. Drinks in the Red Lion.

The name of the pub and then the throbbing from the knuckles of his right hand jogged his memory further.

Had an arsehole of a hippy boyfriend. Not anymore.

As usual, he had gone to a pub where he was not well known and got chatting with a group there. As usual, it had been easy. He was a stocky bloke in his early forties, whose heavy fists indicated he was not to be messed about, but there was also an empathy, a humanity about him, revealed by warm brown eyes. Even in the dives he sometimes frequented, and he liked them rough, from Birmingham to Stourbridge and Wolverhampton, people welcomed him into their conversations. Even the younger ones, the reckless ones, could sense that it was best to stay on his good side, then you would be alright, maybe have a laugh. And these days they were often much younger, both on the football pitch and in the pubs, as his aching body was reminding him now.

Oldest one in there last night apart from the hippie.

He considered again the young woman he had somehow ended up in bed with. She had pulled a sheet over herself and now he could see only her ankles and the soles of her feet, a little dirty. What to do with her? An intriguing phone call from Dudley CID had woken him at six in the morning and it was now six twenty and he should be going. In fifteen years on the beat, this was the first time he had been sent to a possible murder scene. He weighed up the pros and cons of rousing the girl and kicking her out against trusting her to let herself out without taking any of his stuff. He decided he could safely let her sleep. She would not want his albums or sports gear. Anyway,

What we gonna talk about? Depeche fuckin' Mode? Spandau Ballet?

He finished the coffee and hobbled to the small bathroom where he had run a hot bath to warm his muscles and ease his pains, enhanced by his one relative luxury, Radox bath salts. As he passed the bathroom mirror he saw that his black hair was a little long for a copper, the moustache a little bushy, and he briefly considered having a haircut later that day.

Nah. Fuck 'em.

And especially fuck Dudley CID.

***

Old Driscoll answered the door. He hadn't changed. Twenty-odd years on, he was the same shrivelled old geezer that PC Cooper remembered from his own years as a teenage scrumper and trespasser. Old Driscoll, who would chase you from his land but never catch you. Old Driscoll, of the shotgun in his Land Rover, or so they said. Loaded with salt pellets to sting your arse.

Driscoll had called Sedgley police station at dawn that morning to report a dead body near his land. Cooper had got the early morning call, as local officer on the beat, to check out Driscoll's discovery and prevent anybody disturbing the evidence before the Dudley CID came on shift to take charge of the investigation.

As he stood in the doorway, Cooper was aware of the old farmer scrutinising his face intently. Could the old man possibly recognise a former scrumping, cheeking tormentor from so long ago, now grown into a man? Or remember him from that later time, but still twenty years ago, when Cooper's name had been all over the local papers? Driscoll's small face, grinning like Punch, revealed nothing. He brushed past the copper and out into his yard,

- Yer gonna get yer feet wet 'less yer put these on.

He handed Cooper a pair of oversized wellies and strode out, bow-legged but strong, to an old grey Land Rover.

Once they were both in the vehicle, Driscoll drove ten yards to a galvanised steel gate that separated his back yard from the fields behind his house. He jerked up the handbrake, stopping them sharply,

- Get out and open it then.

Cooper had already taken off one shoe in order to put on the wellies. He looked up at the old man. There was the twinkle in his eyes that he remembered from moment-of-truce conversations years ago, exchanges of stalemated banter between the old farmer and bad boys over unscalable fences at the breathless end of a chase by Land Rover.

You know exactly who I am, you old git.

Before opening the gate, Cooper paused to orient himself. He had roamed this land on and off since his early teens but had rarely looked across to the Woods from this side of the fields. Although Driscoll's place was one of a row of large houses that faced onto the busy Sedgley Road West and across it to the suburban High Arcal estate, from this viewpoint at the back of the house they could have been in the middle of the countryside. Driscoll's overgrown fields and hedgerows led down to the old toll road, now a path, known as Whites Lane. On the other side of the lane, after a single row of council houses and the tarmac road petered out, were the bluebell woods. Hidden in the woods were the abandoned quarries and caves. A brook, its waters heard but rarely seen due to the overgrowth of nettles, gorse and elderberry, emerged from the woods, passed under the path and bisected Driscoll's fields. At any moment Cooper expected to see a fox skulking in the dew-dripping hawthorn hedges and bushes that separated the fields. It was the right time of day and they liked it here, where they could hide from man's noise and intrusions and yet easily cross back into civilisation to pillage rubbish bins. But the only wildlife he saw were squabbling crows and a pair of magpies. The grass that was not in the shade of the hedges and bushes was already steaming in the early morning sun.

- Going to be a hot one - he said to Driscoll as he got back in the old vehicle.

- Not for that poor bugger!

Driscoll chuckled to himself until the chuckle became an old man's hacking cough.

After a slow and bumpy ride across two unkempt fields, one empty, one with four desultory ponies and a barn, they could drive no further and got out to walk. There was a low stile to climb next to a galvanised steel gate, then they were on the wet stone and mud of the lane.

- I 'eard 'em thrairpin their motorbikes at about ten last night. Ah wor gunna get aht o' bed!

They crossed the lane into the bluebell woods, following a narrow path through a shoulder-high mass of dew-soaked mugwort, bramble and nettle.

- Ah doh come up 'ere. Tay mah land. But I come up the lane this mornin' to get to the top fields. Bloody dog went doolally. Come runnin' up here, wouldn't come back. 'Ad t' goo 'n look for 'im.

The body was face down and twisted on the path near the base of a thick beech tree, a tragically young and once-strong corpse in muddy clothes and boots. The motorbike, a lurid green Kawasaki 80, lay nearby. Driscoll was excited to share his find,

- E's one o' them punks!

Cooper didn't think so. Yes, this was a rough kid, with his boots, scruffy clothes and cropped hair but there were no signs of his being a punk, skinhead, mod or any other of the urban tribes of the time. Anyway, he thought with a smirk,

Punk's not dead.

- Oo is it? Greebo? Cleaver? Coops?

Jesus, he even knows their names. The skivers. The glue-sniffers and the boozers.

Driscoll moved to prod the teenage corpse with his boot, possibly to roll it over for a better look as if it were a dead fox or badger found on his land. Seeing what was about to happen,

Cooper was startled into action.

- Ey! You can't do that! Step back, Mr. Driscoll.

Driscoll didn't step back. He didn't take orders from a scrumper. But he withdrew his probing foot.

Cooper squatted down to look at the sideways-turned face.

Michael Hickman. He knew him well as a vicious, cheeky kid and a bully, always in trouble. Hard, but not one of the very hardest. Not one of the real nutters who would stand up to and fight a grown man or take on a gang of kids on his own, but still a sly, nasty handful. Cooper felt a twinge at the front of his right knee as he stood up again.

- CID will be taking your statement later, when they get here. That's not my job. But, out of interest, did you hear any shouting last night, at ten?

-Just the bikes.

- No voices or shouting? Nothing like a fight?

- Just thrairpin' the bikes.

- Bikes or bike?

Driscoll grunted noncommittally.

Cooper felt another twinge as he squatted down again to note the frame number of the bike. While there, he scanned the tracks and footprints in the muddy floor. None were distinct, there was nothing that could usefully be photographed to be used in court but it looked like something had gone on around the base of the tree. He knew this land, and the grass and earth there seemed to him more disturbed than a crash and fall-off-your-bike scenario would warrant.

- When your dog found him this morning, did you get close? Have a good look? Maybe turn him over, like you tried just now?

- No. Went straight back to call police.

Driscoll's face was a picture of probity. The upright citizen.

- Did the dog interfere with the body?

- Wouldn't go near it. Went barmy barkin' at it but wouldn't go near 'im.

Cooper sighed. The boy wouldn't have been riding the bike alone in the woods at night. And it looked like a scuffle had taken place around the tree. He would have to speak to Hickman's roughneck friends, all well-known to the police. And before CID got to them, if they even bothered.

He would get them alone, like an old-time copper.

In the woods.

***

The Pup.

- Up in the tree you say?

Aitor was hammering a glowing rod of iron held between tongs, bending it over the jutting horn of the anvil, so Gaizka waited for the interval between clanging blows to respond,

- Yes. Quite high up.

More strikes, then,

- And how old, you say?

Gaizka thought of the little brothers of his friends and enemies in the village. Although they were all rough little tykes, raised outdoors between farm, forest and beach, none of them could have climbed a tree like that. But still, judging from the size,

- About four.

Aitor stopped working and turned to look at Gaizka properly for the first time,

- What does he look like?

Gaizka rallied his thoughts. His father rarely honoured him with a direct question like this. He would try to answer well. But as he thought of the little boy he had to smile too,

- Just a little kid. Quite a skinny one, not chubby like a lot that age. You can see his muscles! I don't know how he climbed all the way up there.

His father was listening to him as if he were an adult. Thinking about what he said too. Gaizka continued,

- He's heavy though. When I chased off the boar with the sling, he let me help him down. I nearly fell over. And he's got red hair. Not bright red like that girl in the village. A kind of dark red, brownish. Mum says he's not one of our people and I should tell you because you'd know what to do but of course he's not one of our people. He must be from the next valley or maybe further. Maybe they were travelling,

trading things...

Aitor interrupted,

- What was the mother like? What was she carrying with her?

- There wasn't much left. The boars had been at her, at whatever the wolves had left.

- How'd you know it was a mother, not a father or another child, then?

- From the screams I heard.

Aitor frowned and dunked the still-hot metal, now the blade of a wood chisel, in the water trough.

- If you heard something screaming last night, it wasn't them. Not from that far up you didn´t. Foxes scream when they mate. Wildcats too, when they fight before mating. Otters make strange noises sometimes. Seagulls.

Scowling, Aitor used the tongs to grab another slug of iron from the pile near the anvil and place it on the top of the bed of smouldering charcoal that was his furnace. The muscles in his sinewy arms twitched as if impatient to start pounding it with his hammer but first he had to work the long handles of the bellows and pump air through the furnace until both charcoal and ingot glowed red.

- Clothes?

- I think she... the woman, had had some... I don't know. There was a lot of blood and mess. He's got no clothes. There was a bag made of hide but it just had plants in it and some pointed stones and a carving.

- Carving?

- Some kind of animal with horns. A stag maybe or a bull. Carved from antler.

- They had nothing made of metal?

- Er... no.

- Does it speak our language?

- What?

- It. The creature. The boy, fool.

- He hasn't spoken yet. I don't think he understands me when I speak to him.

- Tell me about the wolves again.

- There were tracks from a big pack and four dead ones left on the floor. One black or nearly black, the others normal. All big. One had a broken spear shoved through its ribs, coming out the other side. One had bled a lot from the mouth before dying. One had been dragging itself around, its back broken. You could see the tracks it left on the floor.

- What a nice mother she was. And the other wolf? You said there were four.

- The black one had its skull crushed. There was a rock on the ground.

Aitor raised his eyebrows slightly then was impassive again and silent. He turned his back on Gaizka and went back to work. Gaizka waited.

- Tell your mother to feed it. All it wants.

Gaizka smiled,

- She already has.

***

Saturday 17th July 1982 – Afternoon (i).

The woods were not so big. If they were here, not at the baths or loitering in the streets and parks, he would find them. If they didn't see him first. Only a few hours had passed since the discovery of the corpse, but the CID and the body had gone already. The boys he wanted to talk to would not know about the death of their mate, unless they had either been involved or had spoken to somebody who had been involved. Even if they knew nothing about the death, they might know where the bike had come from, which could lead him to whoever had been with Hickman that night.

As Cooper left the path near the brook, and entered the woods proper, he struggled to scale some of the steeper, muddier tracks through the overgrown former quarries, now resembling wooded valleys. The woodland paths were shaded from the summer sun by tall beech, sycamore and even oak trees and so never really dried out until August and even then only in the hottest, driest years. While the hard, physical work of scrambling up and down the slopes occupied his immediate attention, Cooper's mind wandered back to the long-past summers of his teenage years. Had he been happy, playing, escaping with his friends, from the built-up adult world in these woods and elsewhere? The heat and the glorious summer foliage around him reminded him of the hot, endless days and nights of those summers, when, ignored by adults, they had found their own amusements. Some of their fun had been innocent, the stuff of cosy memories to be shared with kids and grandkids one day: scrumping for Driscoll's sweet green apples and pears; fishing or building a raft in Driscoll's pond before the inevitable, but always exhilarating, chase and escape; falling around laughing with your mates as you recounted some detail of one of those life-and-death chases, how so-and-so had run like this (mime actions) and such-and-such had done this (gurn face); swimming in the Marl Hole pool near Himley or the canal at Wordsley; clumsy first approaches to giggly girls or brazen ones. Other memories were much darker, as these were *the woods:* the fights, some relatively honourable one-on-ones, pre-arranged 'offering outs' for a specific time and place (and how sickeningly slow could time crawl as you waited for your opponent and his backers to round the corner), some just cowardly and one-sided beatings of a weaker or helpless opponent. And much that was morally somewhere in between: breathlessly watching the wide-eyed expiration of a thrush shot with a pellet gun; getting laughing-your-head-off, falling-down drunk for the first time, on money stolen from Simon Hughes's bed-ridden granny; a burglary of a friend's house but after booze, not money; roughly handling a drunken girl in an alley, her eyes rolling back, mouth open and gasping because she, shockingly, unbelievably, wanted it, too.

But had he been happy? Had he been conscious of anything, really, or had he just lived like an animal, passing from sensation to sensation guided by instinct, indifferent to time, to friendship, morality? Had he felt any loyalty to, or affection for, those he ran with?

One thing he knew, his body then had been an unperceived and taken-for-granted vehicle for adventure. He had been unaware of his flesh; no twinges had marked the boundaries of the physically possible in those days. When he saw a barbed wire fence, he could either vault it, or he couldn't. The limits of his physicality were intrinsic and fair, not imposed on him by his physical deterioration as they were now.

He paused for breath and looked up, seeking a respite from the monotony of mud, insects, sweat and shadow.

Dappled, he thought.

There was no other way to describe the interplay between the sunlight, the blue sky and the beech leaves high above in the treetops. Even here, in a relatively featureless part of the small forest, there were memories to be harvested: stocky and fearless David Taylor had climbed at least twenty yards up one of these giant trees, hugging it Koala-style all the way and once they had seen two large owls flapping in these tree tops, incongruous in the daylight.

He was approaching the highest part of the woods now, a kind of plateau where the oppressive shade of the woodland opened out into small meadows of tall grass, some of them grazed by tethered horses, before descending again into the deeper, darker chasms that bordered the allotments, and the northern edge of the woods.

Still in the shadows, he stopped, thinking he heard voices. He did, but faintly. Coarse, laddish voices and laughter. And the harsh words and swearing of rough friendship. As he got closer, he began to hear another, nostalgically familiar sound, too,

Phfft.

Phfft.

Pinggggg.

Two teenage boys were firing an air rifle at some beer cans and cider bottles they had placed on a log in one of the sunny clearings. Both were blond-haired. The skinnier of the two, with a burgundy 'chunky' jumper, stretch jeans and black Doc Marten shoes, had unfashionably long blond hair that identified him easily even from that distance.

Darren Westwood.

The other boy had very short fair hair and was much stockier. Alarmingly stocky, in fact, if you were twenty-plus years older and about to have to confront him. A white Fred Perry t-shirt was stretched tight across his wide back and rounded shoulders. Burgundy sta-press trousers stretched over his bulging thighs and fat arse. He seemed to be wearing steel toe-cap work shoes.

Let's get around the side and have a look. 'Coz it might be...

Before beginning a circling movement, Cooper retreated into the darkness of the woods, off-path and downhill a little, his feet crunching on twigs and beechnut litter, keeping his eyes on the boys, ready to freeze if they glanced in his direction. From his own years as a boy-in-the-woods, he knew that it was movement that would give him away, if anything. If they looked in his direction while he was motionless in the shadows they were unlikely to see him.

In profile it was obvious.

Simon Green. Parrot face. Mate of Michael Hickman.

The stocky boy's large, rounded nose was unmistakable. Cooper smiled to himself at the sight of it. You would think that with a face like that Greeny would have no luck with the girls but he knew different. In fact, with his swaggering confidence and his gift for quick-fire piss-taking, this lump was considered something of a ladies' man.

Cooper got as close as he could before stepping into the sunlight,

- I want to talk to you, Greeny.

Wide-eyed, Darren Westwood, saw him first, as Greeny was just beginning to turn around,

- Fuckin' 'ell! Leggit!

He shot off into the undergrowth still holding the air rifle. Greeny was bulkier and slower than his friend but he too began to lurch and crash away through the bushes.

Cooper knew that if Greeny could summon enough adrenaline to get a real sprint on, he would struggle to keep pace with the boy. But he also knew that he was a smoker, and a good fourteen stone of smoker at that. And he had seen him take on a gang of four Parkfielders on his own one night outside the Gate Hangs Well pub, so he knew that one local bobby-on-the-beat was unlikely to scare him very far away.

He'll run till he's knackered, then stop. About one minute.

Cooper started to jog after Greeny and Westwood, pacing himself. All three knew that there was only one viable path for the escaping boys and they soon left the bushes and began to follow the narrow dirt track. To turn right from there would have involved scrambling down the steepest part of one of the old quarries. To the left the undergrowth, mainly hawthorn, was spiky and impenetrable.

Still only jogging, but breathing and sweating heavily in his uniform, helmet and heavy shoes, Cooper struggled to keep track of the gamely bobbing figure of Greeny as the path twisted between bushes and trees, skirting the precipice of the quarry's edge. Then,

Shit, he's stopped.

Cooper felt his heart flutter and, as he slowed to a walk, he felt unsteady on his adrenalin-pumped legs. He removed his helmet and tried to regain control of his breathing as he walked up to the panting, white-faced boy-man in a grassy clearing between hawthorn copse and precipice. The edge of the cliff was still collapsed in places where, years before, somebody had dug away the crumbly yellow soil to get at badgers' setts.

- ...Want.... a... ...word - was all he could get out.

Brilliant. Clint fucking Eastwood.

The young bruiser, gasping for breath, head down, hands on knees, didn't answer.

Cooper hesitated. His plan had been to bully the bully. To shock some answers out of the boy here in the woods away from the niceties of CID and before the inevitable huddling and conniving with moms and dads, maybe lawyers, took place. But this fight could go wrong if the teenager wasn't as tired as he was making out.

He wasn't.

Much faster than he looked, Greeny snatched up a club-like branch of hawthorn from the floor and swung at Cooper's head.

Cooper had been poised to jump back, and began to, but was still caught with a thudding clout to the ear. As he lurched forward onto his hands and knees, a steel toe-cap shoe struck him a glancing blow to the chin.

Getting lamped by a kid. Get up.

Cooper rolled and scrambled to a half-kneeling position in time to raise his hands and partially block another crashing blow from the stick. Small thorny notches on the branch scraped his knuckles and forearm cruelly. His thoughts condensed into one imperative,

You're fucking dead.

Greeny was standing still, the heavy branch by his side just for an instant when Cooper lunged at him. They fell to the ground with Cooper on top, the close-range grappling nullifying the advantages of the boy's weapon and shoes. Cooper manoeuvred into a dominant kneeling position quickly, smacking an elbow into Greeny's eye-socket before rearing up to find the right distance for a barrage of punches to the face. With the slow-motion vision, a sixth sense almost, that came with his rages, Cooper registered the growing inventory of damage caused by his fists: split lip, bloodshot eye, gashed eyebrow, pulped nose, cut inside mouth...

Enough.

He paused. He would speak calmly and the boy would not know how rattled he was, how close to defeat he had been. Still on top, he began,

- What happened last night then? You and Hickman have a scrap?

He looked into Greeny's eyes. Incredibly the facial expression, wide-eyed with panic during the beating, was already reverting to the default cockiness of a young terror. Greeny had been questioned before, Cooper knew. And was there a touch of mockery there? A knowing nod-and-wink to how close this sixteen-year-old had come to beating up the copper? But no answer came.

- Was it about the bike? 'Bout a wench?

- Fuck off piggy!

- You'll fucking well tell me, you little shit!

The blows resumed but Greeny had had time to get his breath back and was struggling and bucking hard, arching his back between Cooper's body and the floor. And Cooper felt ever more light-headed and heavy-armed.

Grunts and thuds. A pause. Heavy breathing. Waves of nausea began to pulse through Cooper's consciousness. His arms felt like useless blocks of concrete and he tasted blood from a cut inside his mouth. Greeny must have got tired again too because he stopped resisting.

Where did that fucking branch come from anyway?

Another surge of nausea.

Going to...

He vomited just to the side of Greeny's head. They lay intertwined in gasping stalemate for long seconds but once he had spat out the bitter last dregs of vomit, Cooper began to feel his head clear and his energy return.

- I said... you'll... fucking... tell me!

He staggered to one knee, then to his feet and dragged Greeny to the edge of the precipice. This was the highest cliff along the top of the old limestone quarry. For most of its length the drop was only about ten yards before the vertical rock face began to level out to a muddy incline but any fall from that point would end on a sharp ridge of limestone jutting out directly below them like a knife.

Pinning down the boy's arms with his knees, he let Greeny twist his head to look down then whacked him hard to the side of the face.

- This could look like an accident. Break yer fucking back. What happened last night? Was it a fight or a crash?

Greeny looked up through bloodshot eyes. Too exhausted now to be cocky, he seemed to be weighing up his options. Suddenly,

- Nah. Just left him. Some fucker was shooting at us. A pellet gun or a catter.

- What you talking about?

- We was on the bike. Got fucking shot. Look.

He pointed to a small bruise under his right eye.

- That fucking nutter, Hickman, wor bothered. I was off. Left him dahn theer.

- You didn't see who shot you?

- Dunno. Saw a bloke. Legged us out o' the woods.

- Legged the both of yers or just you?

- Just me. I'd left Hickman on the bike.

- What was the bloke like?

Greeny's eyes were flicking from side to side. Considering his options again: had he regained enough strength to roll out from under and get away? Could he restart and win the fight? Was it worth it?

- Saw fuck all. Just a bloke.

Cooper knew that while an adult in the woods at night wouldn't see much, teenage boys could see almost as in daylight.

- Don't fuck me about. You could still 'ave that accident. No-body'd see it. Westwood's 'ome 'avin' 'is tea by now.

He eased one knee off Greeny's arm, and still with the strength of his anger, hauled the boy sideways then rolled him so that an arm and a leg were over the edge and locked an elbow around his neck in a tight choke. Greeny's landward arm plucked at tufts of grass and his leg scraped for traction in the turf as Cooper brought his face down close to the boy's ear.

- What was the bloke like? - he growled.

- Can't... fuckin'... breathe...

The cockiness had receded again. Cooper eased off the stranglehold.

- What was he like?

The answer came in gasps,

- A fuckin' nutter... like a fucking ape... fucking baboon or summat... built like a brick shithouse.

- What was he wearing?

The boy's eyes narrowed and he hesitated. Then,

- Nothin'. Fuck all. Fuckin' starkers.

Cooper was now taken aback. The woods had had its share of flashers, gropers and fiddlers but - a naked attacker? A sex killer? The Hickman body had shown no signs of being sexually assaulted. And anyway,

Who'd want to rape this fucking lump? Who could *rape him?*

- Did he touch you?

- Fuck off! Day catch me. Fuckin' legged it back to the street. Back up to the 'ouses. It day follow.

It?

- What else did you see? Big built you say. What else? Long hair? Short hair? Old? Young?

Greeny actually grinned. Through the blood and the exhaustion, the dirt and the sweat, he grinned up at Cooper as he said,

- Plastered with fucking mud. Stark bollock naked. Day see 'is 'air cause he 'ad a mask with 'orns.

Greeny threw back his head and laughed.

***

Cooper let the boy up and he scrambled to his feet, backed away without taking his eyes off the copper, and walked quickly off. When safely out of range, he threw a chunk of limestone that Cooper had to sidestep to avoid, then jogged away with a shout,

- Gettin' old piggy! We'll 'ave yer one day!

and a whoop of laughter.

The policeman smiled despite himself and did not give chase. He liked the rough and daring boys of the woods and the streets, of the wastelands, the towpaths and the slagheaps. Sly and untameable, they reminded him of his youth and the long-gone mates and enemies of youth.

But one rough and daring boy was now dead. And what of the tale of the horned man? He remembered boys from his own youth, just as hardened as Greeny, puffing on cigarettes and telling tales around fires in a dark part of the woods, scaring each other as boys always have: devils and ghouls, escaped mental patients and psychopathic hunchbacks. If you wanted to put a boy like Greeny to flight, that was the way to do it. Had someone stripped naked and put on a mask to scare the boys and separate them? Hickman was a little bastard alright, and would have made enemies, maybe even adult enemies, but who would go to that much trouble?

It was still early afternoon and getting hot now in the clearing. Cooper picked up his helmet and began to limp back along the narrow path, back toward the sun-bleached grass of the horse pasture.

But something was not right. He began to feel sick again. The heat, the flies, the glare of light reflected from the yellow grass all seemed to exacerbate a hideous pressure in his upper chest and head. He could see stars of many colours exploding in his field of vision. Now there was no vision just a field of black, which the coloured stars and impossibly intricate snowflake patterns throbbed and swelled to fill until...

He was flailing and thrashing through the woods at night.

At night?

No this was not real. Even through the panic of his delirium, he was aware that this was some kind of dream or memory, or a dream masquerading as memory.

He fell and rolled over onto his back, glad of the chance to catch his breath, glad of the hundreds of stars visible in the night sky between the witchfinger-black branches of the highest trees. Glad to be young and free again.

As his breathing calmed, he rose to prop himself on one elbow but did not look around him. His gaze went straight from sky to floor, to the grass. He didn't dare look around. As he realised what he would see if he did look, fear kept his eyes fixed on the grassy floor of the clearing.

Not yet. Give me a minute before I have to look. Before I have to remember.

He could look away or close his eyes but other senses could not be denied so easily. He felt the warmth of the fire, not so close, smelt the incense smell of burning hawthorn and heard its crackle.

Look up.

It was a large bonfire, not yet in full blaze. One side burning well, the other still unignited, flames just beginning to lick at the dry branches and splintered crates.

It was the scene he had never been able to remember until now. He had always had to rely on the accounts of others.

Little nutters, weren't you, eh? Built a bonfire in the woods and made a camp in it. In July! Slept out in it. Smokers most of you. Drunk on scrumpy and some said other stuff too. Mushrooms or pills. An accident waiting to happen. Daft lads indeed. Poor daft lads. Not bad lads, really. They'd had their scrapes and scraps, taken their knocks and dished them out but not bad lads. Poor, daft lads burned to a crisp.

This much he had known. Had never remembered but been told. He, the lone survivor, who must have somehow scrambled out of the collapsing pile of flaming wood and tyres. After being treated for alcohol poisoning and shock they had filled him in.

But now he saw for himself. Or dreamt that he saw. Or remembered seeing. A naked, muscular man, his back to Cooper, was watching the spreading fire, a club-like branch in his hand.

A club. Something happened today with a club. Somewhere.

Some pallets near the centre of the pile were moving. There was a blanket hanging like a curtain between them. Three coughing, panicking figures clambered out over planks and tyres. In the flickering light he could make out the features of Scanlon, Kennedy and Braiden, mates from twenty-three years ago.

They were going to make it out! In this dream, or memory, they would make it. This time they would live.

The muscular figure moved forward and began raining down powerful blows with the club. The young men raised hands to defend themselves but he was bigger and the club was heavy. Cooper tried to shout but it didn't happen. He tried to move but felt detached from his body, trapped outside like a ghost. There was a desperate struggle but the huge beast never let them get to their feet and the blows were crashing and relentless.

Once all three stopped fighting back and lay unconscious amongst the planks and sticks, the great hulk raised them one by one and threw the bodies deeper into the burning pile, near the makeshift doorway they had emerged from.

The huge man watched until the flames took hold on the wood around the bodies, then turned and loped away towards a dark path. Then, as the man could be seen in profile for the first time, Cooper noticed the horns. The creature's face was hidden by a mask covered in some sort of fur or hair, crowned by two large horns.

***

Cooper sat up in the long, straw-like grass. It was still warm and sunny and so it was impossible to know how long he had been unconscious. His body felt battered and heavy and he would have liked to lie longer in the grass; to be healed by nature, the warm sun and memories of his abruptly curtailed youth. But CID would have plans for him; no doubt the humdrum task of visiting the friends and family of the dead boy, and he could not risk having long parts of his day unaccounted for should anyone ask about the details of today's work.

He rose and started his walk out of the woods.

***

Complete.

Gorka, as they named the child from the forest, grew bigger and stronger but never fatter despite Maider's best efforts. In the village a fleshy child was a sign of prestige and she thought the family might fit in better if she could take a chubby boy to the market. It had never worked with Gaizka and his thin frame and pointy face and it wouldn't work with Gorka either. She would persuade Aitor to give her nails or fence hinges to trade with farmers' wives for honey and then make from it the sweetest puddings and tarts or use it to flavour their milk but the boy stayed raw-boned. She tried with fatty food too, duck or boar basted in honey and with more boar fat drizzled over it as it turned on the spit, forming a crispy layer that Aitor said was as good as anything the clan chief had in his kitchen. But Gorka would peel off the roasted skin and leave it on the side of the plate, eating only the lean meat. And he much preferred fish from the estuary or big tiger prawns. But who ever got fat eating like that?

He soon learned to speak their language and in the first few weeks of his time with them they also heard a few words of his mountain tongue. Then one day that stopped and they heard it no more as if he had chosen to put away thoughts of his past life and its violent climax.

Maider pitied the boy and frowned at Aitor for calling him 'it'. True, he was different: his body was squarer and stronger than the norm, his wrists and ankles thicker. He would not float if you let go of him when bathing but would sink rock-heavy to the sandy riverbed. And she had never seen a head so broad and brow so heavy. But she told herself and her husband that he was not as strange as some others she had seen or heard of: pink-eyed folk as white as a ghost, the man in the village with a small arm that had never grown, a family in a travelling show whose adults were no bigger than three-year-olds. She could see he was no fairy or troll from the woods but a clever and thoughtful child who would play alone for hours, engrossed with the knick-knacks he found around the house: a wooden spoon, a spool *for wool, carved pegs, bringing them to wondrous life in his own world while narrating the whole story first in the mountain tongue and later, to her delight, in a baby version of their own. When Aitor was not around, Gaizka and his mother smiled at each other to see this frowning little boy and his serious play and Gaizka brought or made him better toys: a twig-legged boar made from a pine cone, a toy man and his wife woven from reeds, little boats and houses of sewn bark. And, because he learnt his words from Gaizka, he called Maider 'mother' and she let him.*

With Aitor it took longer but Maider would sometimes catch him watching the boy's stern play with a smile on his lips or looking on approvingly as the boy carried out some small chore. And at the end of one autumn day spent picking mushrooms in the high forest, when little Gorka was too exhausted to walk all the way back, the smith picked him up and carried him as he would his own and Maider watched as an infant head lolled against brawny shoulder and chest and she knew their family was complete.

Sat 17th July 1982 – Afternoon (ii).

George flopped onto his bed, within reach of the pile of books his father had brought back from his job at the library. He was physically tired, having spent the afternoon at Coseley baths. There had been the usual quota of lean and tattooed hard kids from Tipton and from Dudley's Priory and Wren's Nest estates, including the notorious Cole brothers, but for once they had been too absorbed in their own harsh banter and rivalries to even notice George and his inoffensive friends. And the swimming had felt good. It was true he had no tattoos, was not from a famous fighting clan, and whatever muscles might be growing on his pale body were still well hidden under puppy fat. But his asthma never seemed to bother him in the pool; he was growing taller and he had felt the exhilaration of growing power and speed as he had pulled through the water. Also, he had seen a glimpse of what might be. Some of the Tipton boys, as rough as they come, had been with a couple of skinhead girls. Not shaven headed like the chaps but close-cropped except for a longer fringe at the front. One girl, short but curvaceous in a one-piece swimsuit, had smiled at him then lowered her eyes prettily as she squeezed to get past, between him and the pool's edge.

- Look aht, curly.

There had been no further chat. They both knew that would provoke a confrontation. But 'curly'!

Back in his bedroom now, he imagined himself a little older and bigger, with the girl on his arm. He might have a sheepskin coat. He might wear a union jack t-shirt under it or maybe just a plain white one, tight on a broad chest. He would cut his hair short but not skinned, or maybe grow it much longer. He would not go for the full skinhead look with inches of red or yellow football sock showing between jeans and dockers with coloured laces. He would wear jeans that covered the top of his dockers, with black or maybe white laces. Or just go for black brogues and black socks. It did not matter; he could choose how he dressed and would go where he chose with her: Tipton, the Priory, the Wren's Nest, the Conygre Estate. He had until then favoured the mod look, it was the most stylish and they had the best girls, but after his brush with a skinhead girl from Tipton, he was recalibrating. He thought for some time about the dimpled smile, her long eyelashes, faint freckles on pale skin.

The pile of library books caught his attention. From his earliest childhood, his dad the librarian had filled his life with books. He could still remember his father reading Baba the Elephant stories with him as a very small child, talking about the pictures even before he could read. When George was just a little older they had thrilled together at the heroic and villainous creatures of 'The Wind in the Willows' and 'Toad of Toad Hall', the quaint nineteenth century English not detracting from the experience at all, but enhancing it as they seemed to enter, each night after toast and cocoa, a distinct world created just for them, in which even language was different. Soon, by some miracle, George was reading picture books and comics on his own, then, rapidly transitioning through children's fiction (he loved Just William and Biggles, but, like his father, scorned the work of Enid Blyton) soon began to consume, and eventually exhaust, the science fiction sections of both Dudley and Wolverhampton public libraries.

He was glad to find no science fiction in the pile of books. With the onset of puberty and the transition to secondary school he had lost interest in its other-worldly escapism – how could talk of anti-gravity and rules for robot behaviour help him with the Hickmans and Dean Wilsons of the world? But he did smile to find another type of fantasy, a much-loved and feared horror anthology that, more than once, his dad had had to temporarily ban from the house due to the night terrors it had caused. Then his father would eventually give in and the book would come back only to be banned again. Funny man, really, his dad. Even now, looking at the luridly-coloured abstract patterns of the dust jacket design gave George a mild thrill although the only story he remembered was the silly one of the cat that was bricked up in a cellar wall and whose cries had driven its haunted owner to hysteria and confession. He had been disappointed by that story written for adults. To the savage world view of a child, the murderer's resolve had cracked too easily. A cat squeals so you admit to murder! He knew that he would do better if tested.

What else was there?

'The Coral Island' by R.M. Ballantyne. Another old favourite, possibly his all-time childhood favourite in fact but he realised with sadness that he would not read it again. The tale of three boys pulling together to survive on a deserted island without the help of adults no longer convinced him. He had since read 'The Lord of the Flies'. That was believable.

His dad had brought him a book about famous murderers from the adult section of the library.

He just wants me to keep reading. Doesn't care what.

He would look at it later.

There was a book called 'Sugar Ray', a biography of the boxer Sugar Ray Robinson. Although slight and reserved himself, his dad had a surprising interest in boxing and he and George had recently watched a TV documentary called 'Pound for Pound' about Robinson's career. Normally not interested in sport, George had found himself fascinated by some of the old black and white clips of Robinson's fights. Robinson could unleash flurries of five or six blows in quick succession, all accurate and hard, almost always with devastating results. His tough-looking opponents crumpled down to the floor as if shot. As a child in the seventies, with no mother to send him to bed early, George had been exposed to plenty of late night TV showings of Bruce Lee and Clint Eastwood films but he had always been sceptical of the staged fight scenes between actors. Robinson's power, though, was real and demonstrable and he wasn't even that big and muscular. As he studied the book, it occurred to George that perhaps his father had mistaken his interest in the liberating possibilities of being able to flatten people at will for a shared interest in boxing. He felt suddenly fonder of the old man. Leafing through the Sugar Ray book, George came to a section of black-and-white photos. There were two photos of a Ray Robinson opponent called Randolph Turpin. This man really was muscular. Looking at the chiselled body and tough, square-jawed face, it was hard to imagine anybody beating him, although apparently Robinson had. George wondered if it would be possible for him to achieve something like that kind of physique. He had already begun doing press-ups, maybe if he saved up and bought...

His dad's voice came from downstairs,

- George, do you know this boy?

George went down to the living room, intrigued. Had his dad seen some kid clambering over the wasteland beyond their back garden?

But when he entered the living room, he saw his father looking at the television. He was watching the local news that came on after the BBC news.

- Oh, the photo's gone now. Michael Hickman, they said. Do you know him?

- Er, yes. A kid from the fourth year.

George saw no need to mention yesterday's beating. His face had swollen in places but had not bruised much and the worst cut was hidden by his hairline. While his dad must have noticed something, and had asked a few questions, he had quickly accepted George's answer that he had been accidentally elbowed in a football match.

- What's he done?

Peter Merriman examined his son's face again, better than he had wanted to the previous evening. It seemed unlikely, but he was a kindly man and felt he should ask,

- He wasn't a friend of yours, was he?

The past tense did not go unnoticed. George sat down on a footstool in front of the television but the news item was just ending,

- Nah, just kid from the fourth year.

- He was found dead in some woods. Motorbike accident, they think.

George remembered the black cat squealing behind the cellar wall, spec-less Piggy being stoned in the black and white film of Lord of the Flies.

He felt no guilt.

***

<u>Saturday 17th July – night.</u>

It was night-time in the woods. Pipistrelle bat, fox and barn owl hunted while badger and rat scrabbled for grubs and roots. Deep in the limestone quarry, where a wide cave narrows down to a man-made tunnel, a sweating figure laboured in the darkness.

The bad boys who went into the woods knew of this cave and the tunnel that began at its deepest point and which was said to have once led to the caves near Dudley Zoo and the old underground canal basin. Generations of youths had explored it with torches and matches, egging each other on to squeeze through the narrow gap that led from cave to tunnel and then follow the tunnel fifteen or twenty yards to its blocked-off end. Some, the most daring and agile, could scale the vertical shaft that rose halfway along the now-truncated tunnel but this too was a dead end. Once bravado wore out and honour was proven, none lingered in this place that was sterile, gloomy and cold, inhabited only by woodlice and millipedes. For all of those bad boys, though, those clammy underground struggles would linger in dreams for a lifetime.

Deep underground, a man felt his way through the darker-than-darkness with outstretched fingers using skills and senses possessed by none but his kind these last ten thousand years, neither wanting nor needing light to guide him. Braided with muscle, he hauled his dense body higher and higher up the vertical shaft until, not quite at the top, he braced his back against cold rock and flexed his legs to push a slab of limestone inwards and to one side, opening a gap perhaps a foot wide. By changing position and plunging his arms into the crack, he was able to widen it by pushing the slab, immensely heavy but not fixed, further to one side. He then pulled his whole body into the hidden chamber.

Now he did need light, and felt around on a rock ledge for the old candles he knew would be there. He pulled a disposable cigarette lighter from the pocket of his jeans and lit two of the candles before partly melting the base of both and planting them on ledges at opposite ends of the chamber.

The candlelight revealed a magpie collection of relics from the near and distant past, all either hung from protruding crags or leaning against the cave wall: a short, wide-bladed sword; an ancient pike, its wooden shaft still strong, the iron blade only slightly rusted; an intricately designed steel helmet, like that of a conquistador, with upturned visor edges to deflect sword blows from the face; a three-cornered felt hat; a flintlock pistol; a large musket or blunderbuss; a long-barrelled and finely-crafted shotgun; a charred metal leg brace from a lame man; a broken-bladed lock knife; a Webley revolver; a motorbike chain and a cracked human skull.

The man untied a cheap black pilot jacket that had been secured around his waist during his clamberings and placed it on the floor, near the more modern artefacts. He knelt on the jacket and, in a low voice, he began to pray,

Vuestra merced, dios de la oscuridad y de la alegría verdadera,

Acepte la ofrenda de la antigua hermandad

Y ayúdanos a castigar a los enemigos del elegido

Bendita sea,

   Amén

***

Monday 19th July 1982

Stupid, stupid, stupid bastard.

Stupid, stupid, stupid bastard.

He was chanting under his breath as he walked briskly to school, briefcase in hand, sweating in a prickly jacket, early sun warming his balding scalp,

Stupid, stupid fucking bastard.

Stupid, stupid fucking bastard.

His jaw was clenched. His gaze fixed forwards and down. He had to wait at a pedestrian crossing on the Birmingham New Road and the physical pause prompted a thought. He didn't have to keep going. He could turn and go home, call in sick. It was a kind of sickness that had led him to this. But to stay at home today would only delay his downfall. The lights changed and he resumed his march.

Stupid. Stupid.

He had to do it. Couldn't stop himself. It didn't hurt anybody, either. But why had he done it so close to home?

Doing it there! They were bound to be from the school. Bound to know you!

Stupid. Stupid bastard.

It was a glorious summer morning, fresh and blue-skied with a faint promise of heat to come. Kids were appearing now, on their way to school. It was very early, he thought, but there were already some: sun glinting on blond, brown or still-wet-and-mousy hair, uniforms already loosening on the skinniest and most frolicsome; already running, kicking, jumping past other, slower, folk: the sleepyheads and dawdlers. It was their legs that caught his eye: elastic and tireless, tensile like a drawn bow, innocent of fatigue and wear.

He had to step into the road to pass a cluster of jostling second years.

- Fuckin' pushed me! Yer dick!

A rudely shoved girl with wavy ringlets covered her swearing mouth, wide-eyed as she saw the teacher pass, then theatrically embraced another girl, burying a giggling face in her neck.

What did these careless puppies know of his life, his ordeals? Who were they to bring him down? How could anyone believe that he might be a threat to them? More like the other way around. In their shouting, rosy-cheeked health, even the smallest of them seemed indestructible while he tottered, stiff-legged, toward self-inflicted disaster.

He found himself entering the staffroom, a haven of distorted sofas and armchairs, bookshelves, magazines and instant coffee. He exchanged mumbled greetings with floppy-haired but blokey art teacher, Mr Langley; nodded at Brodie, the smallest and most brutal P.E. teacher. They wouldn't know anything yet.

The mug he found at the sink was stained, needed more washing. Anita, the young English teacher, appeared at his side as he looked for something to dry the cup, and gave him the briefest and shyest of smiles.

Won't be doing that again. Not for much longer anyway. A matter of time.

Soon it was time to go to their form rooms and begin the working day. The school was a modern building and the glass corridor he had to walk was airy and well-lit but seemed impossibly long now that it had filled with kids coming towards him: so many faces to be scanned by him as he searched for signs of knowledge of his crime and his coming shame. But the faces were blank, or sullen, or sarky, nothing out of the ordinary. Some greeted him, but innocently it seemed. The whispering had not yet begun.

As he took the register in his form room, Wenton tried to scan the faces of his pupils for any anomalous reaction or uncalled-for smirk. They were a couple of years younger than the girls from Friday night but they were the kind of mid-stream class, with a sprinkling of popular, well-connected girls, who would be amongst the first to hear of any breaking scandal. He could not bring himself to look at Lisa Stanley. He focused instead on Haley Boswell, relatively studious and well-behaved yet also pretty and allowed into all the best girl cliques. She caught his gaze and held it for a moment without embarrassment before raising her eyebrows and shifting her attention elsewhere. He might be safe. At least for a while.

He began the ritual pretence of teaching nineteenth-century history to Haley and the rest. The vandalised books were handed out then kept closed as he invited the class to discuss the long-dead issue that they would later be reading about. He monitored the resulting off-topic conversations about football both international and local, about who was cock of the fourth year, about who had a good pair on her and who fancied who, this last leading to stifled giggling behind him. As Wenton turned on his heel to face the gigglers, he glanced out of the form room window and saw the panda car pull into the school car park near the main entrance.

His stomach churned and all he saw became slow motion. All he could hear became quieter background noise on another plane. Waves of nausea rippled through his consciousness. He had not expected this so soon. He had thought it unlikely that the girls would go straight to the police. He had half-hoped that they might not go at all. His was not the first dick they had seen, for sure, so why bother? He had known that they would not be able to resist gossiping, though, and that the gossip might reach some teacher or parent who could then go to the police. But a panda car at the school gates already?

He might as well just leave the class to their gossip and bragging and go to the office to meet them, he realised. It would spare him the shame of being pulled out of class.

Miles Wilding, John Kelsey and some other boys with window seats along the side of the classroom had seen the panda car now and were discussing it. Shaven-headed Miles and buck-toothed John were making the most of their privileged viewpoint in the closest corner of the room by craning their necks and moving their heads from side to side as if trying to see through a crowd of tall spectators, although nothing blocked their view. Irritated by the boys' behaviour, Wenton began to focus on the class again. He could make out snatches of classroom conversations,

- Colin Bull most likely, you'll find…

- …burn 'em aht over the woods…

- Campbell's more of a stiff 'un than 'im

- Ard bastard.

- It's Cooper…

- gid im a raht lampin'

- ay cummin fer yow, yer big puff!

So the boys, at least, had no idea what was coming. They imagined the police had come to ask about some fight or robbery. There might be hope in that. It would not be that unusual, would it? Then he became aware of someone looking at him and turned to see that it was Lisa Stanley. She flushed and looked down, embarrassed.

His stomach turned again. She knew.

***

The buzzing Monday morning classroom hushed, section by section, as each group noticed that PC Cooper had entered the room. Andrew Stroud and his innocent friends were the first to hush. Then the silence spread to George's table, populated by kids like George, also low down in the school pecking order but at least aware of it. Next, a table of matronly girls, well-fed and well-prepared with thick-soled school shoes, pleated skirts and bulging pencil cases, ceased their talk of teachers and homework, moms and dads. A couple of tables of more confident boys, the football fans and jokers of the class, soon ceased their jostling and teasing as the quiet spread. Last to desist was the table of the desired: Debbie James, Lisa Stanley, a couple of hangers on, and the new girl, Rosie Betts.

After a brief introduction, the headmaster left, taking Wenton with him and leaving the large policeman alone with the kids.

Adele Gibbons, one of the sensibly shoed girls, thrilled internally. Like most kids in the class, she had heard about the death in the woods already. It had been on the TV news on Saturday. On the news there had been no mention of foul play, but they had made an appeal for witnesses, hadn't they?

Who's he after?

Her eyes narrowed as she looked around at the boys and girls of the class. She had spent last Friday night watching television with her mum and dad, then reading a horror story about some American high school kids who got what they deserved. But she knew that was not typical.

They're out of an evening, most of 'em. Up to no good. Up to all sorts. Could be almost anyone.

She had heard some talk but nothing that would help the police. Kids just seemed relieved that such a prolific and unpredictable bully was now gone. And most were excited like her. Another death in the woods? Twenty-odd years after the first ones, the scandal of their parents' teenage years?

Now a copper had come into their classroom. Who did he suspect? Who had been in the woods?

Cooper sat on Mr. Wenton's desk.

- Alright boys and girls. Let's have your attention.

He had their full attention.

- Now as I'm sure you know, there's been a serious incident. A fatality in the woods off Whites Lane.

Cooper paused and looked around the classroom, scanning faces for reactions.

Some fidgeted, some looked down. Andrew Stroud blinked, wide-eyed, thrown by the word 'fatality'. Adele felt her heart beat faster.

He is after someone. One of them boys. They think they're so clever.

- An older boy. Michael Hickman. Did anybody know him?

Some nodded affirmatively. The copper pursued it but did not single anyone out, continuing to address the whole class,

- Just from seeing him at school or are you mates?

The various answers came,

- School.

Look away.

- Play football with him.

Look down.

- Lives in Hospital Lane, sir.

Fiddle with rubber.

- Right. So we all know who I'm talking about then.

Another pause. Another sweep of the faces. None held his gaze now.

Adele Gibbons, too, looked around her with interest.

Or it could be one of them girls he's after. They're no better than they should be. They've been up the woods a few times, I bet. That Debbie.

- Was anybody up by the woods on Friday evening? See anything suspicious?

There was no immediate response. Some shuffling of feet. Studying of graffiti on desks. Scribbling on inside covers of exercise books.

And yet. Cooper noticed some slight movement at the table of the pretty girls. An almost imperceptible exchange of glances. A raising of eyebrows. A slight nod.

He stood from the teacher's table and walked slowly to the board, his back to the class.

Give it time. It's coming. Keep your back turned.

- Well, I'll write my name and the Sedgley station number here and if...

- Ow!

He turned to see one of the girls rubbing her arm. A little smaller and darker than the others, a Mediterranean beauty in the heart of England, she looked down quickly, but as he turned Cooper just caught the afterimage of a waspish glare she directed at her neighbour, a bigger blonde girl. Dusky cheeks flushed red in a heart-shaped face.

- What's your name?

- Lisa Stanley.

- Let's have a word outside, Lisa. Thank you, boys and girls.

Adele smiled and raised her eyebrows as the pouting schoolgirl followed the big policeman out into the corridor.

***

Monday 19th July 1982 - lunch.

It was lunchtime and the dinner hall cliques were forming. George waited in line with his chipped Formica-coated wood-effect tray. Who could he sit with? Paul Thomas and Steven Evans were alone at a table and perhaps attainable. Paul was always alright with him, was his closest link to kids who dressed right and said the right things. And good-looking Steven Evans, a year older and with similar knock-about credentials, would surely accept his company when Paul did.

Yeah, sitting with Evo and Paul, that would be...

A small freckle-faced boy slid up to Steven Evans and punched him hard on the arm before sitting down at their table. Dean Wilson. A troublemaker and policer of hierarchies, he would never let George sit with them, dragging the level down. George knew from bitter experience that were he to join them he would soon become the target of the little redhead's piss-taking wit.

Better not bother.

George looked around at the other tables. Andrew Stroud and some others had herded together for protection at one end of a table, Andrew himself was gazing open-mouthed at curvaceous Mrs. Pym standing near the door on lunch duty, undergoing who-knew-what initial stirrings. Or possibly just staring as he would stare at an earwig on the classroom floor. No, George did not have to join them, the unaware, the oblivious. It was not that bad yet. It would never be that bad, he would rather...

It could get that bad. You're one step above them, now. One beating. One showing up.

Adding to his depression, he saw Rosie Betts in deep conversation with Lisa Stanley and two others. What did those girls talk about anyway?

Boys probably. Comparing us. Laughing.

They were so unattainable, so steeped in mystique that George could not imagine a mundane word passing their lips. Whatever they discussed, it would be momentous and life-changing.

***

At their table, the four girls leaned in, heads close, three of them listening to Lisa Stanley.

- I swear to God; he was up on Turls Hill Road that night. 'Bout nine o'clock.

Turls Hill Road was the paved part of Whites' Lane.

Rosie Betts appeared sceptical,

- But did you see him yourself? What were you doing there at that time o' night?

The two hangers on, Nicola Banks and Joanne Farrell, were taken aback. They had attached themselves to Lisa Stanley, cultivated her friendship and mirrored her look since the first week of starting secondary school, to the point where they now appeared as pale shadows of her. And here was a new girl, challenging her word on the biggest scandal of the week.

- No. I wor there. Debbie Hackett and Roz Braden was up there. Dossing around. They'd been with Simon Green and Michael Hickman but then they started deafin' 'em out, more interested in a motorbike they'd got. So they was coming back down on their own.

Nicola and Joanne felt vindicated on Lisa's behalf. Because of her looks and coolly aloof manner, Lisa Stanley was welcomed into playground huddles and confidences with wayward older girls such as Debbie and Roz, and the story she told rang true.

Rosie insisted,

- But what did he do? Couldn't he just've been 'avin' a walk?'

For the second time that day, Lisa's dusky cheeks glowed brighter. She looked down briefly at the table, closed her eyes then looked up at the other girls' faces. A beautiful smile formed, then collapsed as her eyes creased into laughter,

- With his dick out? - she managed to hiss before the giggling took over.

- Eugh! - said Nicola.

Joanne had put her face down sideways on the table and was banging her small fist theatrically. A few seconds later she raised her head,

- Did they see it? Was... ...it ...?

She couldn't finish. After some more giggling and gasping, Lisa, more than the rest, seemed to have regained her composure. In recent years, as her blossoming looks had won her the un-sought-for attention of men and boys, she had learned to adopt a reserved, even cold, façade at will. She continued, hushed and conspiratorial,

- They didn't see it much. He whipped it back in quick. But it was out! Anyway, he come out from behind the lock-up garages. 'E'd been waiting there for 'em and he come out with his knob out, *paraletic*.

Rosie had giggled and spluttered with the rest of them but still seemed to be looking for holes in the story,

- Are they sure it was him? He's a pretty normal-looking bloke. Lots like 'im.

- He was their form teacher. In 3R last year. They know 'im and 'e knows them. That's why he put it away quick, when he saw who it was. Then he put the hood of his cagoule on and walked off fast. Bit too late by then, though.

Nicola's eyes widened as she thought of the implications,

- Must be shitting 'imself now. Gonna lose his job, prob'ly.

Joanne looked thoughtful for a moment,

- Yeah. Why'd you 'ave to grass on 'im, Lisa? He'll lose his job now, poor bugger.

Lisa looked levelly at the acolyte, then at Rosie.

- You think a flasher should 'ave a job as a teacher? Dirty bastard. Probably wanking over us all night, every night! Anyway, I wor gonna say anything. Not to that copper. Then Rosie punched me arm n' I...

There was a commotion near the dinner queue, and they all stopped talking to look over. A circle of gaping youth had formed around a sneering red-haired boy, Dean Wilson, who was saying something to a white-faced and apparently apologetic George Merriman. A much wider, blonder boy that the girls recognised as Simon Green walked up behind George then swivelled around to poke him hard in the groin. As George reflexively bent over, Green then held George under one arm in a headlock and with the other started beckoning to Dean to pass him something.

Rosie left the girl's table and strode over. As she approached others did too, anxious to gawp at the latest shaming or upset, swelling the crowd. A few voices, intuiting what was about to happen, began to plead on George's behalf,

- Doh do it, Greeny. It ay worth it.

- 'E's only a third year.

- 'E day do nuthin'.

Greeny grinned, enjoying the attention, as he began to squeeze the tomato ketchup bottle, spraying a thin jet of red sauce onto George's screwed-up face.

George squirmed in the beefy lad's grip, the pain in his groin forgotten, panicking as he realised the enormity of the humiliation he was facing. He tried to reverse out of the hold, even pushing with one arm against Greeny's side but, the grip around his neck was too tight. He tried frenetically pulling his body from side to side as if he might somehow wriggle his way out but Greeny was so heavy that his body was hardly swayed by the movement.

A handful in the crowd still protested as the sticky red liquid spread across the captive boy's face. Some walked away. Most jeered and cawed.

Mrs. Pym had stepped out of the dining hall into the corridor and was chatting with Mr. Langley, the art teacher. The dinner ladies, ladling food from aluminium recipients onto plates, were becoming aware of a disturbance and began craning their necks to see through the crowd.

Greeny jerked back George's head and examined his work with the critical eye of a perfectionist. Not satisfied, he used his free hand to rub the sauce all over George's face and into his hair before throwing him to the ground.

On all fours now, George just wanted to leave and wash his face.

Get clean. Get clean and then it's over. They'll never forget but it'll be over.

But Greeny wasn't finished. A victim was on his knees and that was too good to waste. He knelt and once more jerked George's head back, this time by the hair.

One eye was stinging and watery from the salt in the ketchup but the other worked well enough for George to make out a circle of onlookers, facial expressions ranging from concerned to expectant to amused. Boys and girls. Girls.

- Say sorry.

George said nothing, not understanding. Dean Wilson had bumped into him.

Greeny waited only a moment before crashing a heavy fist into George's cheekbone. The pain was nothing compared to the shock of impact. At a deep, irrational level where logic held no sway, the level of shellshock, cowardice and panic, George felt that another blow like that would end the world.

- Say sorry. Fuckin' apologise, yer cunt.

In a scene that, even as it played out, he knew he would replay mentally for the rest of his life, George said sorry in a high-pitched and sob-racked voice. The crowd was silent by now, then one mocking laugh rang out.

Greeny chuckled to himself as he walked away.

***

Solstice.

The sun had gone down on the longest day hours ago and the dancing, drinking and eating of the revellers was now lit only by the big bon- fire and a few dwindling cooking fires. Moths fluttered amongst the highest tongues of flame and fell singed into the fire or were seized by circling bats. A trio of minstrels wearing crude animal masks - goat, bull and fox - played flute and drum near the big fire but for the moment the dancing was sedate as some the chief's trusted men led their wives through formal steps. Nearly everyone from the vil- lage was here, children and old folk included, and many friends and allies from nearby settlements had walked or ridden up or down the valley for this night on which the chief provided food, drink and en- tertainment for all in a show of wealth and power. To attend was to show allegiance and to acknowledge him as lord. Families and groups of youngsters milled around in the orange half-light of the bonfire, tasting roasted beef or lamb, filling their cups with wine or beer or wandering over to chat with some acquaintance. Children flitted around excitedly, playing a chasing game. Groups had also formed on the extreme edges of the gathering, sitting and lying down in the soft, hummocky grass of the meadow, silhouettes all in a shadowy border- land between village and forest where the smell of wood smoke mixed with honeysuckle, grass, fresh sweat and beer. A murmur of conver- sation emanated from this outer belt, punctuated now and again by the odd good-natured guffaw or shriek of laughter.

Gaizka, twenty years old, was sitting on the edge of the festival with Gorka, about fourteen, as far as they knew, and two village boys, Jokin and Endika. He glanced around. All seemed well, families and friends were enjoying themselves. The chief's fiercest fighters were here and armed as always with short swords and daggers but they were with their wives and families and not drunk yet. Gaizka still couldn't believe that he had been allowed to come to the summer fes- tival for the first time, at the age of twenty. His father always went to these events alone, making his family stay back in the house and even then he came back early and sober, staying only long enough to pay his respects to the chief, in his understated way, by helping to stack the big bonfire, carrying barrels if asked and then watching the evening's wrestling contests and games of strength.

But Gaizka had asked anyway, in the kitchen that morning before Aitor and Gorka went to the forge. Neither of the two boys ever worked a full week in the workshop with Aitor; their muscles could not yet stand it, were not yet tempered. They alternated days, doing only light work on their days off from hammering and bending metal, to give their bodies time to recover and grow into the hard profession.

- Can we go with you this afternoon?

Aitor had looked at him, frowning black-browed for a moment, then turned his gaze towards the broad back of young Gorka, squatting by the side of their great stone hearth, for some reason twisting his neck to look up the chimney flue. Aitor's facial expression was inscrutable as always but he seemed to be thinking, like a man calculating the pros and cons of some transaction,

- What would you do there?

- Help set things up. Watch the games. We could take mother.

Aitor's face clouded,

- And have someone insult her? Those who despise us as outsiders and wait their chance to provoke us?

- It's not like that, is it? You said people dance, eat and drink...

- A man was killed once.

- I thought Gorka would like to see the sports. He's good at them. All of them.

- I know.

Aitor hesitated, looking at the door already. Keen to get to his workshop where decisions were simple and even hard metal bent to his will. Then he spoke again,

75

- It could be time for some people to learn of his strength. Gorka!

The boy rose from the hearth,

- Dad?

- You rest this morning. Gaizka will work with me then you two are going to the chief's festival this afternoon.

And now they were there, lying on the grass under the blue-black sky, waiting for the games to begin.

***

Monday 19th July 1982 - afternoon.

A trace of smoke drifted up from a small fire in a sparsely wooded part of the forest. Near the fire was a crude hut.

The nutter's home, then. Or was recently. Bettsy. Michael Betts.

Cooper scrambled and slid down the last steep muddy bank of several, breaking up his momentum by grabbing saplings on his way down or running full into older trees and taking the impact on his hands and chest. To get to this point had involved skirting the muddy rim of the deepest abandoned quarry, clinging to branches and barbed wire as his shoes slipped on the clayey soil. He was now arriving at a flat area of young birch trees and elder bushes, between the base of the slopes and the overgrown barbed wire fence of the allotments.

Picked a good spot. Hard to get to and doesn't lead anywhere. Only daft kids and glue sniffers ever come here.

This really was as abandoned as you could get, he thought. There were bigger and wilder parcels of post-industrial land in the area, such as Wren's Nest wood or the land around the old

Baggeridge Colliery but those other former wastelands were also ecologically interesting enough to attract the attention of local government in the form of landscaping and grants, a little rubbish collection and signposting as wildlife reserves. These woods, separated from the real countryside by the suburbs and housing estates of Sedgley, were semi-sterile in terms of wildlife and practically ignored by Dudley council. Although foxes and rats liked the place, in years of rambling through these fields and forests, Cooper had never seen a rabbit or woodpecker, adder, grass snake or frog. Even the brook was lifeless, polluted as it was by the run-off from a sewage treatment plant hidden behind brambles and barbed wire. Some people would veer off the old toll-road to walk their dogs in the flatter, relatively accessible part of the woods but no adult ever bothered to scale the slopes that Cooper had just struggled up. Except one.

He approached the shack. Bigger than he remembered, or perhaps it had been extended, the walls were made of wooden planks and plywood boards that might have been salvaged from dumps or taken from building sites. The roof was a mix of different materials: corrugated iron, plywood panels protected from the rain by plastic sheeting and the corrugated transparent plastic sometimes used for factory roof skylights. The floor was partly hidden by vegetation but the whole structure seemed to be raised above the ground on house bricks and chunks of limestone.

The rats must drive him mad. Madder.

Pausing six feet from the grimy curtain that covered the entrance, Cooper picked up a stick and threw it on the roof,

- Come out and 'ave a chat then, Bettsy.

- You come in, Cooper.

The voice was hoarse but strong. Cooper brushed aside the curtain and crawled through the low entrance. Once inside, he could stand up straight as long as he took off his helmet. Although there were no windows in the walls, the corrugated plastic skylights let in enough light to reveal clean, unpainted surfaces, basic furniture and tools hung neatly on nails. On a small bookshelf, he could make out the lurid covers of fantasy and science fiction paperbacks along with some battered school exercise books. Other crude shelves were lined with jars and bottles of what appeared to be herbs and mushrooms. A sleeping bag and some clothes were stuffed under an ancient-looking camp bed. On the bed sat a wiry, craggy-faced man a little older than Cooper, wearing jeans and a yellow t-shirt with a Double Diamond beer logo. He looked impassively at the policeman, who felt the need to speak first,

- Go on then, how'd you know it was me?

- Saw you across the quarry from top o' that hill. Had time to come down and get 'im tied up. Wouldn't want to give you a shock. 'E don't like visitors.

The man on the bed grinned to reveal blocky white teeth as he nodded toward a large brindle and white dog, a mastiff cross, curled up on a heap of blankets in a corner.

- You recognised me, at that distance, after all these years?

- I see you around. And you're the only copper that comes up the woods.

- Can I sit down Michael? I have some questions.

- You can take off yer shoes and sit down or we can talk outside, around the cookin' pot.

Outside there was an area for cooking, roofed over but without walls, where a large pot full of liquid was bubbling on bricks over a fire. Four unskinned rabbits hung from the wall. A polecat ferret peered curiously from a wire-fronted box.

- There aren't any rabbits here - said Cooper.

Betts turned and scowled.

- Day say there was, did I? Been down Baggeridge way. It ay illegal. Vermin, they say. Sell 'em to the butcher in Sedgley, Mr. Rollins. 'E doh think it's illegal.

- I'm not accusing you of anything, Michael. Just got a few questions. Might even come and join you out here to live one day. Get away from it all. Don't you get cold in winter?

- Got an 'eatin' system.

Seconds of silence passed until Cooper realised that Betts had no intention of explaining what the heating system was.

- The kids don't bother you? Here on your own? Some right little buggers around nowadays.

Betts's eyes flashed and one lip curled,

- Don't bother me at all...

He harrumphed the answer, as if offended by the question and then seemed to cut his response short.

Cooper considered the angular and broad-shouldered man before him. He was still as strong and powerful looking as when they had known each other twenty years before. More so, if anything, and nobody had messed with him then either.

I bet they don't bother you. What was it Greeny said about the naked man? 'Built like a brick shithouse.'

- Why's that then? Are the kids scared of you? Do you like to give 'em a fright now and then?

Betts hesitated, then shrugged,

- It's hard to get up here. And there's nothing 'ere when you do, 'cept me, the mud and an angry dog. No way out either but back the way you came.

- Fair enough. And I bet they'd be 'appier takin' on old ladies than a bloke like you.

Silence again.

Cooper paced up and down. On top of the rough shelf from which the rabbits hung was a collection of several fossils. He examined a few, the usual impressions of coral, bivalves and snail shells. Moving to near the bubbling pot, he expected to find rabbit boiling away but saw only plant fibres, half dissolved into a green-tinged, frothy concoction.

- What's that?

- Nettle tea. Want some?

- No ta. You got an air rifle, Michael? Pellet gun?

Betts hesitated, then,

- Got two. Old 'uns. BSA. A 22 and a 177.

Like to scare the young chaps with them, Michael?

- You know why I'm 'ere, doh yer? A chap got killed Friday night. What did you see?

- Day see nuthin'. Wor 'ere.

There was fluttering and cawing high above in the tallest most delicate birch branches as a trio of crows briefly fought then separated. Both men glanced up then back down to the boiling pot.

- So where was yer?

- Upper Gornal. Bouncin' at the Labour club.

He wouldn't lie. Not as daft as he makes out.

- Thought you was more of loner, Michael. Can't see you up there, dancin' to Northern Soul with the mods and modettes.

- Me brother set it up. Got an agency. Gets me door work. Twenty quid a night.

Richie Betts. He had something to do with it all, that night in the woods. Nothing you could prove of course.

- What's 'e up to these days? Richie.

- 'E's doin' alright. Buildin' trade and the agency. Got a big house down Enville way.'

Something had caught Cooper's eye. There was a higher shelf just under the roof of the cooking area that he hadn't noticed before. On it rested a rusty horseshoe, more fossils and something else. A small metallic figure. As Michael went over to stir the bubbling pot, Cooper, without knowing why, grabbed the trinket and put it in his pocket. The hermit turned around quickly and stood up, looking Cooper in the eye and walking purposefully towards him.

Shit.

As he faced the possibility of fighting the beast of a man before him, Cooper's legs felt weak and rubbery and he knew his face had gone white. Yet through all the nauseating fear that dominated his body he felt, at some level, a detached curiosity.

Let's see then. Let's finally see after all this time. Just how strong are you?

Michael held his gaze, trapezoid muscles flared, until Cooper could stand the tension no longer.

- Is there a problem?

Michael smiled then,

- Nothin' important.

Cooper felt his body relax but was now confused. He had been caught taking the object, although by what sixth sense he could not imagine, and the thing obviously *was* important as Michael had seemed, for a moment, ready to throw him about the place. Yet now this act of nonchalance.

He's rattled. Defensive for some reason.

An idea occurred to Cooper. Years ago Betts had been questioned many times about the bonfire incident but had had a flawless alibi. Still, now that the ice had had been broken…

Worth a try.

- I've got more questions. About the bonfire.

Although the deaths had occurred twenty-three years earlier, Michael caught on at once,

- That old one!

He chortled deep in his throat but it sounded false. His teeth seemed unnaturally white in the shade of the woods.

- Yer's not gonna rake all that over again, are yer?

- You were there, weren't yer? Earlier that night, at least.

- So was me brother and me cousin, early on.

He levelled his gaze at Cooper, knowingly, then continued,

- And so was you. All night in your case. It was all gone over again and again back then. It was an accident.

- But why did you and your brother leave early?

- I told the coppers all this at the time.

- Do me a favour. Tell me now.

The hermit kicked a waterlogged tree stump,

- We was a bit older than you kids, remember? Already goin' to pubs and the like. We wor gonna mess about with bonfires up the woods.

- You was always up the woods in those days, day and night.

- Nah. We was growin' out of it by then. We'd discovered women, specially me brother! Anyway, it looked like you was gonna get off with me cousin, Amalia. Accordin' to our ways we're not supposed to stand for that. Supposed to defend 'er 'onour and the like. So we went down the Appletree to 'ave a drink. Left you to it.

- And then? What 'appened?

- Only you knows 'bout that.

- But you know I don't. That's the problem.

- Your problem. Not mine. I wor there.

- But...

Cooper was irritated with himself for showing doubt in front of a witness-cum-suspect like Michael Betts. That was one of the first things he had trained himself out of as a young copper years ago. But that rule did not seem to apply here in the woods.

Just ask him straight.

- Did you ever hear about, or do you know anything about a bloke in a mask? A mask with horns?

Betts' face remained impassive, as if he had been asked about the weather,

- Bloke in a mask with horns? Down Cornwall way they got somethin' like that, a kind of old festival. In Spain, too. Not round 'ere though.

- Cornwall? You take yer bucket and spade?

The weak attempt at banter seemed to irritate Betts' and his eyes narrowed for a second then reverted to normal. He stood taller and looked Cooper in the face.

- You go on like I doh know nothing but then you come to me for answers to yer questions. I've travelled more and read more than most round 'ere, you know. You included.

- I see.

There was nothing else to say. The dream of the day before had perhaps been just a dream: a meaningless hallucination brought on by the blows to the head received in the fight with Greeny. And Betts had an alibi for Friday night, which he knew would check out.

- You let me know if you 'ear anything, Michael. Or if anybody bothers you.

Nobody was likely to bother Michael Betts, he knew, and he had not planned to say anything conciliatory, but they had been friends, or at least acquaintances, in other, happier times. The policeman began to walk back up the muddy hill.

- Wait!

Michael went back into the hut and came out again carrying one of the old exercise books. He leafed through it for some seconds then ripped out a page and gave it to Cooper.

- Tek this.

Cooper looked at the sheet, baffled. It appeared to be a poem written in biro in an elegant hand. At intervals, words had been scribbled out and corrections written above.

- What's this Michael? A confession or a love letter?

For the briefest of moments, Michael looked embarrassed,

- Not a confession. No. It's more... It explains 'ow things should be. 'Ow things 'ave to be.

Cooper kept silent.

Totally fucking cracked. Anyone would, out here on his own all the time.

Michael stared at Cooper for a second then turned away, apparently irritated now,

- Anyroads. You'll do what you want with it. Chuck it if you don't want it.

Cooper put the paper in his pocket. Michael was already getting back into the shack.

- Go on then, what's yer 'eating system? - shouted Cooper. But the stocky figure had already disappeared inside.

- Funny bugger.

Cooper started along the difficult trail back through the woods, clambering up and down muddy banks, clutching at birch branches. It was five minutes before he felt himself far enough away to safely look at the trinket he had filched from Michael Betts' shelves. He recovered it from his pocket and held it in the palm of his hand. It was a small, vaguely human-shaped figurine made of metal, probably bronze, pitted and scratched as if immensely old and so crude in its execution that it was hard to make out what it was supposed to represent. To most it would have seemed like a dog-headed man with pointy ears or a big-eared and not very lovable teddy bear. But to Cooper, after the events of the last few days, there was no doubt.

Horns. A man with horns.

***

Temptresses.

- Hey mountain boy! Billy goat!

It was a woman's voice. Drunken. Malicious.

Gorka looked around from his hiding place between the wheels of the apple cart and some empty barrels but could not make out who had spoken. The midsummer night's festival had run its course and all around him, shadowy fire-lit adults lurched about drunkenly, trying to dance but falling, fighting, vomiting, or scrabbling at each other's clothes in seizures of drunken passion. Kept apart from the village by his father, Gorka was not used to seeing adults lose control. He wanted Gaizka, his skinny, worldly, older brother to explain it all to him or at least to make it normal and laughable by being there with him in his safe place. He needed to urinate but did not want to foul his hideout or leave it.

Gaizka had left with a girl. A grinning girl, unsteady on her feet, had come out of nowhere and whispered something in his ear then taken him, incredulous, by the hand and led him away. Gorka had lost sight of them in the milling crowds and now looked out from his hiding place hoping to see his brother reappear to take him home. But he did not. There was wild dancing near the diminishing main bonfire, led by a shaman, naked except for a bull's-head mask taken from one of the minstrels, and some of the dancers were in pairs, holding hands and spinning, laughing and falling dizzily before dragging each other up to dance again or away to the bushes and long grass. Gorka studied them for a while but none of the boys looked like his brother. His young eyes well-adapted to the dark, he scanned the thrashing bodies in the shady peripheries too: a wavy-haired lass riding her recumbent lover threw her head back in ecstasy. As she twisted, he caught a side view of her swaying breasts, heavy and white. He instantly understood a new facet of life and just as instantly had a burning erection. Was that her? Could that be Gaizka underneath? Nearer to where he hid, a strong, black-haired man, for a horrible moment he thought it was his father, pulled apart the long white legs of a much younger woman and lowered his grinning face to her dark groin as her laughter pealed out to the night sky. Elsewhere other couples and threesomes and foursomes did the same and more and Gorka, who had not seen this before, felt excited but ashamed too. He could not forget the darkness of the laughing woman's groin, which he thought would be soft and mustily fragrant like the cool valley air in contrast to the throbbing erection that stung him like a punishment, made worse by the need to piss.

He was worried, too. His father had not told them to come back early but probably expected it. Had the angry woman he had heard before, but not seen, been speaking to him? Perhaps she or some other harridan enemy of his family would now scold him for spying on the lovers, drag him out by his ear and make him go home or take him to one of the chief's men for punishment.

He would not piss in his hiding place. Whoever had called out had gone. He would stand and piss against the wheel. He jerked it out, still rigid, and pissed up.

- I'm still here, billy goat. Would you show your prick to a lady?

He froze, scared to turn around. There had been no one there.

- Do you insult me like that, billy goat? By showing your cock?

She had been sitting still in the shadow of one of the small oak trees that dotted the cow meadow. Now she stood, a grown woman, short but shapely, well-dressed, and walked toward him steadier than most could walk that night.

- Are you a goat or a mastiff? I know your dad always wanted a dog.

She was a lady, the wife of one of the chief's trusted men, a bully and troublemaker called Borja.

He rearranged his clothes quickly then when that was done had nothing to say or do. He watched her approach.

- I think he got his mastiff, that day they found you, no? A protector for his old age. I saw you in the games and the wrestling today. None

could match you.

She seemed friendlier now. For the first time, he felt able to speak,

- It was just the boys' games. The boys' wrestling.

She stopped right in front of him, smiling, slightly amused,

- But you're a man now. You beat them all so easily. And you don't know what went on after that, what was said.

She was breathing hard, he noticed, inhaling deeply like he sometimes did in the forest in early spring when he thrilled to smell the whole world change and felt part of his mind reawaken. She even closed her eyes briefly and seemed to shudder. But it was midsummer, not cold. She was shorter than him and now that her sharp tone of voice had gone, he felt less fear and was curious,

- What was said?

- My husband and his friends were saying that they were going to have a laugh with the winners of the boy's competitions, strip them, throw them in the river.

She smiled and looked him up and down. She was now very close,

- But when they saw how you won, with those big muscles of yours, they lost interest. They started a stupid drinking game and now they're all asleep or crawling around puking and moaning.

With both hands, she took hold of his tunic near the collar and leaned her forehead on his collarbone, inhaling deeply again. He felt the weight of her body, the press of her breasts on his chest and the cool of her brow on his own sweaty skin. The contrast. Her cool with his hot.

- But what I really need to know is…

Her breathing was more laboured now, affecting her speech, and arousing him,

- …are you… …really…

Her cool and his hot.

-... a mastiff for fighting...

There she would be as soft and moist as his prick was swollen and rigid.

- ...or a goat for fucking?

He felt her left hand moving down the front of his body. She found him, hard, and dropped to her knees.

***

<u>Monday 19th July 1982 - evening.</u>

- What happened to your shirt?

George had been heading straight for the stairs, head down, but was now forced to look up at his father.

As he saw the slim, inoffensive man, librarian by profession, emerging from the kitchen, a look of concern on his face, George felt immensely sad.

- I had an...

The pained expression on his father's face made finishing the lie impossible. So how to explain why he had come home with nothing under his black Harrington jacket, his sauce-stained school shirt screwed up in his hand? How to minimise the suffering that now had to be shared?

- Someone squirted tomato sauce on it.

Peter Merriman came closer,

- Why would they do that?

George looked down.

- Bullies.

The childishness of the word saddened him further. It was a reminder of happier days, when as a six-year old devourer of comics, he had tried to tell his smiling dad about some escapade of the Bash Street Kids or Dennis the Menace.

His father sighed,

- Let's see the damage.

George tilted his head back for examination. The poke to the groin, though painful and demeaning, had done no damage. And the ketchup attack had been psychological in nature rather than physical, but he knew that the punch to the side of the face had left its mark.

- Your face is swollen.

Peter turned away, exasperated, thinking. He paced into the kitchen then returned and put his arm around George's shoulders as he used to years before.

- George. I want you to believe me when I tell you two important things. Believe me in both of them. I know about this from when I was a lad.

George's eyes were blurring with tears as he nodded and sniffed. This was the worst part of the whole thing.

- Ok. Here's the first thing. Never think it's your fault, that you should have done something to stop it. If someone like that chooses to do something like this, it's because they knew you couldn't have really defended yourself. They just somehow know about that sort of thing and they don't take risks. It's like an animal that hunts. They can't afford to lose so they pick their victims carefully. Ok? Understand?

Something deep inside George squirmed at his father's use of the word 'victim' to describe him, even indirectly, but he sniffed out a response

- Yes.

- Ok, then. Here's the other one. Always tell me. Tell me and we'll sort it out with the teachers and the school. Or the police if it happens outside school. That's the right way.

He turned to face his son and look in his eyes, hands on his two shoulders now,

- Don't go thinking about doing it the wrong way, eh? Getting a weapon or something, or getting together a gang of your friends to go and duff somebody up, eh?

My friends. Jeremy?

Peter wanted an answer but none came. He continued,

- Ok? That's the way it gets out of hand.

George nodded and smiled, hoping that would be enough to end the chat. It wasn't.

- So who was it? What are their names?

George felt his stomach turn over. It had seemed like his dad understood. But he didn't. A big fuss at the school, an enquiry, would prolong his shame. Add to it in fact, as the scandal would be amplified that way, become a drama.

It had to be done,

- I don't know. Bigger boys, fifth years.

His father looked into his eyes for long, unbearable moments. George looked away.

Peter removed his hands from George's shoulders and begin to turn back toward the kitchen,

- Well, if you don't want to be helped. I can't help you. But I am calling the school tomorrow. Someone must have seen this. What were the teachers doing?

George was allowed to go up to his room. The stained shirt was thrown on top of a washing basket and a t-shirt pulled on. He knew his father would be making their tea: bacon or sausage sandwiches with brown sauce and a dad's hallmark of finger-shaped depressions where they had been pressed down on. But he knew the maker of sandwiches would be preoccupied, per-haps taken back to his own boyhood struggles, hating to see them visited on the next generation.

Wanting to hide, George grabbed a book from his shelf, almost at random, and flopped backwards onto his bed. 'Outdoor Sur-vival'. It had been a favourite for years. He had once read a book about a poacher, set just after the Great War, and had found the combination of country lore, woodcraft and cunning mesmer-izingly attractive. This book had the same type of content but was practical non-fiction. How to recognise animal tracks, how to distil water, catch fish or build fires or shelter with resources found in the wild. And his favourite part, how to prepare a survival kit. With ingenuity and planning one could fill a small metal box, the type used to hold hot mints, with items that would allow you to survive extreme situations. The idea had appealed to him immensely and he had read over and over the list of contents and pored over the line drawings many a time in the unnoticed solitude of his boyhood bedroom: matches dipped in wax, a small piece of rubber from a bike tyre (catches fire readily), fish hooks and line, a magnetised needle, razor blades.... He flicked through the book listlessly at first until he came to the pages about the kit and began to read again, his interest rekindled. He had never actually assembled a survival kit, though. Even as a much younger child, he would have felt daft carrying one around the suburbs or on walks with his dad in the tame semi-countryside of Baggeridge country park or Kinver Edge. But there was still something appealing about the idea of preparing yourself for survival, doing what you could to arm yourself against whatever nature might throw at you. At least you had a chance.

Lying relaxed on the cool, clean bed, he looked at the faint bulges and hairline cracks in the plaster of the white-painted ceiling and allowed his thoughts to run to where they wished, to the often-cherished memories and longings that he associated with the mother he had never known. We were too young, his dad always told him, just kids and her family were very strict and didn't want her to keep you. They almost didn't keep *her*. But then they did take her when they moved away. Your grandma was still alive then and was happy to help, so we kept you. A simple story that rolled off the tongue: so we kept you. He had accepted it without question as a small child. Never having known anything else, it seemed normal to be raised by his dad and grandmother and then his dad alone. The obvious questions about what was she like, where was she now and why they had not wanted her to keep him were only now beginning to concern him.

There had been a series of substitute mothers over the years, some more satisfactory than others. For years, he had had no idea how his dad could have met these women. He didn't socialise, was not a man for pubs or social clubs except the grim local government workers' club in Dudley, the NALGO club, where he would go to play cards or chess and drink small quantities of Banks's mild, while George drank pop, ate crisps and read. The only women there came with their husbands. Then he had noticed, when scanning through the small ads of their local newspaper, the Express and Star, for second- hand bikes or for friendly dogs free to a good home, he could not now remember which, that on Thursday nights the paper ran a lonely-hearts column. He noticed because often when the nine o'clock news came on and he inherited the paper it was left open on those very pages and once, to his embarrassment, he had seen a woman's ad circled in blue biro.

He only remembered three women well. There had been Patty, large, crude and hard-faced, who liked a drink and a loud, red-lipsticked laugh. She had not bothered to hide her distaste on seeing him, the encumbrance, the deal-breaker. Their simulated family trips to Bridgnorth and Stourport had all ended badly. She was really a night person, a booze and fags person, not keen on walks by the river or through cobbled streets between Tudor houses. One final trip, by coach to gale-wracked Rhyll in spring had ended with a frostily silent three-hour bus ride home and that was that.

There had been a pale woman with frizzy hair who dressed like a buttoned-up old lady, mostly in beige, despite being younger than his father. She had at least tried to smile although she had no idea what to say to him except to ask about school subjects. She must have seemed bland and unattractive after the challenging but buxom Patty and his father had eventually let her drift out of their lives. She had worn those old-lady, skin-coloured tights, he remembered with a shudder of distaste.

Then there had been Sue. Blonde and dimpled with brown eyes and a kindly smile, especially for George. She was divorced and was still self-conscious about the weight she had put on during her unhappy marriage, but George liked her curvy figure and had fallen for her very quickly. Looking back, he associated her with summer, with laughing and fun, and with cool, loose clothes, bohemian almost, including floppy hats and sandals with solid wooden soles, like clogs. Mules she called them. In the hot summer of seventy-six, the three of them had gone on holiday together. He remembered a game of cricket one summer evening on a campsite near a river. Sue was laughing as was usual on that holiday and trying to bat while he bowled and George had glanced at his father, in theory fielding but really just standing there relaxed for once, a can of Double Diamond in his hand. He had been struck by his father's expression and still remembered it to this day: happy, and proud, but also bemused to find himself, there, then, with this woman, on a day like this. George was only eight years old but the expression had worried him and so it was not as big a surprise as it might have been when, a couple of months later, a teary Sue had said goodbye, but that she would visit, squashing him to her soft body before her voice gave out and she turned and walked quickly away down their drive to her burgundy mini. There had been no-one since.

He heard a knock at the door and went downstairs to find his dad had already answered.

- Oh, hello.

Someone outside the door said something.

- Yes. Wait a moment. Uh... come in. George!

He was momentarily puzzled by his dad's flustered response. The friends who sometimes called for him were a polite and unthreatening lot and his father always addressed them by name so why...?

Fuzzily through the frosted glass of the inward-opening door George could make out a tall, feminine figure entering their hallway. He did not fully believe it was her until Rosie Betts stepped into the hallway, smiling. After seeing her giggling and whispering with Lisa Stanley's group, he had assumed she had already found her natural place in the school hierarchy and had not expected to get near her again and yet here she was, aiming a flash of a smile straight at him and mouthing a quick 'Alright?' She quickly reverted to prettily polite again as his dad led her into the kitchen, muttering about putting the kettle on and there being Battenberg cake in the fridge. As they left him alone in the hall, he stood there for a moment, adjusting to reality. She had actually turned up at his home, wearing Adidas Kick trainers, stretch jeans and a grey Y-cardigan. But he couldn't remember telling her where he lived. He was sure he hadn't.

George followed them into the kitchen. His dad was opening and closing cupboards and the kettle was already starting to boil. George was briefly mortified as it seemed like the Battenberg cake was not findable.

Not the finger sandwiches!

Then his dad turned around to face them, the brightly-coloured cake in his hands, the packet unopened,

- George, you never said anything about Rosie.

- Rosie's new. Started last week.

The phrase emerged hoarse and stilted. He could not speak properly finding himself in the simultaneous presence of beings from two irreconcilable worlds: adult versus adolescent, library book fiction versus... what? Real life? He willed the kettle to boil and his father to leave and, after a couple of awkward minutes, it was so. He was alone in the kitchen with Rosie.

Across the small table, over cups of tea and slices of cake, he studied her face for signs of treachery. A trick would explain it all. She was here to lead him into some cruel prank, put up to it by her new friends. She grinned back; mischievous but without apparent malice. An imp, a pixie, maybe. Not a devil.

- Did you tell yer dad? - she asked quietly.

The kitchen door was closed but it was a small house.

- About today? He worked it out when he saw the state of me shirt.

She nodded, still smiling as if they were discussing some pleasant and mundane event not his crushing humiliation. He realised that she was being nice, being matter-of-fact on purpose, for his benefit, but it helped a lot.

- I couldn't help you today, not in front of everybody. But help will come. And the other thing? Meeting my aunt and what happened to that Michael? Did you tell your dad about that?

He paused. He had felt satisfaction at the death of Michael Hickman and was aware that this was exactly what he had asked for that night in the caravan but could not accept that one thing had led to the other.

- That was just messing about. No, I didn't.

Yet he felt intrigued.

A twinkle.

A word from the sludge of literature. But that's what it was. It was in her eyes.

She fixed him with her gaze and spoke slowly like a pretend hypnotist, her face mock serious,

- Don't forget: You – Have - Friends. You - Don't – Have – To - Suffer. Now let's go to the fair.

Before he could speak, she raised a hand, imperious,

- Wait! Let's finish this! It's lovely! We never get this!

She looked straight at him as she fed another slice of Battenberg into her mouth and rolled her eyes up as her face contorted with orgiastic pleasure. Then she nearly spat it all out as her act dissolved into laughter. As George gazed at her, the problems of the day and his suspicions about her motives dissolved. It was summertime and he was going to the fair with Rosie. Rosie of the smile and the freckles and the laugh.

They were nearly out of the door when,

- George, can I have a word? He'll be out in second Rosie.

George faced his father in silence as the door was closed on Rosie.

- That girl...

A pause.

- Have you been... approached by anyone?

George's puzzlement changed to acute embarrassment. Was his father about to give him a sex talk? He looked down quickly.

- What do you mean?

- No, no, not that - Peter snorted out a timid laugh - I mean about the bullying.

A flash of realisation crossed his face,

- It's happened before hasn't it? People picking on you?

- Sometimes. Not much.

George shuffled on the spot, irritated now. Hadn't they already had this conversation? Also, Rosie was right outside the door, waiting. George could make out her angular frame through the frosted glass. He realised that he liked her subtly feminine shape. It wasn't bulgingly sexy like some girls at school. Or Mrs Pym. It was something else. Something better. It was part of her and that was good enough.

His father continued,

- What I'm asking is, has anybody approached you about the bullying? Offered to help or something?

George considered the likely consequences of telling his father about his visit to the caravan and Rosie's cryptic comments about having friends and the like. It would sound mad. It was mad - a series of bizarre comments from Rosie, a strange conversation with a person who made her living by lying to the gullible, and then a stranger coincidence. But what if it were real, not a coincidence? The possibility intrigued him. No, he was not ready to share this yet.

-George?

- Approached? You mean by teachers? They don't even know what happened.

His father gave him a long, serious look then his face softened,

- Go on then. Get out.

A worn-out old catchphrase occurred to Peter Merriman. He called out as George went out the door,

- Don't do anything I wouldn't!

But George had already gone, jogging down the road after Rosie.

***

Accused.

The long grass of the meadow was silver in the moonlight, the orange glow of the bonfire now weak in the distance. She lay across from him on, on her side, one elbow on the ground, arm propping her head,

- So now we know. Goat, not mastiff. Goat-boy. I'll be sore for a week.

Gorka had no idea what to say to this woman.

-What do you mean, goat? Mastiff? You know who I am.

- I know what you are.

She seemed cold again now, like when she had snapped at him from the darkness before,

- I'm not from here. I'm a Vascon, taken from my people as a girl. We know your type and we know what you're good for.

Gorka looked down at the grass.

-My father's a good man. We just want to be left in peace.

She made a small sputtering sound, a derisory laugh without humour.

- That's not your family! Haven't you noticed you're a bit different from Gaizka? That skinny wimp couldn't believe it when my maid offered to suck his maggot. Your lot have got cocks like billy goats and you're only good for fucking and fighting.

- My lot?

- Yes. Don't you know that you're a Basajaun? Or part Basajaun. There's not many pure bloods left.

He had heard of the Basajaun: one of the anti-prey. A strong and fast man-beast from the hills, feared by the hunters of old.

- Basajaun aren't real. They're like the fairies or... or the big wildcats in the old paintings.

She had been gazing at the flickering fire in the distance and at *the human detritus of passed-out revellers lying around it but now glanced across at him again.*

- You've seen those paintings on the walls of caves? The giant cats?

- Heard about them.

- Well those big cats don't live in these hills any more but they're real. A merchant showed me a skin. In the south, where this dress was made – she tugged at the garment – they still have them. Bigger than any mastiff or wolf. It takes six men with pikes and dogs to kill one. Your kind are nearly gone too, here in the north, from plague and hunger but it doesn't mean you're not real.

Gorka was silent for a long time.

- I know I was found. They told me that. And that I spoke a strange language when I was little.

She snorted again,

- Well cheer up! You're going to be as strong as a bear and as fast as a weasel. You're already a good fuck! And all the girls will fall for you, now you're a big boy. It's that Basajaun goat-stink. I brought this, wanted you to wear it while we fucked.

She held up a goat-faced mask that one of the minstrels had worn earlier,

- But you distracted me. Put it on now!

She tried to place the mask over his face but he raised his hand to stop her. Her eyes narrowed. She was thirty years old but for a moment looked like a petulant girl,

- You know what happens where I come from? If a Vascon woman can't get pregnant and she doesn't know if it's her fault or the hus-band's?

Gorka didn't answer. She looked around as if eavesdroppers in the bushes might hear the secret,

- They go to the hills! Find a Basajaun lad or an ugly old one even,

it doesn't matter, we like 'em all once we've smelled 'em, once we've had a few good whiffs. They'll knock you out a kid in one! Course it's going to be all horrible and muscly like you and not properly human, well half-human, maybe, but the whispering soon stops and the husband's happy, proud of his strong little son or daughter and none the wiser.

She had got closer to him to whisper this last part.

- Ugh! Now I'm smelling you again and getting all... Who's this coming?

Four tall men were walking towards them purposefully across the darkened field. All wore the heavy bearskin cloaks of the chief's men and all were armed. Gorka looked at her face and knew in an instant that he had been tricked and that his family would pay the price.

She started to shout that she had been raped.

Monday 19th July 1982.

The fair was now in full flow as word had spread around the surrounding areas and the atmosphere was electric with the tension of suppressed violence and the multiple other possible outcomes of congregated youth. The fairground smell was now more intense and complex after days of fermentation: diesel fumes, fresh grass crushed into mud, candy floss, fatty fried food with fried onions, the tang of ozone from the big electric motors that powered the rides, wet look hair gel and dry ice smoke from the waltzers. And youth, pullulating, seething youth: raucous and unpredictable rude boys from the Wrens' Nest and Priory estates with trilbies and two-tone trousers; tram-lined skinheads with their denim jackets and Fred Perry or union jack t-shirts; skinhead girls in monkey boots and chunky jumpers, scooterboys or mods with their graffitied parkas, loafers and white socks; young black men with wet-look hairstyles and leather jackets - and the hybrids, kids who combined elements of mod, skinhead and rude boy style and couldn't have said what they were. The older kids, maybe at their third or fourth visit to the fair could maintain a look of cool, boredom even, as they puffed on cigarettes, chatted and plotted but the younger boys and girls were bright-eyed with excitement as they made the rounds or loitered, recruiting friends to go on rides or just to be seen with.

The only adults in sight were the fairground workers, the cavalier and scruffy young men who tended the various rides or stalls and took money hand over fist, grinning and winking gap-toothed and sleazy at the girls, cadging or bullying fags from the boys. One of them, spindly, constantly grinning Elvis, always drew crowds with his trick of launching himself into a backflip off the top of the waltzer cars, sending the car spinning madly out of control before landing on his feet. He had no front teeth.

As they entered the muddy walkways between rides, Rosie linked arms with George. Despite the suddenly overwhelming atmosphere of the fair, like walking into a wall of sound, scent, colour and motion, he could make out her subtle scent, fresh and feminine. On seeing so many cropped haircuts and stretch jeans, he became conscious of his own wavy hair and straight-legged Levis but also knew that there was nowhere else, nobody else, he would rather have been at that moment. The hair could be fixed. Trousers could be changed. At least his Harrington jacket was not so bad, some kids around him were wearing them. And he already had the right shoes. He was getting there. Despite everything, here was a chance at happiness. You don't have to suffer, she had said.

They wandered and weaved through the crowds between rides: the Mexican hat, the waltzers, a spinning octopus-like machine, a big wheel, a giant, spinning, turning-on-its-axis drum.

'One step beyond' by Madness was booming out from near the spinning drum so Rosie had to put her lips to his ear to say,

- We don't want to go on that!

She nodded at the big cylinder as it slowed its spin, slowly releasing the punters pinned to the inside surface by centrifugal force. Her mouth was so close to his face that it was like a kiss.

- Why not?

Still smiling, almost always smiling, her eyes narrowed, cat-like,

- They spit.

She squeezed his arm for emphasis as she repeated,

- The silly buggers spit and it comes back and hits somebody in the face!

He grimaced but that seemed weak so added,

- I'd probably puke, then. That'd be worse.

She laughed and nuzzled her head against his cheek, taking and squeezing his hand at the same time.

They were now very close to the powerful sound system of the waltzers. A new track began, a punky classic from years earlier with upbeat drumming and fast, soaring guitars,

- I love this one! Me auntie too!

She beamed at him swinging his hand within hers, moving in fidgety little skips on the spot, too excited to stand still. He froze in embarrassment. Did she expect him to dance right here? A trilbied Rude Boy leaning on the rail of the waltzers cast a stern, appraising eye over the couple. Rosie's eyes crinkled as she laughed at George's embarrassment and grabbed his other hand, pulling him closer, face-to-face. Awkwardly, he allowed himself to be drawn forward, hands in front of him. She had stopped skipping, was nearly still, but was trying to sing along without knowing all the words. Like a child she unashamedly trala-la-ed the start of each line, mouthing the words until the distorted, girl-like voice of the singer prompted her memory,

.... *my natural emotions,*

... . *feel like dirt and I'm hurt,*

...... *if I start a commotion,*

...... *run the risk of losing you and that's worse*

Finally embarrassed, she collapsed into more laughter and rested her brow in the hollow of his neck, hiding her face in his chest. Her scent and touch again became the whole world and made the throbbing, thumping, fairground diminish to nothing.

- Alright Rosie!

Lisa Stanley had emerged from the crowd and was looking at them with one perfect eyebrow arched, amused and not un-friendly. Nicola Banks and Joanne Farrell at her side were look-ing George up and down, unimpressed.

Thinly-veiled disgust wrote the ticker-tape of cliché in George's mind.

- What you two lovebirds up to?

As Rosie turned to look, Lisa gave her the full Lisa Stanley smile, as warm and timeless as the Mediterranean dusk. The two hangers-on took note and smiled too.

- Just dossin' - said Rosie.

- Got any money? - asked Lisa.

Rosie chuckled,

- My aunt works 'ere, remember? What d'ya want to go on?

The fair smell was strongest on the platform of the waltzers, where they waited for the ride to stop. The music was at its loudest here too, 'On my radio' by the Selecter. A few yards away a local celebrity, the journeyman boxer Ronnie Campbell, in black leather jacket and cap, was holding court to a group of black lads, punctuating some long and probably violent anecdote with punches to the air and drawing shrieks of laughter and leg slapping from his crowd. George had read about 'leg slapping mirth' in books but not seen it until now.

The waltzers stopped and a gaunt attendant in a sleeveless denim jacket was lifting up the bar for them to get in when...

As a young child George had been troubled for years by a recurring nightmare in which he heard a knocking at the front door, left his bedroom and, inexorably and against his will, moved down the stairs toward the glass-panelled door, which he knew he must open. He already knew what was waiting behind it: four grotesque dwarfs, one dressed in shabby top hat and tails like a circus ringmaster, the others like storybook tramps. Somehow he knew they were the incarnation of evil, made no less terrifying, in fact more terrifying, by their bizarre clothing and stunted bodies.

Echoing the terror of that childhood dream, the events that

now played out in front of him were so horrific and baffling that they left him powerless to react.

Greeny and three mates had appeared from nowhere next to George and the four girls on the platform of the waltzers. In the spirit of the fair, each had incorporated carnivalesque elements into his appearance that evening: Dean Wilson was wearing his pilot jacket inside-out, revealing the quilted, bright orange lining; Colin Bull was wearing black and white Jam shoes with odd Day-Glo socks, pink on one foot, green on the other, while holding under one arm a lurid yellow toy rabbit, won from a stall or snatched from some weaker kid; in stretch jeans and Italian combat jacket, Steven Campbell was the most normal in terms of dress although his grey trilby was so small that it perched on his head like Pinocchio's Tyrolean hat. But, as he was a mixed-race kid who suffered from vitiligo, the spreading white patches around the mouth and eyes of his otherwise honey-coloured features gave his face the appearance of a skull mask with the colours inverted.

As in the nightmare, George couldn't hear. He couldn't speak. He couldn't move.

He could watch, in slow motion.

Greeny was saying something to the girls, leaning forward, putting his arm around Lisa Stanley and Nicola Banks' shoulders. George realised with a sinking heart that his oppressor was good-looking, in a piratical way, despite his nose. His front teeth were very white but when he grinned yellowing canines were revealed. The girls did not recoil from his clumsy embrace but laughed and shrieked as his weight unbalanced them and dragged them forward.

They like him. Of course.

It seemed incredible but...

They know him and they like him.

Dean Wilson was looking around in his reversed jacket: a small, bored predator. A stealth hunter like a weasel or a viper.

Don't notice me.

Colin Bull. Tall and broad in his camouflage jacket and surreal footwear. Easily led. Drunk or glued-up, or pretending to be, he copied Greeny's two-girl-lunge tactic and grabbed Rosie and Joanne with the added flourish of rubbing the cuddly rabbit in Joanne's face. Surprisingly Rosie did not sag under his considerable weight but both girls shrieked and laughed as they fought to extricate themselves or pretended to do so. Sensing the route of least resistance, he pulled Joanne towards him, holding her body tight to his, face-to-face and said something. She did not struggle except to squirm her face away as he tried to nuzzle her neck with his great head.

Steven Campbell stood back from the rest with his hands in the pockets of his combat jacket. Sullen, perhaps conscious of his disfigured face in the evening sunlight. He had noticed George,

- It's the fuckin' ketchup eater.

Greeny, still busy holding two girls, was now whispering something in Lisa's ear but Dean Wilson was free and still bored. He came over to George, a slow cocky walk, legs relaxed, the grin on his lips belied as humourless by his icy blue eyes,

- Got any money? Wanna get a hot dog? I'll give you a squirt of me ketchup.

Tell him he's a squirt, you coward.

Dean and Steven grinned as George felt unable to answer.

- Yer fuckin' prat - said Dean and, snatching the fluffy yellow rabbit from Joanne, he casually clouted George across the face with it. Then addressing everybody except George,

- Let's 'ave a go on the waltzers, then.

The girls looked variously down or away from George's shameful passivity as they waited for the ride to stop again, then let themselves be pulled into the compartment. George sought out Rosie's gaze but she too was looking down except for a brief, beseeching glance his way as she allowed herself to be dragged into the waltzer car with the rest.

- Sit tight, sit tight. Hold on. Hold on. Get ready for the ride of your life...

The ride operator's amplified patter was drowned out by the opening bars of Donna Summer's 'I feel love' as the cars slowly began to move. Elvis, star of the Waltzers, jogged backwards between cars before grabbing the rim of one and giving it a perfectly-timed shove as it descended into a dip in the track. The momentum gained sent the car spinning wildly to the shrieks of the girls on board.

Numb with disappointment, shame and anger, George wandered off into the crowd, oblivious now to the dangers and attractions around him. An opening door had been closed in his face, he realised. The new girl, by ignoring the hierarchies and limitations of their lives, had allowed him to glimpse a type of existence that might have been.

It's not even her fault. She didn't know. Now she's with them.

He wandered away from the noise and bustle of the waltzers into quieter, darker pathways behind rides and stalls, between parked caravans and trucks.

What if I killed myself? How would they feel then?

Bu the old and familiar fantasy wouldn't take. He couldn't imagine a sad Rosie, sadness didn't seem compatible with her vitality, and the thought of his father's too-easily-imaginable grief soon spoiled the daydream.

If he were to live then, what kind of life could he have?

You don't have to suffer. You have friends.

She had said something like that and there was evidence that, however inexplicable, it was true.

He realised that he was now in the centre of the fairground folks' living area. It was dusk and the washing that hung from lines tied between scruffy, oversized caravans threw long shadows. A mongrel dog looked at him nervously then crept silently into the darkness of the wheel arch of a parked Bedford lorry. The blaring music of the fair had faded to an indistinct rumble that blended with the humming of large diesel generators, punctuated now and then by high-pitched but distant screaming like that of tormented souls in some inescapable adolescent hell.

The fortune-teller's caravan had to be somewhere close. If he could talk to her again, he could probably make her understand that it wasn't over yet, that he still needed help. He soon found it, large and shabby.

There was a light on inside.

***

PART TWO

Enslaved.

In the centre of the settlement there was an interior space of grass, beaten earth paths and small wooden huts, some dwellings, some workplaces, some both. About two hundred households in total. One bigger hut was used for gatherings and there was a squat, stone-walled tower to provide refuge in case of attack. The smallest children played on the grass between the huts. Around this living area were three concentric circles of earthworks and trenches and on top of the earthworks there were log fences and gates with arrow slits. The gates were left open most of the time as that part of the valley bottom had long been stripped of its trees and so any approaching enemy would be seen from a distance. In one of the workshops, the blacksmith Gaizka worked hard to complete the day's quota of axe heads set by Borja, the chief's taskmaster. After fifteen years of forced labour at Borja's forge, his once-weak arms and torso were now well adapted to the jarring, heavy work and his forearms bulged bigger than the calves of a normal man. But still the quota was high. The muscles of his arms were so gorged with blood that they no longer worked properly. His left hip ached from taking most of the weight of his body on his one good leg as he stood at the anvil.

He stopped hammering and stood back for a moment and as he did so saw a child run past the doorway. This was not unusual. He would often stop his work to watch the small children play and remember his own freedom, the time when his father had kept their family independent and proud. Then another small hurrying form ran past. Then another. All going in the same direction. Gaizka thought that perhaps they were rushing to watch a fight or perhaps some angry mother or dog was chasing them. The hammer blows were still ringing in his ears but he thought he heard shouting too. He had to work but was curious and walked to the door, limping heavily as usual.

An old woman dressed in tattered robes had entered the compound and was now surrounded by a handful of women, some of whom seemed to know her, and all of the children. She was tall and straight despite her age and chatted happily with the curious women while reaching into her cloak to give out treats to the children. She had been carrying a rough sack, heavy and bulbous as if full of cabbages or swedes and put it down now to talk and laugh with the others. At one point she said something and one of the women pointed toward Gaizka, standing in the doorway of his workshop, by way of answer. She looked at him for an instant then looked away quickly before continuing her banter with the crowd of women. Then she picked up the sack and two women led her away into a hut. The crowd dispersed, and the children resumed their play.

Tuesday 20th July 1982.

With a grunt of satisfaction, Cooper laid down the heavy dumb-bell for the last time that night, stood up and rolled it into a corner of the darkened living room with his foot. Covered in sweat despite wearing only an off-white vest, shorts and Dunlop trainers, he slid down to sit on the floor and regain his breath there rather than rest his sweaty back on the sofa. He had been circuit training using bodyweight exercises and a single heavy dumbbell. Should one of his many fights one day go bad, either at work or on one of his pub crawls, he felt he would be ready. Each workout seemed harder than the last but he would be as ready as he could.

Now what?

He wasn't going out. He never went out after exercise, based on the belief that he would surely end up getting in a fight and los-ing if he left the house in a weakened state. He had listened to his LPs too many times and could not face them again. Nowadays they were for the girls and women he brought home, not for him anymore, if they ever had been. And that last girl, the Red Lion one, Haley? She had hated his old rock albums, he recalled with a smile. She had screwed up her face in disgust at the sight of them.

That was a disappointing night all round for young Haley.

Getting old. Too old for that game. For everything.

He would eat beans on toast and drink a bottle of Pale Ale. There might be something on telly. He couldn't remember if it was the night for *Dave Allen* or *Not the nine o'clock News.* If not, he had his small library of books and his collection of Boxing News back issues.

So that's a fucking treat lined up then.

Then he remembered the poem that Michael Betts had given him outside his hut in the woods.

He found it in the pocket of his uniform jacket, hanging in the bedroom and sat on his mattress bed to read it. It was handwritten in biro with many scribblings out and only became legible when he smoothed the crumpled paper flat before him, and turned on the lamp,

In the Woods you will find him.

Your shackles will bind you and keep you from harm,
in factory, council house, schoolyard and farm,
But dare you slip chains and consort with the master?
Drink nectar, cavort, let your poor hear beat faster?

In the woods he awaits you with servants from hell,
(Turn back at the sound of your factory bell!
Deny your true nature, original joy,
Shun the woods and back lanes you caroused as a boy!)

Caress a young maiden or fight for your life?
No, we'll always find you at home with the wife,
Blood vengeance and sport, rough unplanned love,
All now denied by your meek god above

Rebel while you can, and embrace the true way,

Hurt him what hurts you, have a roll in the hay!

And should someone slight you, trouble your clan,

At night in the woods let true God possess man.

Cooper looked at the paper for a while.

What had the hermit said? Something about the poem explaining 'how things should be'? Whatever he had said, the poem was not evidence and the hermit was neither witness nor suspect. In fact, according to CID, there was not even a crime to investigate.

There was wicker waste paper basket in the corner of his living room and he crumpled the paper again and tossed it in that direction. It bounced in off the wall.

- Must've been on the wacky baccy. Daft bugger.

His joints aching and his muscles tired, Cooper limped into the kitchen, looking for beer and baked beans.

***

Cast out.

- *I'll tell you a tale, then, if that's what you want.*

There were large fires at each end of the longhouse. Children played with their wooden toys in the flickering orange glow of one great hearth. Because dusk was the best time for hunting and for sinking the eel nets, the men had not yet returned and it was mainly women and children who sat on seats and rugs near the other fire listening to the stories of the old folk. Here in the long shadows on a rainy autumn evening, no line was drawn between rich and poor and the wives and daughters of powerful men sat near serfs, menders of clothes and those who relied on handouts. It was the tall old lady from outside who had spoken, encouraged by the women who knew her,

- *A special tale. Of travel and love. With meaning for this place.*

There was a murmur. Some looked around and grinned, faces glossy and flushed in the close heat of the fireside. This might be good. None said no to the offer of a story.

- *It began with a beating. A horrible, unjust beating of a boy for a crime he had not committed. They cracked his skull with clubs studded with iron and had their horses trample his unconscious body. He was dragged out from his village behind a horse and his broken body left for dead by the road.*

A girl's voice came from the darkness.

- *Who was the boy? What had he done?*

You were allowed to ask questions and sometimes the story would change as a result, the teller moulding her tale to the audience,

- *You have to listen well, my girl. I said he had not committed the crime. His family's enemies wanted him cast out so they invented a crime for him and did what they did.*

All were silent now. Even the children at the other end of the long hall seemed to be playing thoughtfully, subdued perhaps by the thrum-

ming sound of rainfall on the thatched roof and the unaccustomed late evening darkness that had arrived with autumn.

- He was found by a woman, old but not as old as me, and taken in. She too was an outcast from the village and she used her pony to drag his heavy body to the shack where she lived alone. She was a wise woman, an expert in remedies and the ways of the old ones.

- How did she live, an old woman alone outside the village?

- If you are different you have to find your own way and she had done so. The villagers did not understand her for she had been a woman who loved women, when younger. But the woman who had first loved her, long dead by then, had also taught her the lore of plants and their uses. So although she was despised by the men, and by all in public, when the hunters and fishermen were away, the women would come to her with their sick children or their own ailments and pains and she would help them and be paid well. It was said she could both stop the birth of unwanted children and help the barren to conceive. Women from rich families kept sending food, salt and clothes for years afterwards, either from gratitude or to pay for her silence perhaps. Anyway, she cleaned his wounds and used her medicines and poultices to stop infection. She hid him from the women who came for help or to leave gifts and slyly questioned them to find out what had happened. She heard the tale of his supposed crime but also enough about his accusers to allow her to guess the truth. She fed him and gave him milk from her goats. She couldn't do anything about a cracked skull but to her surprise that and all his broken bones, the ones she could splint, healed in a month, faster than she had seen before in many years of healing. When she saw this, she realised that he was a Basajaun and laughed at herself for not seeing it before.

A little girl's voice came from the darkness,

- What's a Bazawon?

There was laughter. Then a boy's voice,

- They´ re fairies from the forest. They take children and leave their own in their place.

117

The old lady smiled indulgently,

- That's not exactly how it happens.

Some of the adults chuckled now. The woman continued,

- The Basajaun are just the old ones, the people who lived around here before us, hunting and finding food but not growing crops or keeping animals like we do. They are not little fairies or big monsters but look a lot like us. They are clever, strong and very, very fast. Now they only live in the highest hills, sometimes in caves, and there are less now than there used to be.

- Why?

- The answer to that is coming later in this story.

- What happened with the boy? The Basajaun boy that she saved?

- He got better. After weeks of groaning and puking, one day he started to speak. He explained what the old woman already knew, that he was the son of the blacksmith, a man she had heard of, and had grown up in that same valley but in the hills, on the other side of the river.

On hearing this part of the story, some of the old folk, the out of favour ones, skinny in their poor clothes, seemed troubled. They looked at each other sideways or glanced at one woman in the group, the wife of a warrior, still attractive in her middle age. Some looked at their feet. The storyteller had not stopped,

- Once better, or nearly better, the boy told his healer that he had to return to protect his parents and brother from enemies. She knew he was not the birth son of the blacksmith but she understood that he had to go. She warned him to go straight to his father's house but by night and avoiding the village. She went to her hoard of treasure, the unused gifts of many years of payment, and came back with a cudgel and a short sword for him. That evening he left.

Friday 23rd July 1982.

Old Driscoll did not feel so old as he walked back down to the stables through one of his own fields. There was a juvenile bounce in his step as he traversed springy mattocks of grass or skirted clumps of nettles. A boyish twinkle in his eye reflected the mellow early evening sun, still at treetop height, still warm on his bristly chin and hooked old man's nose despite the rain drops that were beginning to fall. Rain was good. It would keep them in the barn. He quietly rejoiced in the prospects of the evening: the golden glow from his fields and the smell of fresh summer air, rain, grass and mud; the thought of the two girls waiting for him in the barn; the clink of cider and beer bottles and cans in the plastic bag he clutched in one claw-like hand.

- ´Ere I am, then. ´Oo wants a drink fust?

Due to his own excitement his voice came out louder than he had wanted as he ducked into the musty gloom of the small, roughly built stable where the girls were sheltering from the rain. The smaller, darker one arched thin eyebrows and rounded her Cupid's bow lips in a timeless caricature of innocent surprise. The taller, blonde one turned to face him, raised a cigarette to her lips and narrowed her eyes mischievously as she drew on it. The blonde looked him up and down then coolly held his gaze,

- You said we could ride the osses.

She knows it ay abaht osses.

- You'll 'ave to wait a bit. I told yer, that's for later. When the owners ay abaht. They ay my osses, them just on my land.

She sighed, theatrically,

- Lets 'ave a look at that bag ´o booze then, Driscoll.

Rosie Betts flashed a reassuring, sparkly smile at Lisa and they both spluttered into laughter.

***

At first the fumes were too strong and made Greeny jerk the freezer bag away from his face to retch and choke. But already, just from that first aborted inhalation, he was aware of a shift in his mental state. Somewhere behind his eyes he had felt an almost physical transition, like a turning inside out, and he was already starting to perceive some aspects of the world differently: his sense of touch was instantly changed. Numbed. Tingly. His hearing seemed somehow sharper and the sounds he heard seemed more interesting. More relevant. He felt that he should focus on them, concentrate on their deeper meaning.

Sitting opposite him, on the other side of the small fire they had made in this hidden corner of the woods, behind dense thickets of elderberry bushes and bramble, was Colin Bull, big, burly and affable. Bully also coughed and spluttered,

- Fuckin' good stuff innit?

Greeny didn't bother to answer at first. The 'stuff' was always exactly the same. From the same factory. There was no good or bad, like with beer or whatever. That was bollocks.

- We talkin' or we doin' this? - he finally snapped.

He had never done it with Bully before and the 'good stuff' remark just confirmed his suspicions that the big chap didn't really get it. Probably didn't even have dreams. Some glue sniffers didn't get dreams, just talked about getting a 'buzz'. So they were pricks. Why do it and put up with the headaches and the drowsiness afterwards if not for the dreams? Others, too scared to really have a go, would hold the bag somewhere near their faces for a couple of minutes, pretending to inhale but not really, then stagger around as if drunk. But this stuff didn't make you drunk, that's not what it was about. You did it for the dreams.

He continued to glare at Bully over the smoke of the burning hawthorn branches on their near extinct fire, pointedly not putting the bag to his mouth again until he felt satisfied that he would be quiet and let him concentrate. He really wanted to listen, but not to Bully.

The choke reflex now past him, he began to breathe deeply into the freezer bag again, concentrating on the rhythmic rustling sound of the thin plastic as it filled and emptied, filled and emptied.

**

Driscoll hurried back down through the field toward the barn once more. He had been sent on an errand but it was all to the good. It was a sign that his plan was beginning to work. His excitement, expressed in a kind of internal monologue, made him grin. Made him want to rub his hands together in anticipation and jump up and click his heels together with joy,

Saddles eh? Little sluts! Little… vixens! I'll give you a ride! Too stuck up to ride bareback! Not too stuck up to knock back me booze, smoke me fags!

Such was his state that his bandy legs could hardly carry him properly over the uneven, downhill terrain. He stumbled but caught his stride before falling then was brought to a halt anyway by a fit of coughing.

Won't be easy, now, steady up. Game's not won yet! They're spoilt nowadays with their school dinners and their free milk… Not like in the war! Rationing! They were grateful, back then. Knew the value of things.

He stood still, bent over, hands on knees, until he regained his breath.

I've got a chance though. Their mums and dads and little boyfriends don't give 'em everything. Not Bulmer's cider! Menthol fags. Five-pound notes! Oo's gonna give 'em all that, 'cept me? And oss rides! Not all at once, mind. Not at first. Up the stakes, bit by bit. But up the rewards, too. Let's get that pretty little one on an 'oss.

He had reached the barn.

It was empty. Empty of girls. Empty of booze.

***

As Greeny focused down on the sound of the plastic bag filling and emptying, it became louder, warmer and more comforting, like a mother's heartbeat to a baby in the womb, shutting out all else. Within seconds he felt the thrilling deep shift, the shift of perception as sound became image, image became sound. He was in a world of blackness, warm and secure, hearing nothing now but transfixed in contemplation of a pulsing web of multi-coloured light that expanded and contracted rhythmically before him. The fighter in him rebelled for a moment, instinctively refused to succumb, and he snapped back to real-world consciousness, becoming briefly aware that he was sitting on a log, near a fire, in the woods. With Colin Bull. Finding no danger and irritated with himself for messing up his own trip, he resumed his deep inhalations. Soon the colour dream returned. Now between the gaps in the main web of light, he could see other, distant universes of light, themselves pulsing with light-life, and within their gaps, in turn, were other…

He slumped and then fell sideways off the log, by chance away from the fire, coming to a stop with his head resting on one arm near a bank of nettles and his side and rump in the ashy remains of an older fire.

He stared into the nettles and became aware of the strange, sad music radiating from them. He began to wonder why he had never noticed it before but then suddenly knew the answer: because it was thought-music not sound-music, of course. Not everyone gets it. He then understood that there were small and gentle beings living in the undergrowth. Unseen and unseeable, he nevertheless felt their benign presence. Touched by their innocence, he wished them well. In full communion now, they responded: they wished him well in return. All was harmony in the undergrowth world.

- What the fuck's 'e smiling at? - muttered Colin Bull but Greeny was too far gone to hear.

Now that Greeny was out of it, Bully had given up pretending to glue-sniff. He liked a fag, a bit of booze, not breathing in chemicals. It made him choke and if he were honest, he would admit that he never had dreams. Of course, being a teenage boy he was far from honest and, if pressed, could and would effortlessly make up the most lurid and bizarre dreams at will, just as routinely as he would exaggerate any of his sexual experiences, arguments and fights. He had a salvaged half-fag in the pocket of his jean jacket and he didn't fancy sharing it with Greeny so he began to walk back toward the path, picking his way carefully between bush and bramble. He'd be back in a minute.

Greeny lay smiling in the ashy clearing in the bushes. But the smile gradually faded from his face and a frown furrowed his smooth young brow as he slowly became aware that evil stalked the land. The little beings he had communed with sensed its coming and tried to warn him, their sad music becoming urgent then frenetic as they fled to ancient hiding places deep in the nettle forest.

Then it happened. All hope and joy in the world was extinguished and Simon Albert Green plunged into a black mindscape of dread. He could not move, hear or see but felt the presence of the Minotaur moving nearby. Without seeing it he knew that steam rose from its rough black fur. Hideous gore dripped from its wet muzzle. Its dark eyes swivelled, searching for him, malevolent beyond reason, getting ever closer.

Suddenly they were face to face.

Panic surged inside him. He couldn't move and was helpless before the immense hatred and ancient cruelty of the giant beast before him. It snorted then screeched with rage as it began to rain down clubbing blows from gorilla-like arms and fists.

The rules of existence changed suddenly and Greeny could move, but only his arms, and they were weak and floppy. Horrific, shuddering impacts to his head deepened his panic and he felt the approach of oblivion in every blow until...

Got yah. Yer fucker!

By force of will his strength was back and he had the beast by the neck. Had grabbed some matted fur or flap of skin there. The creature bellowed and writhed and a musty stink filled his nostrils, but he had it! Greeny began to pound the meaty head with the power of a man fighting for his life. Soon the animal weakened enough for him to get hold of both lapels of its jean jacket and spin them both around so that he was now on top...

- What the fuckinell? It's me, Greeny! Bully!

Greeny stopped punching. He remained sitting on Bully's chest for a few seconds, breathing heavily, allowing reality to re-establish itself in its own time. Pinned underneath Greeny, Bully looked up, trying to judge whether the bad dream had receded enough for him to talk and move again without provoking another flailing attack.

Stiffly Greeny rose to his knees then manoeuvred sideways so that he was sitting back on the log again. He hated the bad dreams but at least he had them. They were the price you paid for the good ones. He glared at Colin Bull for long seconds then,

- What you dream about then?

- Me? Er, I dreamt about a great big fuckin'...

Bully had no idea what he was about to say but he knew it would come to him. He could always come up with something plausible,

- ...big fuckin' factory, man! Fuckin' suck factory that makes all kinds 'o sweets, chocolate and stuff. An' there's all these different big rooms with giant machines in for making the suck and there's these little blokes what work in the factory...

Greeny was sceptical,

- That's a film ay it? That was on at Christmas.

Bully stood up and made a show of knocking some of the ash off his clothes before Greeny's unsympathetic gaze.

- I dunno. I never sid that one. Look, before y'went off yer fuckin' head and jumped on me, I was coming to tell yer. There's two wenches comin' up the path. They've got a bag o' summat. Looks like booze.

***

Revelation.

The tale went on. A boy had a question for the teller,

- Did the fairy boy find his family?

- Not fairies, I've told you. People. A lot like us. A bit squarer of head, much stronger of limb and fast like a polecat, but people. Some think them handsome. Yes, he found them. He found his father's house empty of furniture, the workshop gutted, the anvil gone. High in the pastures behind the house, near the edge of the beech forest, he saw something new and climbed through the overgrown meadow to find two earth mounds, graves with flowers on top, and there he cried.

A girl of twelve, pretty and well-dressed, gasped,

- His mom and dad?

- Yes. The blacksmith and his wife. The ones who had taken him in and raised him.

- What happened?

- He knew what had happened as soon as he saw the graves. Those jealous of his father's skills and independence had made their move and now his parents were dead and their forge was in the village. But he needed to know how they had done it and what had happened to his older brother, also a blacksmith.

A black-haired girl of fourteen, shiny-faced from the heat of the hearth, called out,

- It's Gaizka, our blacksmith! The crippled slave. He's in the story!

Younger children let out exclamations of delight. Could it be true? Someone they knew in a story? Someone who spoke to them? Made them toys? They fell silent when an old man, a once-great hunter long fallen out of favour, spoke sternly, his deep voice filling the hall,

- Let her tell the tale, young lady. She says we'll learn from it.

The other old folk, the thin ones in poor clothes, looked unhappier still. The girl who had yelled was the daughter of a storied warrior, a rich man, and it was asking for trouble to scold her in public. But the old woman was shaking her head and smiling, eyes closed.

- There are many villages with a blacksmith, my pretty. Let's not draw morals from this tale till it ends.

The girl turned her head away with a mock pout before breaking into a sideways grin at her friends. What did she care? The world was hers. The story went on,

- So the boy made his way toward the village. He did not walk on the path but followed the treeline high above it, so that he could see any travellers who might pass below but his own silhouette would be masked by the darkness of the forest behind him. When he dared get no closer to the village, for it was not yet full dark, he came down and hid in a copse of trees and fern right by the path and waited there. After not too long a wait, a figure came into view, walking slowly, carrying something heavy. The boy grasped his short sword. If this was a man who had killed his parents, or even an innocent man who would not give answers, he would plunge the sword right through his chest. He felt the power latent in his body like a drawn bow and knew he could do it. He wanted to do it. Then he saw that this was no warrior, nor even a hunter, but a fisherman carrying a wicker basket that would be full of gasping eels from the traps. He hoped that the man would speak and that he would not have to kill.

- Were they traps like ours and eels like ours?

The young daughter of a fisherman had blurted it out.

- Yes, exactly the same. But don't worry about your father. This happened before you were born. No one lies in wait for him tonight.

There was something about the way she said it. Had a surge of emotion or excitement slightly constricted the old lady's speech for a moment, before being willed away? Or had she lingered on the word 'him'? The powerful man's wife, until then smiling golden in the firelight, aware of her splendour, now frowned and looked about. But the story continued.

- When he saw the sword and cudgel, the young fisherman thought it was a roaming thief that stood before him and dropped his catch so the robber could help himself. He said with disdain that he was unarmed and would not be getting killed for a few fish. Take them if you need them, he said. But when the boy stepped further from the shadows into the moonlight the fisherman knew him as the one from outside the village who had been killed and was ready to run from the ghost before him.

- Woo ooh ooh oo ooh!

A cheeky boy, bored with this slow story that led nowhere, had made his best ghost noise and his friends all chortled in support before being shushed and cuffed into silence by their elders so that the story could continue,

- I'm not a ghost but answer my questions and do not shout or you will be, he said as he grabbed him. The fisherman felt the strength of the grip, and saw the blade before his face and began to speak: when you were thought dead, robbers, outsiders, began to raid your father's house at night. One night they killed your parents and fought with your brother, wounding his leg. They were taking the forge and all the tools when some of our hunters happened by and chased them off. Then the forge was moved to the village so your brother could work in safety and for the good of all.

- It's our Gaizka.

But no one was listening to the whispers of the black-haired girl. All watched the woman, all listened to the tale,

- You insult me by repeating these lies and I would kill you now, said the boy, but I need you to carry a message. You will speak to the men who killed my parents, their leader and his wife. Especially his wife. Tell her that tonight you saw a spirit, a god from old times in the form of a goat-man. He promised revenge for those killed and will return when the moment is right. He will return at the head of a host of demons like him and none of her men shall survive his revenge.

At last the noblewoman, the Vascon, rose to speak, her face pale, her *voice trembling,*

- *We welcome you to our fireside from pity, old hag, and you spread gossip against our best families? Against warriors who have saved this village from enemies and made it rich?*

The older woman's face did not change,

- *I was invited here and asked to tell a tale, that's all. Don't fear me. I shall not beat anyone with a cudgel nor drag your children under horses. Not I.*

The Vascon turned to the old hunter.

- *Drag her out. She insults our house. Strip her of her rags and leave her in the cold.*

His deep voice rang out again,

- *I'll not harm a woman. And if her tale is just a story, not the truth, then she insults no-one here.*

The storyteller addressed the old man,

- *That one talks as if my poor tale could bring destruction down on her. When bad things happen it's not because of old women's stories but because our own wrongs come back to us. Or that is what I believe. Now I'll continue if you don't mind.*

Friday 23rd July 1982 – night-time.

The interview room of Sedgley police station was small and the neon lighting reflected harshly off its pale, blue-tiled walls. While the corridors and halls of the old building brought to mind a Victorian primary school, this sterile room was more reminiscent of an operating theatre in some obsolete and inhumane hospital.

Greeny was seated, elbows resting on the table, his head in his hands. From the other side, moving slowly and deliberately, Cooper planted his meaty fists in front of the boy and leaned towards him. But when he spoke, it was quickly, urgently,

- Right, Greeny. Yer stepdad's done us a favour and fucked off and CID's not coming in for a minute so you just fuckin' listen. I know you and I know your fuckin' bollocks and I don't wanna hear any of it. You're in the shit. There's a fourteen-year-old girl unconscious in hospital and her dad's tryin' to call it rape.

He paused. Greeny looked up and stared. His face was pale, blemished by cuts and bruises. The copper continued,

- If she comes round and confirms that, and the forensics match up, you're lookin' at five years minimum: DC first, then prison when you're eighteen. So none o' this 'I day do nuthin', I day see nuthin' ' bollocks, right?

Cooper lowered his voice, the tone was milder now, conciliatory,

- So if you were there but didn't do it, best to start talkin' and we'll try and turn it round for yer. As much as is possible. 'Cause if yer mate did it, he's bound to try to put it on you so yer best bet is to tell your side of things first.

Cooper sighed, unclenched his fists and sat back in his chair.

Greeny continued to stare blankly, noncommittal, then shifted his wide body on the hard plastic chair. His left cheekbone was numb and throbbing, beginning to swell and close his eye. His lower lip was bulging and with a crust of congealed blood on one side and there were other cuts inside his mouth so that it would hurt to talk. But he didn't want to talk. His head throbbed and felt fuzzy, he couldn't think but he knew what he had to do. That fucking tart would pay for this. He would see to that. Pay more than she could imagine. He just had to get out of here.

Footsteps sounded in the hallway. Cooper glanced at the door,

- She's comin'. CID. Remember, none of yer bullshit or it'll be you and me again.

A woman entered, nodded at Cooper and sat down at his side, across the table from Greeny.

She was smartly dressed and young for the police, Greeny thought. He was used to scruffy, overweight beat coppers, plug fucking ugly most of them, not the likes of her. It hadn't mattered before, but seeing her, he wished he was wearing one of his white Fred Perrys not the stinking yellow t-shirt that stretched too tight across his chest and belly. Or the black one with red and white trim on the collar. That was smart. He looked hard in that. That's what he'd had on when he'd gone out that afternoon. Before that silly cow started messing them all about. She'd explained about the booze, robbing Driscoll and all, but what was she doing with a smelly old t-shirt? Did she find it lying around?

The detective flicked open a notebook,

- Hello Simon.

- Alright.

His reply was almost a grunt.

- I'm Detective Sergeant Yvonne Halstead. You are Simon Albert Green of 54 Upper Ettingshall Road, is that right?

- Ar.

- And you came here this evening voluntarily to help with our enquiries and to make a statement, right? You understand that you are not under arrest at the moment?

- Me stepdad made me.

She flashed the briefest and coldest of smiles,

- Be that as it may, do you understand that you have not been arrested or charged with a crime but that anything you say may be used as evidence in a court of law?

Greeny sighed and looked around the room,

- Ar, I spose so.

- Pardon? I need you to say 'yes' or 'no' and to take this seriously. This is an investigation into an alleged rape, which carries a sentence of at least five years.

Greeny looked at her face with interest for the first time. Her voice had become harsh. And had there been a spark of ferocity in her eyes? She continued,

- So which is it? Yes or no?

- Yeah. I understand.

- Good. Now I'm going to ask you some questions about this afternoon and this evening and we'll make notes, then we'll write it up in a statement for you and your dad to sign.

- Right oh.

She was a bit broad-shouldered but might be a decent shape. Even with that loose-fitting, buttoned-up blouse, you could see there was definitely a good-sized pair in there. And that lipstick. And being bossy like that, like he was supposed to be scared of her. He felt his head clearing.

Halstead picked up her biro,

- Let's get started then. So, Simon. Were you in the woods off

White's Lane, otherwise known as Turl's Hill Drive, this afternoon or early evening, today Friday the 23rd of July 1982?

- Well, yeah. You know I was. Me stepdad told yer.

- We need to hear it from you. This is your official statement. What time did you get there and who were you there with?

Greeny did not own a watch and had no need of one.

- Dunno. After school.

Greeny was studying at her face now. Something was going on with her. Something he'd seen before but hadn't expected to see here. He glanced across at Cooper. He seemed to be sleeping.

- Shall we say five o´clock?

- Could do. Could 'a been about that.

He smiled, lopsidedly.

- With a mate.

- Pardon?

- You was askin' who I was with. It was a mate. A chap I know.

- The girls have already given us his name, Simon. You can say you were with Colin Bull.

Like he'd fall for that one.

- Cor remember this chap's name. Doh know him that well.

It was mad but… Her eyes were wide, like she was a bit scared. But she wasn't scared, not exactly. He'd seen it hundreds of times. She fancied him.

- Let's get on with it. What were you and this mate doing in the woods?

- Conkering.

She looked up from her notepad,

- Did you say 'conquering'?

- Ar. Getting conkers. For conker fights.

Greeny began to smirk but Cooper had woken up, or perhaps had never really slept. His chair skidded backwards as he rose then lunged forward, slamming heavy fists onto the table just in front of Greeny, who flinched back,

- Look. Fuckin'. Greeny.

He seemed too furious to string words together, then,

- I've told you about your bullshit and about taking this seriously. We're gonna come back in five minutes and you'd better have something useful to say about what happened in those woods tonight or I swear I'll get you on yer own again and fuckin' lamp it out of yer.

The detective and the copper left the interview room

***

She came back in and smiled the quick smile again as she sat down,

- So. Conkering. Get any good ones?

The boy was slouched sideways in his chair now.

- Nah. Rubbish. 'Ardly worth putting a string through 'em. Where's Cooper? When's me stepdad coming back?

- Your dad's playing the game. Let's not waste any more time. Tell me about the girls. Did you give them the alcohol?

- Nah.

- I suppose it fell from a conker tree, did it?

- Nah. They come with it. A bag full o' bottles and cans.

- Stolen?

- Wouldn't know.

She was looking at the table top and her notebook, not at him.

- Right. ...what happened? Tell me in your own words, from the time the girls came.

- We was just drinkin', 'avin' a loff, 'round the fire. Smokin'. As yer do.

- Did you have sexual intercourse with either of the girls?

- I fucked 'em both.

She stopped taking notes and looked at him,

- I day fuck both at the same time. It was separate, like.

- Tell me exactly what happened.

Her face coloured.

- For the official statement.

His eyes still on Halstead, he flexed his legs, he knew they were thick and strong, and slid his chair away from the table. Relaxed, he began to talk.

- Well Lisa'd had a bit too much to drink by then and she got all tearful, like. Cryin' and sobbin'. Says her dad's so strict and all that. So I said come here. And we was 'avin' a bit of a cuddle, as you do, and she was *nuzzlin'* like with 'er 'ead against me chest and I thought I'm in 'ere coz I was kissin' her neck by now and she started like... groaning. And so I put me 'and...

He had stopped.

- Yer like it doh yer?

- I...

- Yer like 'earing about it, doh yer?

- I don't...

His eyes widened, incredulous,

- *You* want some doh yer?

He was now touching a bulging erection through his jeans. Grinning at her.

Pallid, she stood on shaky legs and began to walk around the table.

The door opened.

- What the fuckin' 'ell?

Cooper was back.

***

Dark Harvest.

It was now pitch black outside the longhouse and one of the two fires had been allowed to die. The biggest of the children who had played near it had come to the other fire to listen too, while the smallest now slept in the arms of the women and girls. The Vascon, furious at the tale that so enthralled the others, had sent two big girls to look and listen for the returning men. But the girls had not returned. The wise woman's story had continued,

- So the boy, knowing himself friendless and outnumbered, left the eel fisher with that warning to carry and set off to wander in search of a new life and allies, that he might one day return and exact his revenge. He vowed to himself that when he did come back his attackers would die, that they would know why they died and that his brother and his brother's descendants would be raised up and protected so that none could attack them with impunity. The story of all his wanderings after that is a tale too long to be told well here but I can tell you that for months he avoided the villages of the plains and valleys and hunted in the forests, running down and killing large prey like none of our men could, eating raw meat like a wolf. When at last he came to the lands of the Vascons, far from the sea, in the foothills of the big mountains, he was taken in by a woman at first, and, being a good hunter and good at their wrestling and games of strength, very similar to yours, he was soon accepted by all. Over the years he became one of their chief men and, as their blacksmith got older, took over the forge from him and was better at it and much valued, having learned when a boy.

Something was bothering the Vascon. She stood up, pale and wide-eyed,

- It's time for the story to end. Something must have happened to the men. We should get ready to go to the stone tower.

The old lady paused in her storytelling. Despite the warm light of the fire playing on her bone-grey face, her look and voice were cold,

- But you cannot know what has happened except from hearing out *my story, pretty lady. Your scouts, those girls, will not return, I think. I said my tale had meaning for this place. Don't you wish to know your fate?*

The Vascon woman, until that night still handsome in her middle-age, looked older, uglier, as the shadows played across her face,

- What's in that bag you had? Open it!

But the bulging, lumpy sack lay on the floor somewhere in the darkness at the foot of the old lady's stool. A crowd of children and women sat, squatted and lay all around her and they weren't going to move.

- Let her finish – said a sharp-tongued widow – Your men will have gone too far and had to make camp. Or taken wine off some merchant and got legless.

A younger voice came from the darkness,

- What happened with the boy? Or man, now. What's his name?

- Yes, he was a man by then. Where as a boy he was as strong as a man, as an adult he became something more than a man, a full-grown Basajaun, more powerful even than the strongest of the Vascon stone-throwers, faster than their best sprinter, able to hammer at the forge all day then beat them at their own sports in the evening. And he was clever too. He learnt their strange language in a few weeks and could argue a point with the best of their wise men and convince them to follow his counsel. But he was not happy.

- Why?

- He knew that his brother was enslaved, or as good as, and that his parents' murders had never been avenged. And there was something else. He could have taken Vascon hunters and warriors with him and gone back to the village on a mission of vengeance, they would have followed. But he also knew that the Basajaun people, the key to his own origins, lived right there in the high mountains above the lands of the Vascons. If he could find the Basajaun, though none had been seen for years, he would know who he was, be able to explain his difference.

The Vascon woman sat muttering to herself in the darkness at the edge of the group but no-one listened and the story went on.

- He made trips into the high mountains but could not find them although he thought he saw them in the distance sometimes, disappearing into the forest or behind rocks. When he realised he would never catch up with them, he said goodbye to his woman in the village and made camp in a rocky valley and lived there, wearing no shirt or tunic, hoping that they might recognise his strong body as one of theirs and come to him. And come they did, in time.

- What were they like? Giants?

- Not fairies, nor giants, I have told you. A family came to him. Mother, father, boy and girl. Perhaps coming like that was their sign of peace. They were straight and strong like him but the few clothes they had were of deerskin not cloth and they had no use of metal, just antler, bone and wood. The man's spear was tipped with sharpened flint, glued with pine resin. They spoke their language to him and he was surprised to find he understood some of what they said, in a strange way, like seeing something through cloudy water, but could not answer them except with gestures. He shared some food with them and showed them his iron knife. He followed them a day's walk into the forest to their camp.

- Were they his family?

- He thought of them as his tribe maybe, or clan. He lived with them in a group of a few dozen and learnt, or remembered, more of their language and they told him that they had once been many more until, in recent generations, disease and enemies had diminished and scattered them and the few that remained had been chased into the highest mountains where they vied with the bear and the wolf for survival.

- Enemies? Who?

- Us. Men. Like your camp dogs snarl at and fear the wolf so our men dislike the Basajaun. And when the Basajaun were weakened by a disease that killed nearly all the men, their enemies had come with

iron weapons and mastiffs to finish them off and had nearly done so. Perhaps that is when the boy had been separated from his birth mother and came to live with a blacksmith.

One of the oldest boys, a twelve-year old, spoke,

- You say they are strong but they sound silly and weak. Getting sick. Chased away by enemies. They don't have metal or proper clothes...

- You can be so strong that you are weak. They were strong enough to do without the things that we need to survive. Strong enough to not feel the need to fight. And they had their wisdom too, knowing the ways of plants and animals better than us. At night they would take potions that let them dream and seem to travel while they dreamt. They communed with the old gods. The gods of forest and weather that you still remember only for feasts and bonfires are, for them, still alive and move amongst us. And when they drink their elixirs, those gods possess them and speak through them, or so they believe. But none of that helped them when the sickness came. Sicknesses that bother us but only kill our weakest killed whole families and left them at the mercy of their enemies. He pitied them and tried to help.

One of the girls sent out to look for the men had returned. She had entered the hut through the stiff, cowhide door and was walking towards them, strangely slow and languorous, her clothes dishevelled. The Vascon rose and hurried toward her. Some of the listeners glanced in her direction but then turned back to the storyteller. A boy asked,

- Did he teach them to fight their enemies?

- That was part of it. But first he taught them to work metal and brought them the tools to do it. And he taught that if they were to live in one place now, not follow their prey, they should grow plants in that place. He taught them to trade with the Vascons, so they could swap game for metal and other things they needed. And when he smoked and drank their potions with them, he too was possessed by their gods and those gods used him as an instrument to talk of vengeance and pride. And the gods spoke so well through him that the

Basajaun listened and understood for the first time and believed him the incarnation of their oldest god, the horned one.

A peal of hysterical laughter came from the darkness then the sound of a slap. It was the big girl, now on the floor from the Vascon's blow, but still laughing as if drunk. She was talking,

- Don't worry, you'll like them! I did! Better than our men. They kept me happy...

Her voice broke up into laughter again. The old woman looked beyond her to the door,

- Ah. I believe he is here.

All were watching the door now. The Vascon woman backed away from it, towards the others and the fire.

In they came, advancing toward the seated group. Rough and sturdy in dark clothes, masks and helmets covered their faces and firelight reflected from the leather cuirasses of their torsos and the blades of their weapons. The leader wore a helmet of polished bronze with great curved horns, the front of it a mask like the head of a goat but flattened to follow the contours of a human face. He stood over the cowering Vascon and his voice thundered,

- Do you know this goat face, witch? Do you know why I am here?

She did not answer but looked down. He spoke to the old teller of tales,

- Show her our harvest.

The old woman reached over and pulled the rough sack toward her, dragging it. The women and children at her feet scrambled away, making space around her but still watching as she held a corner of the sack with one hand and pulled at a cord with the other. The cord fell away and the bag was open. She let go of the open end and the severed heads of men rolled out onto the beaten earth floor.

Friday 23rd July 1982. Night.

Cooper parked the Austin Allegro panda car on wasteland opposite the Greek chip shop in Roseville centre. Even under cover of darkness, he preferred to cross the main road and enter the fairground in Jubilee park on foot rather than arrive at the fairground in the ridiculous, underpowered vehicle.

Detective Sergeant Halstead had gone home sick after whatever had happened in the interview room with Greeny – the dirty little bastard – and now he would be working alone for the rest of the evening. It was better like that. From the moment he had first heard that the girl in hospital had mentioned a Betts, a Rosie Betts, he had pulled strings and used up favours in order to get in on the CID's rape investigation but now he wanted to work alone. Although the interview with the girl would have to be tomorrow, when Halstead was back at work, he could make initial contact tonight on the pretext of asking the girl in for interview. And he had a few questions of his own for her about the Betts family and about Greeny and events in the woods.

As he left the Panda behind him next to a half-filled skip and some scrubby vegetation, he vaguely wondered if it would leave an oil stain on the gravel as it had in the car park of Sedgley police station. He made his way toward the main road. Some youths who had been hanging around outside the chip shop walked away a little too fast and he heard laughter as they rushed around the corner, already running no doubt, guilty of some minor crime that did not concern him.

After crossing the dual carriageway, he entered the formal old park. It was pre-war, he thought; a pleasant and orderly space for most of the year, with its trimmed hedges, tennis courts and bowling green, except for these few weeks when the fair moved in and other rules prevailed. It was past eleven o'clock now. The rides and stalls had been shut down for more than half an hour and the final stragglers, couples and small groups of young people, were making their way out of the park, some still holding drinks or candy floss on sticks, all of them unusually quiet, some of the impulses and lusts of youth satisfied for this night at least.

Some fairground workers were turning off generators, folding up shutters and screens and locking up. Lights on in the rows of caravans behind the attractions suggested that others had already finished for the night. A group of young men, black and white, sat on the steps of the waltzers, smoking, drinking from cans of Castlemaine and Tennants and watching some kind of action going on in the trampled mud and grass at the foot of the steps. In the growing darkness and at a distance, Cooper could only make out two dark forms writhing in the deeper darkness of the shadows. As he drew close, he began to discern muscular brown arms and torsos entwined python-like and glistening with sweat.

- Me fuckin' chain, mon!

White teeth laughing, eyes rolling. It was wrestling but without malice. A test of strength. One black youth released the other and scrambled to his feet quickly, shaking his finger in mock threat at the man on the floor,

- I'll stamp yah rasclat fuckin' chain in the fuckin' mud next time, mon.

He grinned up at the group on the steps.

Seeing that some of the drinkers were also smoking fat joints, and not wanting a confrontation, Cooper skirted the muddy clearing between rides, avoiding the drinkers and smokers and entered an area of caravans and small mobile homes.

All the caravans were different in size, shape and level of disrepair. Some were self-propelled, some towable. Some were probable MOT failures while some appeared new and had powerful Toyota pick-ups and, in one case, a new Mercedes parked outside. But none had the look of an office or headquarters or of being a good place to start asking for a girl called Rosie Betts. He was preparing to knock on the closest door when a slim man with wavy blond hair came out of a medium-sized, medium-scruffy white caravan. Obviously in high after-work spirits, the man strode across the grass, the cocky, legs-relaxed walk of a hard man on the move. As he raised a cigarette to his lips he saw the copper and in a comically unsubtle manner ducked his head and changed the trajectory of his walk slightly so as to head for a gap between vehicles rather than pass close to the policeman. Cooper needed to speak now or he would melt away,

- Evening.

- Alright.

The head went down more, the cocksure walk quickened rather than slowed.

- Wait there a minute. Police want a word.

The man would either run now or stay, depending on what unpunished crime had driven him to the itinerant life: how serious, how far away, how long ago.

He turned and stood his ground, squinting at Cooper through narrow eyes as he took a long drag on a stubby cigarette. Somewhere close, generators still thudded away and the smell of diesel hung in the air around them, although as Cooper approached the thin man, the fuel stench was overpowered by the smell of aftershave and fags,

- Yer what?

It was a challenge not a question and was delivered so confidently as to cause Cooper to reconsider his tactics. It was hard to believe that one so skinny could really be dangerous but somewhere this one had learnt how to at least act hard. To Cooper any bluff along those lines was a challenge to be met,

- I'm looking for someone.

The narrow eyes flitted side-to-side in an otherwise impassive face. Cooper continued,

- A teenage girl called Rosie Betts. Lives with a woman, probably her aunt.

The thin man expelled cigarette smoke through mouth and nose and then flicked the fag-end into the mud between caravans.

- Don't know 'bout that. Lots o' girls and women on the fair.

Cooper gazed at him levelly for a moment,

- Name?

- Uh?

- What's your name?

- Why? Fuck all to do with me.

But the fugitive was already backing away, twisting his centre of gravity to begin to lean into a run. Cooper grabbed the collar of his denim jacket with one hand and pushed with him in the same direction, launching him sideways faster than he had intended. The thin man's feet slipped on the mud and he flailed his arms for balance before he was slammed into the side of a darkened caravan, Cooper's forearm across his throat. Outweighing the carny by about three stone, Cooper kept him pinned against the caravan with his body weight and brought his face close to his,

- It'll fuckin' be summat to do with you if yer doh tell me which. Fuckin'. Caravan.

The man was twisting and writhing with unexpected strength, causing Cooper to struggle for breath already, yet, in the physical language they had been forced to learn from childhood, they both knew that this was now a dialogue not a fight. By limiting himself to wrestling and not trying to escalate things with a head-butt, knee or bite, Cooper's opponent was already acknowledging the policeman's dominance and accepting the deal being offered.

His eyes swivelled again,

- They live in a big white ´un. Back row, near the generator trucks.

Cooper eased off the pressure on the man's neck first, then stepped back, not taking his eyes off his hands and torso,

- Show me.

The narrow grey eyes flashed: he could not go along with that humiliation. Cooper sighed,

- We doh ´ave to ´old ´ands. Walk past it and I'll follow.

Cooper walked several places behind his new informant, who was now muttering and spitting angrily, now kicking out his legs in an exaggerated manner as he walked, trying to reassemble his shattered façade of cockiness.

As they passed a large beige and white caravan, the man hacked and spat a gob of phlegm just short of its door and looked at Cooper significantly before turning and walking towards an unlit path between caravans and tennis courts. Just before disappearing into the warm darkness, he stopped,

- Play yer cards right and yer might get yer end away - he jeered - Just don't drink the cider.

He was sliding away but Cooper got a final question in,

- You've bin there, then?

A voice from the darkness,

- We've all bin there mate!

was followed by a laugh and the drifter was gone.

***

A woman of Cooper's age, or a little older, opened the caravan door. Her face was strong-featured and handsome, at first reminding Cooper of sixties actresses, like Julie Christie or Britt Eklund but as they were now, years after their pristine glory, enhanced by age and experience. When she smiled, though, a warm and ageless femininity transformed her appearance and he realised that they had met before. Somewhere.

- Yes?

He hesitated slightly. If they had met, how could he not remember?

- Er, good evening.

A little formality helped get results when giving people the knock. He would not be speaking in dialect,

- Does a Rosie Betts live here?

Her smile didn't waver but the twinkle of her eyes intensified,

- Yes, she does. I'm her aunt. Come in and have a word. That's what you want isn't it?

She was actually laughing at him, teasing him, he realised, as she opened the door fully then turned her back on him and walked down a short and narrow corridor. She passed some closed doors towards what looked like a living room area of shadowy sofas and cupboards, lit by the flickering glow of a small television. Her white, hippie-like dress was also evocative of the sixties, a transatlantic and bohemian variant of the sixties, but it was the sway of her walk that triggered the memory. He knew who she was. Amalia. Amalia Betts, Michael's cousin.

She turned quickly, noting his confusion and also the direction of his gaze,

- Come on then, we won't bite.

Cooper coughed and looked down, focusing his efforts on not

tripping on anything as they made their way through the darkness into a small but comfortable lounge area. The temperature in the room was several degrees higher even than the warm night outside. A fit-looking teenage girl sat on a sofa, stroking a cat. She seemed to be wearing only a long white T-shirt with large black letters on the front, long legs curled under her unselfconsciously. She smiled lazily, expectantly, at the policeman, her expression open and pleasant. It was a gaze he knew well.

Pissed. Or something.

The older woman turned to look at Cooper, also smiling faintly.

- Rosie's my niece. We were having a drink and listening to some old records. Remember this one?

The LP was between tracks and there were a couple of seconds of hissing vinyl before the song began, a huskily whispered sixties ballad,

> *Remember,*
>
> *walkin' in the sa-a-and.*
>
> *Remember,*
>
> *walkin' hand in ha-a-and...*

Cooper again felt the need to clear his throat,

- Doesn't ring a bell, no.

> *Your lips were so invite-in'*
>
> *The night was so excite-in'*

He took out a small notebook and pen,

- I won't take up much of your time. And if you'll both agree to cooperate, I'll turn a blind eye to the fact that she's been drinking. Or whatever.

> *Softly, softly we met with our lips....*

The aunt sat in an armchair, legs crossed, elbows on sun-tanned knees, brow furrowed in mock seriousness,

- Fire away, officer. I told you, this is my niece, Rosie Betts. Ask her what you like. And sit down if you like.

- Then turn off the music. And you, girl, sit up straight.

Rosie sat up, stretched the t-shirt almost to her knees then held it there clenched in her fists as she answered the questions matter-of-factly. Yes, she knew what rape was and understood that this was a serious investigation. Yes, she had been with Lisa Stanley and two boys in the woods that evening. Yes, she agreed to voluntarily attend Sedgley police station to make a statement at ten o'clock the following morning.

Cooper closed the notebook. He was intensely uncomfortable sat on a spongy armchair in a stuffy caravan and very aware that the original pretext for his visit was now spent.

Rosie and her aunt knew it too. He would have to leave unless he had a reason to stay.

Rosie looked at her aunt and relaxed back into her languid cat-stroking.

- That's it then, is it? - asked the aunt - I expect you'll want to be off, won't you?

Part of Cooper's mind was racing despite himself: long white legs and a white t-shirt. What's the chances of her knickers being black? Pure black cotton stretched on firm, pale flesh? Black and white. Firm and soft.

- Are yerz feelin' alright in y'self, Sor? Would yer be loikin' a cup o´ tea before yer off?

Rosie spluttered into laughter at her aunt's Irish accent.

- Just a joke we have between us, officer. We´ve got family in Ireland.

- Wouldn't mind a cup.

- Rosie. Will you be gettin' the nice policeman a drink and no mistake, at all, at all?

The girl swayed between them on her way to some concealed kitchen.

- Pretty isn't she?

- Delightful.

- They say she takes after me, you know.

Her voice had taken on a purring, self-consciously flirtatious tone. Unnoticed by Cooper one of the two had turned the record player back on, but quieter. The same song was playing again, but with the volume down. She leaned closer,

- You don't remember do you?

- Remember what? I don't know what yer on about yet.

- A girl like her? A bit older? Twenty odd years ago, in the woods?

- You talking about you and the night of the accident? I don't remember much, you know. I was young, foolish and pissed out me head.

Her face was now inches from his, her wide, full-lipped mouth slightly open as she gazed brightly into his eyes. Her strong, mature features and finely arched eyebrows over deep liquid brown eyes seemed to expand to occupy all his thoughts.

What a fuck this would be.

Bend her over the arm of this chair.

Lift that hippy skirt up.

With the girl watching.

But it wasn't happening for him. There was no stirring. He remembered Haley from the Red Lion.

Better not.

Don't want another fiasco.

Rosie had come back in from the kitchen holding a steaming drink on a tray,

- Didn't have proper tea so I got you some camomile.

Cooper had only the vaguest idea what camomile was. In his frustrated state, all he could manage was to take the cup with shaking hands.

- Don't spill it on him, tipsy girl. We'll make you clean it off.

Rosie chortled.

The aunt leaned back in her armchair, resignedly, her eyes rolled up as if at some pleasant memory,

- We had a bit of a snog, was all. You and me. Back then. But it could have been more. There was a proper mattress in that camp my cousins built! Then I had to go. You never met our dad, lucky for you, but he was strict, 'specially with us girls. Be in bed by ten or come home, he used to say!

She grinned at Rosie, now back on the sofa, who chuckled at the old joke.

- I told the police all of this at the time, you know. It was nothing. A kiss and a cuddle. I'm not surprised you don't remember.

- No. I kind of remembered. Remembered better when I saw you.

Anyway, they reckoned I got bashed on the head. Either that or I wanted to black it all out.

The camomile with sugar and lemon was a revelation.

- What do you call this stuff again?

- It's camomile, amongst other things - the aunt seemed colder now - Should help you sleep tonight.

Silence. The old-fashioned china tea cup was only half empty and what remained was still too hot to swig down quickly. Better make conversation. See what comes out. He'd got some good grasses like that and some of them lived in caravans like this one. He nodded at Rosie, reclining against cushions, eyes closed as she listened to the music or to their conversation,

- That's not tea she's drinking. Or camomile. And what do you do about school?

- We live on a site in Essex when we're not travelling with the fair. She goes to the school there. And they send her stuff to do when we travel. Tests and everything.

- And the booze? Who sends her that?

- What? That she's drinking now? That's home-brewed. Barley wine. Won't hurt her. Didn't hurt you when you were her age. You were pretty keen for me to have some that one time, as I recall.

- Like I say, I don't remember much about that.

- Do you want some? Take off them big shoes and sit on the sofa with me and Rosie?

Inadvertently he glanced at Rosie. Her eyes opened and fixed on him instantly without having to scan or zero in. Even drunk, her smile held a heart-breaking promise of innocence and youth. Which was all he needed,

- Well...,

Cooper rose stiffly from the yielding armchair, pushing hands on knees,

- ...I'm a copper now not a young chap in the woods. I'd best be off.

Amalia raised her eyebrows.

- I'll see you tomorrow at ten, young lady.

He drained the last of the infusion from the china cup, placed it on a low table and made his way carefully down the darkened hall. To his middle-aged eyes the short corridor was as black as pitch but he found the handle by touch.

***

Logroño Witch Trials. Logroño, Spain. 1611 A.D.

A stocky jailer led the adolescent girl by the hand onto the high wooden platform, nearly as high as the box where the inquisitors sat. He did not bother with chains for one so slight and let her stand free although the woman next to her was loosely chained to a post. A man was chained to another post but lay unconscious at its base. The girl was perhaps fourteen and skinny for her age. Some in the crowd craned their necks trying to decipher the symbols and pictograms embroidered in black onto her yellow robe, to illustrate her unmentionable crimes. But the garment hung so loose on her that the pictures were lost in its folds. Was that a dog? Could that be a star? She's up for murder, murder by witchcraft amongst other things, could that be a dagger?

Behind the platform where they were left standing there were three pyres, stacked high with dried-out pine and beech logs bleached ash-grey by the sun. A pair of buzzards called to each other as they wheeled high in the cloudless sky.

The chained woman was about thirty years old, dressed simply in a skirt and blouse. She had red cheeks and wavy blond hair, a little frizzy. She said something to the girl in a language that most there did not know but was shouted down by a lean-faced priest, Salazar, who sat in the box,

- Speak Christian, woman! If you want your end to come easily not hard!

An older, bulky man in rich church robes, the Bishop of Pamplona, said something inaudible to Salazar, who looked at some papers on his table for a moment then addressed the girl,

- You are Zuriñe Garay from Gernika, are you not?

- Yes sir.

- And you understand my language do you not?

The girl hesitated, then,

- Yes sir.

- Do you know the woman beside you?

-Yes sir.

- Can you identify her?

The girl looked pained and did not answer.

- Can you tell me her name?

- Ziortza Goikoetxea

The bishop, watching intently, his face resting on ample chins, spoke to Salazar sharply without taking his eyes off the girl,

- What? What's that name?

- Ziortza, your excellency.

Salazar continued, addressing the girl again,

- Now you will recount for us the events you saw on the night of this last summer solstice in the house of Jon Errementari in Gernika, with particular reference to certain acts and ceremonies carried out by Ziortza Goikoetxea and others present.

He paused for effect,

- Who was there? Was it a Christian gathering?

- I would not say so, sir.

Salazar waited then realised she was not going to continue,

- Well go on, girl, why not? What was not Christian about it?

- It was all women and Jon, in his field outside his house. I wouldn't say there was anything Christian about it. They were drinking a lot and talking about the spirits of the forests and the mountains.

Salazar turned to the bishop, raising his eyebrows,

- Spirits she calls them, mind.

Then addressing the girl again,

- What was the reason for this so pleasant a party and why were you there?

Zuriñe lowered her eyes,

- The women asked me. I don't know why.

- And the reason for the gathering?

- Jon was in trouble. Everyone knew. Gonzalo, the fat one, had taken a dislike to him, was borrowing money without paying it back, insulting him in the street, following his daughter around...

The bishop interrupted again to question Salazar, not the girl,

- Gonzalo?

- A local drunk and bully.

- I see. Jon Erri...?

- A blacksmith and wheelwright. The man on the platform, charged with them.

The bishop snorted,

- I know he's here, I'm just trying to establish who he is and why we are bothering with this gossip.

Salazar closed his eyes for an instant then continued,

- I asked you about the reason for the gathering and you said Jon was in trouble. What does that mean?

She looked around again, like someone sharing a secret, with two hundred pairs of eyes on her,

- Well, it was to help him you see. To conjure up help and get rid of Gonzalo for him.

At the word 'conjure' a ripple of excitement passed through the crowd.

- *How did this conjuring happen?*

- *Well, it started like a party. They were drinking till late. Jon had two sides of lamb roasting by the fire and some flagons of wine and they were all drinking, telling funny tales, then saucy ones, specially her – she nodded in the direction of Ziortza – very saucy ones of people dancing naked and kissing the beast's arse in a Sabbath…*

Now there were laughs from the crowd, two distinct types of laugh, one from the men, another from the women,

- *…and women going with women and two men going with one woman and doing it up the bum…*

More laughter. It was the way she said it a little embarrassed, a little excited and so young. Now it was the bishop who had closed his eyes. Without opening them again, he said something to Salazar, who then interrupted,

- *Yes but, aside from the stories, what actually happened? What did you see?*

- *When they was all well gone, a stranger came. A big strong feller. Thick black hair and eyebrows. Walked straight out of the fields and lay in the middle of all them women and they made a right fuss of him, snogging and kissing, after all those stories and all the wine they'd had. Married women, too, some of them.*

Some more chuckles from the crowd, mainly the masculine type with only a few girlish trills. Older women clucked and tutted. The bishop remained impassive, bored perhaps, but Salazar seemed more alert now. A glint of anticipation in his eye,

- *And I believe a type of ceremony took place then, did it not?*

Zuriñe looked flustered. He tried again,

- *A ceremony or mass. They did something special, like you see in church but all wrong.*

He could not resist glancing across at the bishop now and then. The girl continued,

- *Mass? No. Just the snogging and the kissing. One or two women might have done a bit more than that, specially that Marie, the Frenchie. I wasn't watching. Went home.*

She raised her chin primly. There was a guffaw from a large blond man in the crowd, his huge belly bulging through an open white shirt.

- *They all stayed there and I went home.*

A flush of colour came to Salazar's cheeks and he spoke hotly,

- *But you have said in other interviews, on pain of death, that the beast was present and a mass was made in his honour.*

- *Well that black-haired feller was a bit of a beast, I should think, but except for him, no, I didn't see no animals.*

The fat blond man raised his cup and laughed loud again. It rang a little false this time but was enough to set them all off, even those matrons who had frowned before. Salazar folded his hands in front of him, his knuckles white.

- *Take her down. Forty lashes and food withheld.*

Ziortza Goikoetxea shifted on the spot, awaiting her questioning, scanning the crowd for allies.

Saturday 24th July 1982 - morning.

He is sipping tea in the kitchen. His breakfast toast is finished.

He hears heavy and slow footsteps on the pavement just outside their front room window. They come to a halt and there is a sigh and a cough, some rustling. Something is muttered then the footsteps change direction and get even closer, echoing now, and he knows it is the postwoman entering the side passage, bringing mail to the side door, not the front, as instructed by his mother.

His heart speeds up a little and something sickening turns over deep inside him. He feels it is not going to happen today but he also knows it might.

He waits until the footsteps retreat again. He doesn't have to run to check. He can walk, take his time. He takes another sip of tea to prove it to himself.

As he enters the narrow hallway, he can see that the three envelopes strewn on the inside doormat and carpet are all brown. All are official, none personal. So it is not what he hoped for, he knew that anyway, but could still be what he fears.

Hands unsteady, he bends and picks the letters up. All three have transparent rectangles that show the address printed on the bill or giro inside. None of them are from the police or the courts. One day that will come, though. He saw the slight girl talking to the big policeman in the corridor that day.

He considers fate. The gods. He imagines them, silk-robed looking down on events as in Sunday-afternoon films like Jason and the Argonauts and stifles a shrill giggle. Both retribution and redemption have been delayed by some wave of a divine arm. But that delay is just further punishment. Now he will face the same drama tomorrow, and the day after, spared only on Sundays when the postwoman never comes.

Still, there is the hope, too. The good thing. The impossible hope that sustains him.

Back in the kitchen, he leaves his plate and cup unwashed in the sink. He doesn't need to leave for work yet. There's time to read it again before he has to get ready.

Passing the airing cupboard at the top of the stairs he sees that his shirt and trousers are ironed and waiting for him. His mother was always proud of him being a teacher. In the bedroom he takes a crumpled letter from a drawer and smooths it out.

It is not the original, that is gone, but a copy he made before posting. Scrunched up and thrown away, then retrieved, more than once.

Now he doesn't want to read it. But he flattens it further, pressing it onto his desk top with his palms, and begins despite himself.

There are thank yous and explanations. He understands that it only started because she felt sorry for him and for herself too since breaking up with the other person. He knows that it wasn't as important to her as it was to him. But for him it was the most special time in his life and she must have felt something too at least that first evening, looking out over golden fields (they were golden in that light).

He understands that sex is important to her and that she misses what she had with the other person.

But he misses her a lot so much that it hurts and doesn't see why they couldn't continue going slowly.

He hadn't known it could do that, physically hurt. Heartache.

They could meet again perhaps

And see how she feels then

Things might change

She didn't answer this or the others. Over the years.

The others explained how special their two meetings had been to him, and why.

Interludes in a bleak and solitary life.

Maybe ending like that was for the best.

But now there is nothing to look forward to.

Unless the reply comes.

And comes before the other.

***

<u>Saturday 24th July 1982 - morning.</u>

As she entered she saw Cooper pouring himself a cup of tea in the shabby kitchen-cum-staff-lounge area of Sedgley police station,

- Mornin´ Detective Sergeant.

- Morning Constable Cooper.

- You want to get some o' this down yer.

He looked across at her as he sipped tea from a stained white mug. Amused. Quizzical.

He can't know how bad it was. What I wanted to do. He only saw me stand up.

- You 'ad a bit of a funny turn last night, didn't yer?

Bastard.

- I couldn't concentrate, that was all. There's something about that room or I was ill or something. I'm fine now. I will have some tea. What's that you're...?

- Fried bread. We 'ave bacon sandwiches of a night then save the dripping for the next day.

Everything about you disgusts me.

- Here's yer tea then. Help y'self to sugar.

She was still conscious of his facial expression and the attitude it suggested. She felt the need to direct attention towards the challenges of the morning,

- Do you think she'll turn up?

- Stands a good chance. Probably with the aunt. Had to give them a knock last night – no phones in bloody caravans. If not we'll 'ave a ride down Jubilee Park and 'ave a word there. I suspect she'll contradict young master Simon Albert Green on a

161

good few points.

She nodded. This was better: back to the routine of witnesses and statements, contradictions and corroboration.

- And then this afternoon I'll pop over to hospital and see if they'll let me speak to Lisa Stanley.

- Right.

He slurped tea.

- Do you believe there was a rape?

Cooper grunted,

- About as much as I believe that daft apeth had sex with both of 'em. That's just the dad. Nah, somethin' funny went on but I don't think it was rape..

And something funnier went on in the interview room last night.

-There's some dripping in that cup if you want to spread it on some bread.

He put his plate and cup in the kitchen sink and lowered himself onto the misshapen sofa to read the paper while they waited for Rosie Betts and her aunt.

***

Saturday evening.

The evening was warm and cloudless. It was still daylight as Cooper walked down Bourne Street but the blue sky was darkening in the east. The houses here were big. In their gardens, the rampant early summer growth was subdued into neat privet hedges and well-trimmed lawns. Sprigs of pampas grass in coloured glass vases decorated some of the porches and front windows. As well as the usual Ford Fiestas and Austin Allegros, cherished Rovers and plush Ford Consuls lay fat-tired on the tar-macked or paved driveways. Just visible through lace curtains, large televisions glowed in living rooms.

But the policeman was troubled. The lords of misrule were al-ways close; this frontline of cosy suburbia was within a mile of the council houses of the Wren's Nest estate and the terraced houses of Hospital Lane. Even in this quietest and most genteel of Coseley streets, he could hear the rumbling music and distant shrieks of the fair at nearby Jubilee park and smell the flowery summer smells of 'the Cornice' a small wooded copse between Bourne Street and Driscoll's fields, a favourite haunt of teenage drinkers and shaggers. Now, however, the usual, fragile balance seemed to have shifted further than ever toward entropy and violence: a boy had died in an apparently minor accident; a local bully had told him a story of a masked prowler that was too bizarre to not be believed; and then there were the still un-clarified mysteries thrown up by last night's rape allegations. On becoming coherent, Lisa Stanley had cleared it up: it wasn't rape. She had sex with Simon Green because she wanted to, at the time. Her dad had made up the rape claim after finding her dumped on his doorstep. It probably fit in better with what he wanted to believe and gave him a target to focus his anger on. But the two interviews in Sedgley police station, of Greeny last night and then Rosie Betts this morning both perturbed Cooper for different reasons even though they were both more or less consistent with Lisa's final version. What had happened be-tween Greeny and Halstead in the interview room? He had seen the boy rubbing his groin and leering and seen Halstead move towards him as if she were up for it. That stuck up cow! She didn't seem the type to like a bit of rough. Also, why had Greeny been so subdued at first and who had bruised his face for him? Not the weedy stepdad, surely? And that scruffy old t-shirt he turned up in? As for Rosie Betts, her manner had been open and helpful and her side of the story had been relatively believable: finding a stash of booze with Lisa, bumping into the two boys and getting drunk with them, Lisa going off with Greeny. Her story was plausible, it was her surname that bothered him. The Betts family tree was complicated but Michael Betts was her uncle, apparently, her mother's brother. There was nothing else to link Michael Betts to the rape-that-wasn't or the recent death in the woods but to find another member of the Betts family involved in strange goings-on in the woods, twenty-three years after the bonfire deaths... So now he was going to Upper Gornal Labour club to properly check out Michael's alibi for last Friday night. The flashing teacher was another potential suspect, in theory, as he had been seen in the area at the right time, but Cooper had seen the man and could not imagine him killing Michael Hickman.

Let the teacher wait. Let him sweat for now.

And CID still considered Hickman's death to be accidental.

Don't know their arses from their elbows.

By now he had passed two pubs: The Brook in Bourne Street, a pseudo-country pub on the edge of Coseley with a grassy beer garden that bordered Driscoll's fields and a brook, and the Radcliffe Arms, a scruffier, grimmer establishment where, in a vain effort to compete with The Brook, someone had installed picnic tables in a corner of the car park, near clumps of nettles and doc leaf. Cooper made a mental note to visit The Brook one of these nights and get in with the regulars to see if he could find out anything more about the movements of Michael Betts or old Driscoll. Arriving at the Tipton road, he continued through the still pleasant suburbs around High Arcal school and crossed into the council estates of Upper Gornal.

***

They were showing 'Quadrophenia' at Upper Gornal Labour

club. There were Vespas and Lambrettas in the car park and a Mk. 2 Cortina with fur dice hanging from the rear-view mirror. The main room was packed: all the chairs had been pushed into rows but kids were also sitting on tables and on the floor. As well as the young adult Mods, younger hanger-ons made up the numbers, wide-eyed and admiring: boys self-consciously sweating in their oversized and over-decorated parkas, teen girls blinking doll-like and excited in too much makeup.

There was just one bouncer on the door: Cisco Smith. Cooper knew the gypsy of old and felt a certain fondness. He was a thief and a rogue but not a troublemaker. He would try to make money by taking scrap metal from abandoned factories or power tools from building sites, or might get into a fight over a girl, but didn't cause trouble out of devilment or boredom. The last time Cooper had seen him, maybe a year ago, he had been a skinny, floppy haired youth in jeans and jean jacket, riding a horse up White's Lane with a girlfriend on the back. Now he was much more heavily built, to the point of being barely recognisable, sweating just outside the door in his bouncer's dinner jacket, wide neck bulging in a white collar.

- Fuckinell Cisco, you bin on the weights?

Cisco actually smiled as he recognised Cooper and then Cooper remembered another thing he liked about the gypsy: he was a free spirit. He didn't follow the rules that surrounded him, not automatically, not even the rule that says you don't talk to coppers.

- Ar. Got some old uns. Rusty. Set 'em up in the garage. You alright, Cooper the copper?

Cooper expelled air from pursed lips,

- Y'know. Older than God's dog but cor complain. Ahd yer get so big, though? Yer was a skinny 'un.

Cisco grinned,

- Weight gain powder. An' a fuckin' shitload o' food. Fuckin' Sunday dinner, chips, gravy, whatever, just shovel it dahn 'n train. Weight piles on. 'Course some of it's flab but yer tek that off later.

- Maybe a young 'un like you would. At my age, I'd just stay fuckin' fat. Yer bin working the doors long?

- Baht six months. That's why I started training. Said I was too thin.

- You ever worked with Michael Betts?

- Ar. A few times. 'Ere or in Dudley. It's usually either 'im or Marlon Campbell. Doh know which ones 'arder. Either one'd pale the shit outta me.

His eyes creased with mirth. Cooper continued,

- What's 'e like, Bettsy? Lots o' scraps?

- Nah. They teks one look in his eyes 'n that's enough, nine times out of ten. When 'e does ave a fight it doh last long, I can tell yer. Fast as fuck. Strong too.

- Right.

- Doh like it, though. Avoids a fight if he can. Knows 'e'll 'urt some bugger one day. More of a lover, 'im.

Cooper could not believe his ears,

- Yer what? 'E´s an ugly bugger.

Cisco chortled, looked around theatrically, then lowered his voice,

- 'E does alright. Got a face like a bulldog chewin' a wasp but they'm all after 'im!

- Bettsy? In 'is vest and 'is wellies?

- Goo in there 'n ask the barmaid if yer doh believe me. Ask 'er what she did after knockin' off last Saturday 'n if she doh say 'shaggin in the car park with Bettsy', tell 'er she's a liar.

Cooper laughed incredulous,

- Doh believe yer. Yer'm 'avin me on.

- Ask Marlon. Been after that barmaid for years. Brings her chocolates and everything, got a flashy car, smooth talker, dresses well, Armani aftershave, muscles on his muscles, got nowhere. Not a smile. He reckoned she was either a lezzer or racist. Along comes this scruffy bugger with cowshit on his fuckin' wellies and his old yellow t-shirt and she's the one goin' after him. Follows 'im out the door! Bent her over the bins 'round the back o' the car park.

They had to move away from the door to let two modettes out. One girl, wearing a boating blazer and with long red hair held back by a white Alice band, was sobbing.

Cisco continued, enthused by his subject,

- I've sin it before too. From wenches as young as them two to grannies. *They* go after *im.* He doh 'ave to do nothin'.

For a moment the gypsy looked startled, his eyes widening as he remembered he was talking to a copper,

- Course, 'e doh touch the young uns. Jail bait, like. Nothin' like that.

***

A God.

- Some see him as a man, that's true enough. The innocent, like that young girl, who don't have the knowledge of the world to see things as they are, even when they drink a good potion, or don't want to see.

Ziortza Goikoetxea had been asked to give her version of the mass of Hondarribia.

- Some, more corrupt, see him as a great black goat with a huge cock. Or a goat-man. That's the closest they can get to what he really is.

There were some sniggers at the word 'cock' but they were soon stifled or shushed. The court had reconvened after many hours away and now soldiers had been posted at the foot of the interrogation platform and around the fringes of the crowd and they stared out stone-faced at the people, looking for trouble. The three great pyres of fire-wood loomed bigger now, black hills against a dark blue sky pocked by the evening star - and their mute presence also quietened the mood of the mob. In the twilight Salazar's lean face was cadaverous,

- How did you see him?

- A god. An old god in a young body. A horned god of vengeance and passion.

At this, some in the crowd turned to look at the inquisitors, waiting for their wrath: denunciations or barked orders to ignite the pyres right now but the fat bishop did not react at all and Salazar seemed almost to smile,

- A horned god you say? A demon then, not our lord Jesus Christ?

Her eyes gleamed in defiance but she spoke quietly,

- A spirit much older than your lamb god. Much truer to the spirit of a noble man or woman. He doesn't claim to suffer for us, but he will make your enemies suffer if you can summon him. And the mass we gave him was better than yours too.

Almost imperceptibly Salazar glanced across at the fat man to his left.

He was listening this time.

- Please explain to the bishop how this mass differs from those you have seen in churches. Perhaps the wine is taken differently, or the communion wafer is of a different type?

- But I don't think you would want me to do so, sir.

- Ha! You are suddenly humble or shy but at least you do not try to lie your way to safety like the girl before you. Perhaps you shall avoid a whipping like she got if you tell us the truth about this great mass for your great and important demon. Don't be shy with us about the details, we are used to this testimony and cannot be shocked.

For a moment Ziortza's ruddy features were obscured by straw-coloured hair that fell in her face as she looked down at her feet, seeming to gather her thoughts. Then she looked up again at Salazar and spoke to him,

- Like yours, our Sabbath has wine but not just a miserly sip. Rather, as much as you want and with it a feast of food, not one crumbling wafer. Only when your stomach is full can you drink the nightshade potion without vomiting. And our mass is open, in a clearing or a cave, and our acolytes willing.

The bishop said something to Salazar, who then spoke to the witch,

- The bishop would like to know why you think our acolytes unwilling.

- You force boys to serve you, to service your needs like they were girls! In the vestry and in your chambers, from what we hear. Our Sorginak are free to come and go, not bound into seminaries that twist and pervert them by men fouler than any demon.

She had been staring at the bishop, who, until then impassive, looked paler now and smaller. Salazar, not seeing this change, continued,

- I see. I'll remind you that your best hope to save your soul from eternal torment is to confess your own crimes honestly before you are purged by fire, as you know you must be. To accuse others falsely will not help you. Tell us what happened in the mass.

She snorted, almost laughed,

- Everything you imagine and more. Maybe more than even he can imagine – she nodded at the bishop – It started with drinking and stories, the girl was right about that, and some kissing and cuddling. This was mainly women, mind, plus poor Jon. Then the singing and clapping to get us in the mood to dance, and the drinking of the elixir. And soon the clothes came off and they were dancing naked, she was the first to strip off, that young 'un, and they danced like they didn't know where they were and like dancing was all they knew, because that's what it's like with the potion at first. Then they fell down and was kissing and touching each other all over and that's when our lord came.

- How did he appear? From where? And what form did he take?

- He was just there in the middle of it. I've told you his form depends on the seer. That young 'un saw him as a handsome young man as she took his great cock in her mouth while another woman kissed and licked her down there to get her ready for him. Then they all took turns to feel his shaft in them, helping each other along the way with their fingers and mouths till each one could do no more.

- Did you do this?

- I was one of them, yes.

- Did you not fear for your soul?

- No. We summoned a true god, all willing, all enjoying it, so he could honour an ancient promise and right a wrong. We harmed no-one except one troublemaker. The bully Gonzalo was punished that night, mauled by a bear on his own land, it looked like.

The bishop gestured to Salazar to come close and they began a whispered dialogue, growing heated at times, the bishop hissing something insistently, not quite audible to the crowd below. As the crowd gave up trying to understand the discussion, for it was in church Latin anyway, a murmur began. Despite the shadow of the pyres and the presence of the guards, some dared to joke about the bawdy tale they had just heard. These country folk! What these Basque women get up to when the men are away after whale and cod! You know what they need, said the men, to keep 'em out of mischief. Others in the crowd had noticed something happening around them. While the soldiers posted around the square to watch the crowd for dissent or impertinence were big, and had probably been picked for that very reason, each was now faced with or surrounded by several even stockier men, strangers all. They were a rugged-looking lot, the newcomers; some had long, wild hair and some had it cropped short, most had dark hair but some were ginger or blond. All had broad, square heads that topped wide backs almost without neck and every body part bulged with muscle: thigh, buttock, chest and back. Their faces were heavy-browed, cruel-looking. It was difficult to tell with their crude and baggy clothing but most or all carried heavy, short-handled axes. They looked relaxed and chatted good-naturedly in their own strange tongue, kicking at the ground as if impatient and glancing up at the inquisitors with interest now and then. The guards' eyes swivelled about in quiet panic, hoping some officer would notice and send for reinforcements soon or that the pyres would be lit and the prisoners burnt, to draw attention away from them.

Up on the platform, Salazar suddenly rose and stalked off, his face black with fury. The bishop called his name but he continued down the wooden steps without answering or looking back. He was going toward the city gate that led to the cathedral quarter. The crowd parted hastily to let him pass then he was lost within it.

The bishop appeared comically nonplussed for a moment but none dared to laugh. No verdict had been delivered, nor had Jon the blacksmith spoken, but there was no-one to speak for the church except the bishop himself, who did not seem able to. The verdict would be death by burning for somebody, it always was. But the sentence had to be read out first.

Eventually the bishop called across to the jailer who had brought the prisoners up onto the platform. That jailer came and listened to brief instructions from the bishop then took the same route down from

171

the platform as Salazar had and likewise disappeared into the crowd. The bishop took a quill pen and began hastily writing on paper while the crowd waited in near silence. Some of the rough axemen grinned at each other. Others, fiercer, from who knew what untamed regions, scowled and spat.

Eventually the guard returned with a young priest, white-faced. He seemed impossibly thin and weak and when the bishop beckoned him over and whispered in his ear, he swayed for a moment like a man about to faint before steadying himself by putting a hand on the purple cloth of the inquisitor's table. But he took the paper, yellowing and brittle, and walked to the front guardrail of the platform, also resting one hand there as he raised the paper before him to read out the bishop's verdict. His voice rang out surprisingly clear and strong over the crowd,

- The verdict of the bishopric of Pamplona invoking the power vested therein by papal decree and thus by divine right, incontrovertible and infallible, is as follows: the charges against the blacksmith Jon Errimentera of Gernika of celebrating a false Sabbath or Akelarre , of bestiality, idolatry and the committing of lewd and blasphemous acts are withdrawn due to lack of reliable evidence or testimony.

There were gasps in the crowd. If one were let off, it usually went worse for the others.

- All charges against the girl, Zuriñe Garay, also of Gernika, are also withdrawn due to lack of reliable evidence, testimony or confession.

This brought a sigh of relief. They had liked the girl. But now they feared the more for the witch. Or thrilled the more.

- Due to the false, preposterous and salacious nature of the testimony given by the woman Ziortza Goikoetxea, it is ordered that all such testimony be struck from the records and proceedings of these courts this very day. All charges levelled by the church against this woman too are herewith withdrawn. Moreover, the final sentence of the court is that the three accused be immolated in the purifying flames of the three pyres for that purpose here erected...

More than one rough warrior grabbed the handle of his axe.

- ...in effigy this night and without delay as a warning to all who maintain pagan traditions.

As the cheering and jeering of the crowd died down and the dry wood of the bonfires ignited, long amber tongues of flame licked the night sky, attracting first moths then small, demon-faced bats that fed on them.

Saturday 24th July 1982.

Driscoll's house was big, turn-of-the century red brick, set well back from the road in a large, neglected garden, one side wall encased in a nest-like thatch of ivy. The doorbell seemed not to work but when Cooper stepped inside the scruffy porch and rapped on the door, there was still no answer.

You're here. Your car's here and your dog's here.

The old man's Border collie had slunk from under or behind the old Land Rover and was snarling quietly at Cooper, sometimes pacing forward, sometimes retreating toward his hiding place, never taking his eyes off the copper.

- Fuck off, fucking animal. Where's the old perv then?

It now struck Cooper that he could not for the life of him imagine what Driscoll might do on a Saturday night, alone in the house. In some old man's pub, alright, it was possible to imagine him talking to the other old codgers about horses, or the war, or people they knew or had known. But in the house of an evening? He didn't seem the reading type (racing tips and dirty magazines aside) and even if he had a television, Cooper couldn't imagine what he might watch on it. 'One man and his dog' maybe?

Ignoring the cowering dog, Cooper strolled along a gravel track between nettles and tall grass into the long back garden that gave onto the fields. There he saw the old man leaning against a wooden gate looking out over his own land towards Whites Lane. He waited until he was nearly within touching distance then,

- Ooh, Mr. Driscoll, never 'ad you down as a birdwatcher.

Instead of jumping as Cooper had expected, the farmer turned around slowly, not before taking a moment to stuff something into an inside jacket pocket.

- What d'yow want? Yer'm 'ere without my permission. That's trespass.

His eyes were glazed and bloodshot, slow to focus.

- Just here for a friendly chat, Mr. Driscoll. I'd have thought a respectable landowner like you would want to be friendly with the police.

Still moving sluggishly, Driscoll grunted and turned back to face towards his fields.

What's that smell? Like a plastics factory. Or nail varnish.

- You might even be able to help us now and then.

No answer came. Cooper realised that Driscoll was leaning on the fence for support, to stay upright.

Pissed? He's not a drinker.

He pressed on,

- Thought you might know, for instance, who gave a load of booze to a couple of teenage girls last night.

A stifled, spluttering sound came from the old man, his back to the copper.

Is he laughing, the old nutter?

The conversation wasn't going as planned but there was no other plan, so,

- Because if someone did that, trying to get some young girls drunk so he could 'ave 'is way with 'em, I reckon he'd deserve a good arse-kicking, the dirty old perv.

Driscoll had managed to turn around again and, either due to the laughter or his intoxication, was now sliding slowly down to a sitting position, his back against the fence. As always, the laugh soon deteriorated into coughing.

Well done, Charles Bronson. He's obviously terrified.

Driscoll was trying to say something,

- Great... big... fuckin'... knockers she 'ad.

Without breath to speak more, he made a timeless gesture with cupped hands in front of his chest. Yelping foxes could be heard but not seen in the darkening fields. Driscoll slowly got his breath back,

- Like melons. Big round uns.

Despite his current handicaps, Driscoll was a consummate mime. The movements of his still-cupped hands were suggestive of pendulous, globular weight. But then his eyes narrowed and his head tilted to one side. He was going to drift off unless Cooper kept him talking,

- Who's that, then? Who yer talkin' about?

- Blondie. Bettsy's niece.

- What did yer see?

- Big bouncing tits. Big knockers bouncing up and down. Riding him! Riding Greeny!

Rosie Betts did not have large, round breasts, was in fact slim and athletic, but this could only be a garbled version of last night's events and Cooper needed to hear more,

- The blonde one? Not the little one?

- Nah. He shagged 'er fust but yer day see nuthin. Kept their clothes on. A quickie. Then it was Rosie's turn. Ah sid it all. Found 'em and followed 'em after they took me booze.

Driscoll became animated again,

- Riding 'im she was, n' throwin' 'er 'ead back 'n screamin' in gyppo language or summat... then she... she...

Again he was overcome by cackling laughter and coughing. But he was eager to continue,

- She lamped 'im! She made fists and started paling the 'ell out of him! Big lump like him! 'E tried to fight back but she was faster than him, stronger, too!

- Then what happened?

Driscoll seemed almost back to normal now. Telling the story he needed to tell had required him to concentrate, to overcome his intoxication. He would not try to stand up yet, but he would finish the story,

- She saw me. I dunno 'ow. Impossible at that distance, me in the bushes 'n all, but she'd picked up a bloody big rock and she looked all around 'n saw me watching 'n she stopped dead. Dropped it 'n rolled off of 'im. If she 'adn't seen me, she'd a killed 'im. Then and there, with that bloody great rock.

His story shared, Driscoll seemed to relax. Cooper waited a minute, then seeing the old man's eyes closing, began to walk away.

He can put himself to bed. Or stay here. I'll have a proper word tomorrow.

He was halfway back to the house when the farmer spoke again,

- Wait. I day tell yer the best bit... - before sliding sideways into sleep.

***

Driscoll woke up. It was very dark and Cooper had gone. He sat up and rested his back against the garden fence for some minutes; re-orientating himself, gathering resolve, then pulled himself up and began walking stiffly toward a small shed in one corner of the garden.

Why you go out, this time of night?! Why you always go out to fields this time of night, when you have wife and son in house?

177

The sudden reprimand, delivered in a grating East European accent, was loud enough to startle Driscoll into dropping the keys to the shed. At some level Driscoll knew that Marta was long dead but that didn't stop her nagging. He groaned pitifully as he bent down to retrieve the keys,

You a crazy old man. No, you not man. Not been a real man for years. You crazy old goat! Want to be like the young goats!

The door open, he turned on the light and scanned the highest shelf on the far wall. If he had any, it would be up there, with the creosote, the WD-40, the bottles of turpentine and methylated spirits. The effects of the first bag, a stale old one picked up in the woods had worn off, after his sleep in the garden, and Driscoll had a dream to chase.

wife and son in house.

- Yer'm dead, woman! Done away with yerself years ago. 'N 'e doh come 'round 'ere no more neither!

Then he saw it. A half–pint tin of Evo-Stick.

You think you do like them, you be young like them, but no, no!

In his mind's eye, he saw the wagging finger and the mocking smile, cold of eye, that were so characteristic of her later years, the barren years after his young bride became the bride of disappointment and bitterness.

The old freezer bag was all stuck together, and stiff in places. Reluctantly, he dropped it and looked around for a replacement. Bin bags! Black plastic bin liners. He fretted for a while over whether they would work as well as the freezer bag had, whether they too would be able to transport him, despite the protests of his wife, to the old places, the old times.

Needs must as the devil drives.

With shaking hands, he hadn't eaten since breakfast and it was now nearly midnight, he opened the tin and poured a dollop of the creamy, honey-coloured liquid into the bin bag. The new bag was obviously too big for his ends but by gathering and scrunching he was able to create a bulging pocket of fume-filled air in one corner. He put the bag to his lips and began to breathe in and out. He inhaled and exhaled, standing up in his shed, for some minutes but no dreams came, only dizziness, and he realised he would have to sit down somewhere and concentrate, concentrate on nothing, on emptying his mind, if the spell were to work.

He must have recovered his keys and he must have opened the gate leading to his own fields. He found a barn that he knew would be empty and sat down in the musty straw, back to the wall. Bag to mouth. Breathe in, breathe out. In and out.

That's the only in and out you do, old man! Weak, shrivel up old man!

He could see Marta now, as well as hear her. The sound, and the look, of Marta in her last, harridan years was still enough to make him cringe but also to sadden him. That was not the Marta he wanted.

He was new to this game. Could he control what it did to him? Where it took him? He suspected not, it seemed too powerful to be controllable, the way it unleashed memories and dreams that overwhelmed the conscious mind. He would have to take his chances. He put the bag to his lips once more.

For a while there was nothing, only darkness and his own rhythmic breathing. Slowly twisting black shapes formed in the blacker void. The shapes swirled and pirouetted for him, blossoming into colour until a new reality formed. Not images, not sounds, this was not a picture show but a reality first experienced long ago, now resurrected in every long-forgotten detail.

He was young again, very young. He was in a sunlit summer field, blue skies above. He knew the field. It was the meadow in the high part of the Woods.

But something was wrong. He was a boy. A boy in a field in

the summer with his first love. Mary! It was wonderful, this return to a time of innocent childhood happiness, but he sought a different, later happiness. The other reality faded.

The animal smells in the barn were too strong he decided, when he eventually regained a kind of consciousness, they took him back too far.

Get into the woods. She liked the woods. At first. The first few years. The bluebells in spring. Reminded her of Poland, she said.

He found himself in the woods.

He was on a narrow path somewhere in the high part of the woods, near the quarries. The vegetation on each side was dense, nettles, bushes and elder grown to head height. It was a humid summer afternoon and he had to brush midges and flies from his sweating face or swat them as they buzzed around his ears.

It was round here we did it! The first time! She wor stuck up! Not bloody ungrateful like some round 'ere! 'Appy to bloody be 'ere, after what the Germans did!

He knew what he would see if he parted the bushes and looked. He could hear the gasping and breathing now, the little moans. He smiled.

That's 'er. She loved it, she did. Loved me, in them days. We 'ad a few good years after that. She 'ad friends 'n' all. 'Er English got better. Liked goin' to Bilston market and the like, or up Sedgley to the pictures. Robert Mitchum! Dirk Bogarde! Then the friends started 'aving babies.

The world rippled and he could see Marta, lying on her back in a clearing, head held back, mouth open, eyes closed in devotion to the sensations of her body. Her legs were parted and raised, skirt thrown back, to make easier the entry of...

An abomination. Their own son. The big blond baby they had adopted when natural means had failed, now grown to a big brute of a man, hammering away between his young mother's legs. The impossible vision swelled and spun, offering Driscoll graphic close-ups from various angles before settling on one image, the contorted face of his son, laughing in his face as he thrust away.

The image receded. The world reverted to darkness and quiet. Driscoll was conscious of his heart rate slowing back down to normal.

Our cuckoo 'e was. Is. Thought she'd be 'appier with a little 'un to look after. We both did. Enough going spare after the war. Took 'er about six months to realise 'er mistake. Never took to each other. 'N 'e was a real 'andful from the start, with his screamin' and 'is tantrums. She kept trying to be a mother to 'im but 'e just sent 'er more round the bend. She started goin' on about 'ow we should've picked a girl, that it would've been different with a girl but that I 'adn't wanted one. So then it was my fault and I 'ad that every day 'till she done away with 'erself.

Then the harridan was back. He sensed her presence and the gist of the onslaught before it arrived,

Ah, girls! We all know about you and girls! Dirty old man! Touching and feeling in your fields and your barn!

I never forced no one.

One day they lock you up! Take farm off you!

Then there was silence. He was lying on his back in his own back garden again. In the sky he could see stars and the glow of the moon behind a cloud. Bats flitted around the tops of the trees. His experiment had been a partial success before it went so disastrously wrong. He had seen Marta, conjured her up, but would never regain his young wife. Now he was tired and hungry. There was an open tin of Spam in the fridge. He trudged uphill through the fields, back toward his garden gate.

The broad shape of a man, made silhouette by a light on in the side porch, barred Driscoll's path back to his house. Why wasn't his dog there, barking?

Driscoll did not believe in devils or ghosts. He knew it just a man, despite the mask, despite the horns, and he guessed that, after his years of unpunished crimes, retribution had finally come. Some girl's dad. Some brother or boyfriend.

Time to pay the piper!

He didn't want to die. He wanted to run, to save himself, but he was puzzled and had a question, although it came out as an affirmation,

- That's the mask. 'Er mask. She put it on. Before she started bashing him.

The dark figure spoke,

- Run, old man.

***

The Teller and the Listener

In the darkness of the damp cave, the listener briefly stirred. Then a sudden, chilling conviction roused him to full consciousness: the bargain he had made was not worth it. He had been tricked into forfeiting everything, he had a job and a life up there on the surface, in exchange for these mad and impossible tales of witches and, what? Cavemen? He had swapped his life for this? He tried to move but couldn't. He was not surprised at this failure and realised he had grown used to failing.

The voice of the teller had never paused so the listener began to listen again.

West Hampshire – September 1939

- You feelin' better now, buddy?

Leonard ignored the voice. The pain pulsing through his pelvis and right femur had a sickening sensation to it, separate from the pain itself, like an aftertaste. The pain alone was bad enough, the worst he had known in his thirty-four years, but the grating, splintered sensation that came with it was worse; a horribly unnatural feeling that something essential was permanently damaged. Words like ruptured, maimed, crippled came to mind but he could move his toes and feel them.

He was lying on wet concrete looking at a wet brick wall dotted with tufts of damp, green waterweed. He dared not roll over, or even move much at all because of his injuries and the fear of making them worse. Part of the brickwork in front of him was dull in the shadow of some unseen obstruction but part was in faint sunlight and even in his pain he noted that the thinnest filaments of the grassy water-

weed glistened like living emerald where the sun caught them. That meant his glasses had survived the accident or whatever had happened. He could hear the sound of trickling water somewhere behind him and smell the dank canal. He had fallen in a lock.

- Can you hear me? Help's on the way. We'll get you out of there, bud.

He now became aware that the voice belonged to an American, the first he had heard in real life, outside of film and radio. Not a cultured American. It was more of a tough guy accent like that of George Raft or Jimmy Cagney. It also had an aftertaste, like his pain, a slight residual accent from somewhere else. He experimented with moving his head and it didn't feel too bad so, careful to not twist his torso as well, he lifted his gaze slowly up the wall until he saw the outline of the speaker, silhouetted against a summer sky. All he could make out was a bulky, square-headed shape. The American voice continued. Somehow, it didn't even sound out of place,

- You're lucky you got that concrete ledge to support you. Part of a sluice. They don't normally have those. Or unlucky somebody let most the water out, I guess. Anyways, I sent the negro kid to get help.

Leonard just groaned. Then after some time,

- There aren't any negroes here.

There was a pause.

- Sure looked like a negro to me. Like I say, he's run for help. I told him we'd need a ladder, police, a doctor, whatever he can get.

Where at first the voice had been steady and matter of fact, this part about the negro was delivered in a forcedly jocular tone like it was not the man's real voice but one he would put on if interviewed on the radio and wanted to make a good impression. A disturbing thought occurred to Leonard: if there was a negro, maybe up from Southampton or down from London for some reason, he would not know the area, would not know where to go for help,

- Which way did you send him?

- Toward the bridge. If he gets up on the road he should come to a

farmhouse and they might have a telephone or a car, I reckon. I'll stay with you till then. I'd have gone but that feller looked like he could run a bit better'n me.

- *There's a gypsy camp, or tinkers or something, near Lyndhurst house. They've got a horse. Somebody could go for help on that.*

- *I didn't see them. Guess they moved on.*

From down in the lock, Leonard squinted up at the American again but with the light behind him it was impossible to discern anything except a general impression of bulk.

- *Say, there's a kind of ladder built in the wall. Looks kind of slippy, no good for haulin' you up, we'll need a stretcher for that, but I can get down to you. Keep you company. Gotta get back to my ship tonight, back to Southampton, but I don't like to see you left on your own down there.*

The big man started to climb down into the lock. When he got to the concrete ledge, he squatted down where Leonard lay and the injured man saw him properly for the first time. As well as sounding like a film American, he was dressed like one, not flashy like a Jimmy Cagney gangster but still smart, like James Garfield as a gutsy reporter or fight promoter. He was much bigger than Garfield but had that same tough but friendly smile and unruly black hair.

- *It's best if we talk. Keep your mind off it, keep you awake. You were kayoed for a while there, pal.*

- *If he can run to Lyndhurst House, they can send help.*

- *What's that buddy?*

- *I work there. It's the closest place.*

- *You work with those kids? The Basque ones?*

It was true, talking did take his mind off the pain.

- *Yes. I mean my real job is in the town. The cement factory. But I help out there in my free time.*

- I heard something 'bout that. So you help them, do you?

That sounded like the real voice again, not the radio one, but Leonard didn't like the tone; cold, sarcastic. Still squatting, it was too damp and dirty to sit, the American continued,

- They thought I was a Basque, some of the merchant marine guys. They'd read about Paolo Uzcudun, the fighter, in the papers and because I was from that part of the world, and was built like him, they said I was a Basque too.

- The merchant marine, like Jack London.

Leonard felt embarrassed as soon as he said it. The American didn't seem to notice,

- That's right! It's a hard life but you see the world. Singapore, San Francisco, all the ports, Santiago, Buenos Aires. Tough places, tough guys. Lots of strange guys, too.

He had been looking around the slimy walls as he spoke, only occasionally catching Leonard's eye but now looked him in the face,

- Faggots and queens some of them, you know what I mean?

- Well, yes. Homosexuals.

- Jack London write about that?

- No.

- So how'd you know about it? Nothing like that around here, right?

- No. I shouldn't think so. Do you think he'll be able to find his way back? Now that you're down here. They won't see us.

- Your bike's up there. They'll see it.

- Oh.

- Course there's fags and there's fags.

- Yes.

- If they're only messing with guys that want to be messed with, leave 'em to it right? Who are we to judge? We don't have to watch, right?

- *That's right. I suppose.*

- *So if it don't happen around here and it ain't in Jack London's books, how come you know so much?*

- *The fellows talked about it in school.*

- *I bet they did.*

The hard tone again.

- *Or you see cases in the newspapers. We call them nancies or pufters.*

- *I see. Then you've got the other type. The ones that pick on the weak. Force themselves on young guys or kids even. Did you see that in the newspaper, too?*

- *I think so.*

- *Court cases?*

- *Yes.*

- *Well they deserve what they get. Then they get some extra justice from the fellers in prison and they deserve that too.*

The American sprang to his feet. He had been squatting on his haunches for five minutes and he was older than Leonard, in his forties probably, but the movement was swift and fluid. Leonard couldn't see but it sounded like he spat into the water.

- *So you work with the Basque kids, eh? How they doin'? They gettin' used to the old place? I thought they all got adopted by now?*

The cheerful voice had returned.

- *They're doing as well as can be expected. Maybe you should go and look for him.*

The big man turned to look him in the eye, his face blank. Then, stone cold,

- *Who?*

There was an instant of silence.

- The black boy.

- Yeah. Him. He'll be comin'. Must have had to run to the village. So do they talk about it, Guernica and all? Some of them were there, right?

- We're told not to bring it up. I'm just there some evenings to teach music. To provide therapy through music and movement. I think some were at Guernica, though.

- I'll bet they were. Been through a lot. You know at first they thought it was leaflets they were dropping? There was no reason to bomb the town. Didn't make sense. Whose idea was this music and movement?

- It's a new technique. As you think about the music, something pure...

- No. I mean here, now. Did somebody ask you to come in and do this with the evacuees or was it your big idea?

- I approached them. I have some training in music and I wanted to help.

The dark-haired man shifted stance to stand square in front of Leonard, planting his feet a little wider than before.

- I'll bet you did, you son of a bitch. Like they ain't had enough already without your groping and grabbing.

He was unbuttoning the fly of his trousers. His penis, a fat cylinder of silky brown skin, emerged between stubby fingers and he started to piss down on Leonard. He swayed his hips so that the stream of dark urine spattered and skittered into droplets on the damp concrete and then soaked noiselessly into Leonard's clothes before circling back to the concrete and around again. When Leonard tried to speak, the heavy stream was directed onto his face, making him splutter and shake his head.

- Piss on you, hijo de puta. The gypsies told us all about it. Let's see how you swim.

He began to kick at the head of the prone body before him. After the first two kicks all shouting stopped and each heavy kick after that moved the shuddering body closer to the edge and the dark green water below.

PART THREE

It was early evening and Dean Wilson was standing on the concrete roof of one of the World War Two air raid shelters, converted into changing rooms for footballers, at the top of St. George's Park, Hurst Hill. In the depths of winter, the long, grassy slopes of the park below him were so popular with sledging and sliding boys and girls that the snow would get polished into a diamond-hard veneer of ice, and fearless showboaters could slide down for a hundred yards, standing up on dockers or Sellatios, while a heavy metal-runnered sledge could gain enough speed to fly over the last, and steepest, ten yards of the slope and land on the football pitch at the bottom. But on this warm evening the only other kids on the parkland were a pair of girls, about ten years old, lolling and swaying on the swings in the small playground at the top of the steeper slope.

- ´E´s ´ere again, 'e 'ay come. - mouthed Dean to himself. He had mischief in mind, a plan for the evening and was finding it hard to keep quiet, to keep still, even. Hundreds of yards away, at the bottom of the park, a tall and square-shouldered youth in faded jeans and a red jumper emerged from a gap between the concrete-panelled walls of a pub car park and began the long walk toward the shelters. In one hand he was swinging a plastic Asda bag, filled with something bulky but light.

Fidgeting and spitting, Dean watched as Colin Bull got closer, one step at a time, patient by his standards until, to his disbelief, Colin paused to say something to the two girls,

- Come on Bully! - he shouted down the park, adding under his breath - Yer bell-end!

Allies rather than friends, Dean and Colin usually greeted each other with a nod or a muttered, 'Alright' but, as Colin finally hauled himself up onto the roof of the shelter, after throwing the Asda bag up first, Dean couldn't be bothered with even that.

- Bored out me fuckin' box up 'ere waitin' for you.

Colin was a head taller and despite being too good-natured to have ever been a real contender for cock of the school, he had shown his lanky, big-knuckled power in just enough fights to be ranked in the top five, by most reckonings. He didn't need to explain himself to Dean and they both knew it. He nodded at Dean's black Fred Perry t-shirt, black Sta-press trousers and Adidas Kick trainers,

- What yow come as? A fuckin' ninja? Fu fuckin' man-chu?

Dean looked down at his dark clothing. A ninja. Not a bad quip for the big lump but totally wasted as they were alone.

- We'm gooin up the woods, remember? Gonna shit somebody up? Blend into the darkness? 'N'yow come in a fuckin' bright red Slazenger jumper? Ronnie fuckin' Corbett.

Colin grinned. The plan for tonight was a good one, would be a real laugh, and Dean was the perfect evil little fucker to make sure it got carried out. He pulled a long-jawed face as he looked down at his own jumper,

- Doh matter. It'll be pitch black by the time we do it. Did yer bring the tights?

Dean tossed an unopened packet of Playtex tights onto the concrete roof at Colin's feet, and nodded at the bag in Colin's large hand,

- Why's yer bag so big? That ay a sheet.

- We day 'ave any white sheets. They're all yellow or blue with flowers or whatnot. Brought a quilt instead.

Dean's eyes bulged,

- A fucking quilt? Yer´m gonna come out from behind a tree in the middle o´ the woods wrapped in a fuckin' quilt? They'll piss 'emselves laughin', yer dozy twat.

- It's a thin un. It'll look like a sheet when it's on.

Colin picked up the tights and put them in the Asda bag with the quilt. His face flushed red as he considered whether to let Dean's use of the word 'twat' ride or not. Kids had been lamped for less. Dean changed the subject quickly,

- Come on, let's 'ave a fag while we wait for 'im.

He sat on the edge of the roof, facing down the park. He wanted to know some details, the dirtier the better, about what had gone on with Greeny, Bully and the two girls. He had managed to get Greeny alone already and ask him but had not been able to get more than a laconic, 'Fucked 'em both. Slags'. Colin would at least be more talkative than that, you just had to read between the bollocks was all. He tried to make his question sound casual,

- So… er… what happened the other night then, with them girls?

Colin sat down next to him and accepted a fag,

- We'd been on the glue up the woods, just comin' off it like. 'Avin a fag and there they was, with a load o' booze. Couldn't believe it.

Girls and booze. Up the woods. Stories didn't start much better than that as far as Dean was concerned.

- Was they pissed?

- Lisa was a bit tipsy. There was some o' them Babycham things? Bloody horrible. Anyway she was drinking one o' those so she was a bit gone already. Do tek much with a little 'un like 'er I s'pose.

- Wasn't just that though, was it?

- Nah, there was big bottles o' cider and Banks's. Bout twelve cans too.

- 'Oo went with 'oo?

Colin exhaled quickly, dismissively,

- We day even get that far. I day any road. Coz o' that nutter, Greeny.

- What did 'e do?

Colin paused to think before continuing, as if still trying to puzzle it all out for himself,

- It was all a load o' bollocks. I think that Rosie wanted me to go with Lisa, so she could be with 'im. Yer can tell, like.

It was true. Dean had to admit that despite being a big dozy lump, Bully did know his women. Known for it. The big youth continued,

- I wor even bothered, I fancied 'em both. But he was watching that Lisa like...

He seemed to struggle.

- ...a hawk?

- Ar, that's right. A dirty bastard of a hawk, though. And then, yer woh believe this...

He had Dean's full attention.

- Rosie took aht this scruffy old t-shirt 'n said I should try it on.

- What, like women's clothes or summat?

Colin looked at his friend for a moment.

- Er, no.

- Never mind. Goo on.

- A bloke's t-shirt. Yeller. But then o' course when Lisa said she wanted to see me in it, too, gigglin' an' the like, course Greeny 'ad to start actin' the prat.

- What'd 'e do?

- Grabbed it off me. Put it on himself. Looked a right twat. Then there was a bit of pushin' and shovin' and I said fuck this and I was off.

- Yer left 'im up the woods with two wenches and a load o' booze?

- I can get wenches. Doh yow worry.

That was also true. At least he had revealed a bit more than Greeny had.

- Remember when Farrell used to jump the see-saw on his bike?

An older kid, Chris Farrell, had become a local legend by sometimes bombing his powerful two-stroke Kawasaki along the football pitch and then up the first, steepest slope fast enough to sail high over the see-saws of the play area.

- That wor the best. On the way down 'e'd jump the goal posts.

But they both knew all of this, had had the same conversation many times during the interminably long and hot days of the summer holidays when they found themselves here in this park with nothing to do. As they stared ahead, drew on their fags and spat, the long daylight hours of the summer evening ahead of them, probably devoid of booze, violence or saucy girls, seemed as extensive and bland as the green parkland before them. At least, and at last, daylight would eventually fade. Nobody was expecting them to go home. And they had some fun planned for that night in the woods.

***

- George! Can I have a word? It's important.

George had been reading Papillon on his bed but he came to the top of the stairs and saw his father looking up at him from the doorway to the living room.

- Come down George, into the kitchen. There's tea in the pot. I want to ask you about something.

There was no Battenberg but there was malt loaf. They cut themselves slices and spread butter on it. Peter Merriman poured tea for both of them. It was too hot to drink for the moment. They sat facing each other at the small kitchen table.

- It's about this bullying, George. No, don't worry. I know you don't want to talk about it and that's natural, I wouldn't have either. I mean, I didn't when it happened to me. It's just... what I tried to ask you the other day. I'm worried about over-reaction. I'm thinking about some things that I've seen, or heard about, that I wouldn't want to happen again... er, in your case.

George didn't answer. He wasn't going to lie unless he was forced to.

- I'll explain what happened to me, should've told you before really, and what went on with your grandad and if it rings a bell...

- Grandad! What's Grandad got to do with me being bullied?

He had not known his grandfather and had never imagined him as anything other than an old man.

- Well that's what I'd like to know, really. It's probably nothing but I've seen some connections, probably coincidences. I don't want history to repeat itself. Not if it involves...

He struggled for words,

- ...things getting out of hand.

Again, George said nothing.

- I'll tell you about me first. You'll probably wonder what all the fuss is about. Anyway, I was the victim of bullying, quite serious bullying by some lads, local tearaways, you must know the sort.

He was toying with a square slice of malt loaf, trying to squeeze it uniformly along two of its edges to make a rectangle. He sighed,

- I wouldn't even bother you with this normally but it's important to what we're talking about: it was a really bad assault, not just bullying, I should have said, being honest. They beat me badly and they stripped some of me clothes off and did other things. They'd probably get life if they were caught doing that today. And, of course, being what they were, they did it publicly.

- Jesus, I'm sorry dad.

- It's alright, though – he actually smiled - That's not the problem. It's what happened later.

- What, they got you again?

- Well, no. I think somebody got them. Got them for me.

***

In the post-industrial village of Roseville, about a mile away from Whites Lane and the woods, three young men emerged from the wasteland of bramble, broken concrete and thistle that rose from the canal towpath, and crossed the road, walking purposefully toward a near-empty car park behind a block of flats. It was half past eight on a Sunday evening and the road was deserted. Of varying heights and builds, all three were big and all three walked with a rolling, springy gait suggestive of great mass, agility and power. They were dressed scruffily in old boots, jeans and jumpers.

They walked through the car park toward the high street, looking at each in turn of the handful of cars that had been parked up for the night but paying particular attention to the biggest and most powerful: an old Vauxhall Victor. As they reached the low wall separating the car park from the high street, one vaulted over it effortlessly then sat back on top of it to watch out for passers-by who might emerge from one of the two pubs or the Greek chip shop on the corner. Another walked back through the car park to the road they had crossed earlier where he too kept watch.

Seeing no signal from the others to detain him, the third youth took a bunch of dozens of keys from a pocket and tried them one-by-one in the door of the big Vauxhall, twisting and forcing the worn old lock with a practiced movement of the wrist until, at only the fourth attempt, he was able to open the door and slide inside. Less than a minute later the car was being slowly reversed out of its parking space.

***

- Got them for you? Like beat them up?

George suspected that it was going to be more than that.

- A lot worse. You must have heard about the three boys that died in the bonfire up the woods a long time ago before you were born?

George nodded.

- It was them. Those three that did that to me, they were all dead a month later. The only survivor was their mate, who hadn't touched me.

George spoke too quickly,

- And you think you caused that. Caused somebody to get them.

Peter looked confused for a moment,

- No, not caused it. I'm not saying I caused it.

- You didn't, like, ask anybody to get them or anything?

- No. Well, I mean that's what I'm getting to. There was this old bloke. Like a tramp, almost, with scruffy clothes and a big bushy beard but he was a cobbler. He had a little hut, a workshop, that they let him keep on some wasteland near the Birmingham New Road, near the school. Some of the kids used to swear that he lived in it but I don't think that would have been allowed. Probably had a caravan or a council flat somewhere. People used to bring him shoes to mend. They did that a lot more in those days, that was a proper job then. And he used to talk to the boys and girls on their way to school or coming back. That was more normal in those days too. He even took them into his hut. But it was alright, nothing funny, he was just a friendly old bloke. He'd chat and joke with 'em about football, or birding or motorbikes even, with the boys, and who knew what with the girls but it must've been quite innocent. There was never any suggestion that it wasn't, anyway.

- Okay.

- So he must have heard about what happened and he called me over a few days later.

- He knew your name?

- He knew everybody's name and all their family and a bit about every one of us, like where you lived, who you knocked about with. Anyway, he called me over and he said they was right buggers, I think those were his words, and he said that they should get what they deserve, ain't that right? He didn't talk Black Country, he was a bit posher or from somewhere else, so he said 'ain't that right?' not 'ay that right?' And I can't remember but I think I probably said 'yes', like I was agreeing that they should get what they deserve.

- And then what happened?

- Nothing, that was it. Those boys died, though.

- And you think he did it.

- No not at all. He couldn't have. He was an old man about seventy-five. With a gammy leg.

George felt relieved,

- This is nothing, dad. An old man who speaks to everyone spoke to you, 'cause he heard you got beat up and he wanted to sympathise. Then the three kids that bullied you got killed in an accident, doing something stupid.

- I know it's nothing! And the police at the time didn't think it was anything. I think they looked into it a bit, but it was treated as an accident. But then if you put all that together with what happened to your granddad and what I think's happening now, it all looks a bit too coincidental. There must be something.

- What happened to granddad then?

Peter Merriman had finished the malt loaf. He had been swilling what remained of his tea around the bottom of the cup with one hand but now stopped that and began picking with his fingernail at a solidified smear of brown sauce on the checked tablecloth.

- He would never say exactly what started it. It was just before the war, when him and some of the other Spanish evacuees were in a kind of home, still waiting to be fostered out, the older ones like him or the ones with problems, you know. Down South. And somebody, one of the staff I think, had been molesting him...

- Grandad?

Peter glanced up from stain for a second,

- He never said exactly that but reading between the lines I think that's what it was.

- Right.

- So they were in this big country house, like a stately home type thing, like Himley Hall, donated by a rich lady, a Duchess or something, for the evacuees, and it was in the middle of the countryside, miles from the nearest village. But there were some gypsies camped nearby, he said.

- Gypsies or just travellers?

George had recently learned about the difference from talking to Rosie.

- Well your granddad said they were gypsies but I'm not sure he distinguished between Romanies or whatever. Anyway, it was a group of families camped in the fields for some time, it must have been, because the kids from the camp used to play with the Spanish kids, became friends.

- The Duchess just let them go out and play in the fields with gypsies?

- No, daft lad. The Duchess didn't live there, she just donated the house. There were staff. The kids were just being looked after before they were fostered, supposedly, and I don't think there was that much supervision. Well, obviously there wasn't, that was the problem.

George snorted a little, like it was funny, but his father was serious,

- Apparently the man that had been doing it, the molesting or whatever, was found dead in a canal lock one morning. It looked like he'd fallen in, got injured and not been able to get out again. Your granddad always reckoned the gypsies knew what was going on and that they did it to help him and as a kind of punishment.

- But it was probably an accident as well, right? Nobody was arrested or anything.

- He said they questioned the leader of the gypsies, a bit of a hard knock apparently, because they started packing up and getting ready to leave just after it happened and that made it look a bit suspicious, of course. Turned out he had a really good alibi, though. He'd been away, in an illegal fight, prizefighting for money at some big horsefair in Essex. Hundreds of witnesses and not the kind of thing you'd make up to tell the police anyway.

George made a sound, exhaling quickly to express disbelief.

- Of course, he learned that part from his friends, the gypsy kids, if they were gypsies, not the police. Then they finally did leave.

A pause.

- So you see what I'm getting at, right? On their own these stories don't sound like much but if you put them together, it might be something. And then that Michael boy, what was his name?

- Hickman.

- He dies. And then I find out you're being bothered…

Peter stopped and sighed. There was no tea or cake to fiddle with. Even the stain had gone,

- And you're knocking about with a lovely girl, that Rosie, but I heard her name is Betts and that's the name of a very rough family, travellers too, going years back. So I've got to ask you…

George prepared himself, while trying to look unaltered outwardly.

- Have you been offered that kind of help? To fight your battles?

***

The dog that came bounding through bush and birch toward Cooper was the lurcher-mastiff cross that Cooper had last seen sleeping in Michael Betts' hut.

Shit. Where's the fucking caveman when you want him?

He looked around for a branch or plank to swing. His eyes widened with panic as he realised that the thin sticks of birch that littered the forest floor were useless as weapons and that even the thickest of the young trees around him offered neither shelter nor purchase for climbing. He was out of uniform and without his truncheon. The brindle beast was close now and had slowed slightly. Cooper knew from a lifetime of confrontations like this that if it began to bark warning and pace from side to side, it was not ready to attack and might be content to hold him at bay. But the dog kept coming, not barking or changing direction, just somehow lowering itself into a low-slung ready-to-pounce position while still charging.

You fuckin'

Cooper crouched to grab a chunk of damp limestone from the leaf litter,

Ugly

then half rose as he thought better of it.

Bastard

He slipped on the muddy leaves

Piece-of-shit

and found himself, to his horror, sitting defenceless on the floor

Fuckin'

As the dog raced toward him, preparing to spring, he fumbled in his jacket pocket for the familiar, heavy cylinder, forming a fist around it as he scrambled to his feet

Hound!

His punch, a flailing roundhouse right hook, was timed to perfection. He felt the eternal thrill of the perfect contraction as the loose muscles of his arm snapped whip-tight at the moment of contact, magnifying the force of the blow.

The beast's head was knocked sideways, causing the airborne body to twist, its momentum wrapping it around Cooper's torso before it dropped to the ground, limp and heavy amongst the mud and leaves. Cooper gazed at the twitching body at his feet as he struggled to regain control of his breathing and his trembling limbs.

A curtain moved in the doorway of Michael Betts' hut and the hermit emerged into the fading light of the glade. The sun was now behind the ridge that separated Betts's patch from the quarries and the long shadows of the birch trees had now merged into a general gloom. He was wearing an army-surplus work shirt and faded jeans with a large-buckled belt. To Cooper's great surprise he grinned,

- Yer've gone and killed me dog, ay yer?

- I think he's breathin'.

Betts approached then squatted down to have a closer look at the hound,

- Nah. 'E ay got long. Yer cracked his skull.

- We can tek 'im to the vets.

- They cor do nothin' for him now. Can't put a cast on 'is 'ead. There'll be swellin', bleeding on the brain, the lot. 'Is time's up! What did you 'it 'im with?

Betts seemed intrigued, amused, rather than angry.

Cooper held out his open hand to reveal the roll of coins, old sixpences, bound together with duct tape.

Betts's smile widened,

- I've seen them before! Some o' the boys on the doors use 'em. Best with leather gloves, good tight uns or you 'll break yer own 'and, nine times out of ten.

Cooper flexed his fingers, he could still open and close the hand, but the area behind the knuckles was already ballooning.

- You ay bothered 'baht losin' 'im? You had 'im all trained up for rabbitin' and the like, day yer?

Betts looked Cooper in the eye quizzically,

- Rabbitin'? 'E' ay a ferret! Or a lurcher for chasin' 'ares, although his dad was. But 'e could beat any Staffie in a fight. Some said I was daft, crossin' the two breeds, that you should keep like with like or you end up with the worst of both. My own brother laughed at me when he saw this one as a puppy, big 'ead on a skinny little body. But I know you can improve the breed by mixin' the blood a bit. This one was a case in point. Took 'im a while to fill out but when 'e did was more of a terror than any mastiff and as fast as any lurcher. It's not a secret either, the vigour of the hybrid, they call it. Sometimes you 'ave to do it, to keep the breed 'ealthy.

Cooper had never heard Betts speak like this, making small talk. Was the lonely cabin life getting to him? It was almost disappointing to think that this rocky island of a man might feel the need for human contact. Cooper had also come to talk, scrambling through clay, mud and hawthorn on his day off, muddying his denim jacket and ripping the knee of his jeans to try to get answers to some questions that troubled him on a personal as well as a professional level. So if the nutter was in a good mood for some reason, he would let him talk, then feed his questions in. Betts continued,

- Sometimes the gyppos come up. They knows there's badgers live near the top meadow and they try to dig 'em up for their dog fights. Send their little dogs down the holes and put up nets. There's more bettin, yer see, when it's dog against badger. More prestige for 'im what sets it up when they 'ave a big meet. I doh like it but our people's supposed to be friends with the gypsies so I cor chase 'em off. What I´d do in that case is pretend to keep out of it but set 'im on their dogs, in the dark, like, so they doh know nothin' about it, just find the dog all mangled. Makes 'em think twice about comin' up 'ere, it does.

He nudged the expiring dog with the toe of a boot,

- 'E'd rip the neck out of any of theirs, big or small.

They both looked down at the animal. Its breathing had quickened visibly for a while but had now stopped.

- 'E was more of a guard dog. Companion.

- I'm sorry. Yer should keep 'im under control.

- 'E did what he was bred for. Defend the master. And you fought back when attacked. Nothin' wrong with that, either. It was either that or 'ave him chew yer balls off! Cuz 'e would yer know…

Betts' laughter turned into hacking as he spat into the lush summer grass, not yellowed yet by the sun here in the shade of the birch forest,

- Day yer read the poem I give yer? It was all about that. Doin' what's right. Ancient breed like 'im, the mastiff part, the old Spanish part, not the greyhound, he knew what's what by instinct. They was bred to fight the wolves. Protect the flock. Kill or be killed.

Betts was studying Cooper's face.

Cooper's principal memory of the poem was that he had read it quickly and thrown it away. Had there been something about dog fights? Wolves?

- I read it… er… Not much of a poetry reader, me.

Betts seemed disappointed,

- Well you 'ave another read of it when yer can.

A silence. Betts leaned forward and scooped up the dead dog, sliding it over his shoulder so that when he rose, he was carrying the animal on his back. He had lifted the heavy corpse as easily as if it were a pillow. He stood there grinning expectantly, the carotid arteries bulging in his thick neck,

- So to what do I owe the pleasure? Or did yer come 'ere just to punch me dog?

Perhaps because of the white-toothed smile, or the release of tension caused by physical effort, Betts looked younger for a moment, fresh and virile. What had Cisco Smith, the other bouncer, said about Betts and women?

They go after him.

- I've got some more questions.

- Police business or your pleasure?

It was disorientating the way Betts could slip in and out of dialect at will. Did he do that with everyone? With the butcher who bought his rabbits? The gypsies? Or was it some special tease just for the police, to remind Cooper how little he knew of the man, of where he went in the winter for example?

- It's a...

Bit of both? No point lying. You're here out of uniform and he'll get the gist from the questions anyway.

- I'm off duty, ay I?

Betts turned to walk toward his cabin.

- Come on in, then. Beans for dinner.

***

They were walking hand-in-hand down the rocky part of Whites Lane, coming from the Sedgley side down towards the brook. The trees and bushes either side of the stony lane blocked most of the moonlight and made it too dark to see much of Rosie's face but from the way she squeezed his hand and the tone of her voice he knew that she was smiling,

- You glad you snuck out then?

Glad?

He was very glad, head-over-heels glad. The summer night smelled of lush new vegetation, flowers and pollen, damp clay and limestone and he was with Rosie. Many years later, he would look back at the early part of this evening as the time in his life when he had felt most alive and, briefly, happy.

She had been waiting on the corner as she had promised on the phone and they had walked to the top of Sedgley Beacon, the highest point for miles around. Hair tousled by the warm summer wind on top of the hill, they had taken in the view that spread out before them: to the east and north-east suburbs, council housing and industrial estates; to the west the rolling south Staffordshire and Shropshire countryside as far as the hills of Clent in the blue-grey distance. Until then they had been chatting about school: what would happen to the flashing teacher, who fancied who, who was hard, who was alright and who was a laugh. Seeing a chance to impress, George had pointed out the Clee hills, once pointed out to him by his father on childhood kite-flying trip.

- That's right - she said - and there's yer Malvern.

She pointed to another bluish mass.

- And you're not even from here.

They had never discussed where Rosie was from. George had never thought about it either. She didn't have a strong Black Country accent so she wasn't local, she was just from the fair, semi-magical and itinerant. Her eyes narrowed, one of those smiles again,

- I´m from all over. *We're* from all over.

Had her voice lowered slightly on the word '*we're*'? She had certainly looked him straight in the eye for an instant then looked quickly away. Who is 'we'?

He felt sure that this had something to do with what his dad had been talking about earlier, in the house. He began to formulate a question, but Rosie spoke first,

- What about you, Georgie, would you like to travel? Get out of this hole - with one hand she dismissed the huge conurbation to the east - See a bit of the country?

She had then turned to face him, standing so close that their bodies touched as she held the sides of his open jacket. He was conscious of the warm softness of her body and, somehow equally exciting, the fact that she was as tall as he was.

- You could just leave your problems behind, come on the fairs with us.

The freckles that framed her brown eyes were perfect for her, he realised: perfect in their imperfection. She continued,

- Nottingham Goose fair. Yorkshire and Lancashire.

She was playfully nodding the affirmative, now, as if trying to enthuse a small child: eyebrows raised, exaggerated smile, mouth open, a caricature of persuasiveness,

- Can you ride a horse? I'd show you. It's summer now. We could ride on the beach in Devon or Cornwall. On Bodmin or Dartmoor. France! The Camargue! Spain! Cantabria! They have beaches you wouldn't believe. Just leave all of this. Leave Greeny and that lot to rot in this shit hole. They'll have shit lives in this shit hole and you'll be the winner.

Although at that moment he would have followed Rosie anywhere, he found himself saying,

- Leave me dad? Leave school? They'd bring me back. It doesn't make sense.

She seemed about to speak, about to continue trying to persuade him to travel with them but then stopped and shrugged,

- You're right. Thought I'd have a try. Could have saved some trouble.

Her eyes began to narrow, on the point of crinkling into one of those smiles of hers, his favourite vision in the world. She always did it and he loved it but now George watched in amazement as it didn't happen. She abandoned. Before it was even formed, she turned off the smile that he had thought so natural and typical of her.

She seemed to shake herself as if preparing to enter some new phase.

- You remember that song? At the fair? About falling in love with someone you shouldn't have?

He didn't answer. He had heard lots of songs at the fair and he was thinking about smiles that could be turned on and off. She went on, speaking more quickly but less assuredly than before,

- Well... I like it a lot. So I borrowed the single from the waltzer people and copied down the words. For you.

She handed him a piece of graph paper folded in two. He opened it up to see five short stanzas, the verses of the song, written neatly in blue biro. One verse was underlined in red.

- Don't read it now, pillock! Read it later.

She flashed a brief smile at that but the smile quickly faded when he didn't smile back and then she pushed his hands together, closing the paper like a book.

- You can read it another time. It's just about when people can't be together.

- Right.

- 'Cause that's normal, you know? That's why there's songs about it and the like 'cause it happens all the time. Then people get over it. It's not forever. Or it might be but you're not sad forever. That's what I mean.

She paused. She seemed flustered. Unsure. He studied her face, trying to interpret her feelings. Was that sadness or embarrassment? Was it another part of the act? Then she spoke,

- You can kiss me if you like.

Her skin and lips were firm and fragrant with the promise and strength of her youth. Everything around him at that moment, girl, evening sun, the scents of summer, would stay alive in him into adulthood then old age and oblivion.

***

- We can get her tits out! After we shit 'em up. We'll tie 'em up and get her knockers out!

Dean Wilson was trying to elicit some enthusiasm from Steven Campbell and the rest, but Campbell just looked back, impassive. Here, in the darkest part of Whites Lane at night, he would at least hold your gaze not look away, but the boring black-and-white bastard seemed like he couldn't be bothered. Even Greeny, sitting on a log in the shadows, looked grimly resolute rather than excited, and the trap had been his idea. Of the four of them waiting in the shadows that night, only Colin Bull looked to Dean to be appropriately alive to their plan's potential for humiliation and hurt. The big lump, cheerful and easily-led, was chuckling to himself between nervous drags on a fag as he pulled part of his improvised costume, the thin bed quilt, from a plastic bag.

Dean persevered with Campbell,

- Tie 'em up man! Get 'er tits out! Pinch 'er nips, fuckin' slag!

Campbell still seemed unmoved but it was difficult to tell. In the deeper darkness under a giant horse chestnut tree, where the brook went under the path, only the white parts of his face were visible. Dean kept on with his haranguing, trying to get a reaction,

- We'll tie 'er 'ands with the quilt! 'Old 'er arms behind 'er!

No response came. No movement from the white mouth and eyes, suspended in the warm, honeysuckle-scented summer night. It was the pointless waste of talent that irritated Dean. Campbell was nearly always sullen and moody but, perhaps embittered by his own disfigurement, could usually be relied upon to play the game, to add his own dose of joyless vindictiveness to whatever Dean or Greeny got them into.

The previous summer, in the aftermath of one of the regular running battles against kids from the rival school, Parkfields, they had managed to isolate and capture a terrified younger boy, dragging him off the street into a derelict factory by the canal. Dean had set the bar high from the start: knowing that the worst part of any beating was the gut-churning prelude, he had stayed Colin Bull's hand just as the big boy was about to launch into a cheerfully unimaginative pounding of their captive. Instead, Dean had prolonged the waiting. Backed up by the presence of his three larger friends, he had carried out a kind of one-man good-cop-bad-cop routine, sadistically alternating between taunting and friendliness ('Doh worry mate, we ay gonna lamp yer!' he cooed in a put-on baby voice, putting his arm around the kid's shoulders before shoving him into a clump of nettles). Confused and frustrated, the little boy's bravery finally ran out and the tears came. Only then had Bully been allowed to hit him. To the amusement of the others, Campbell had added an unexpectedly imaginative finishing touch. As the small body lay trembling amongst the half house-bricks and dock leaves of the concrete floor, he had extracted his (long, mottled) penis from his jeans and pissed on him. Explain that to yer mom and dad, Parkie.

Now, Colin Bull was trying to wrap the white quilt around his shoulders but could not get it to stay in place,

- Gimme an 'and with this fuckin' thing. I know! We'll tie 'im up too. Get 'is dick out!

Thrown slightly by this unexpected contribution from the big lad, Dean decided to use it,

- Er... yeah. We can make *'er* get 'is dick out. Make 'er play with 'is maggot. Be a right fuckin' loff. Where's the tights?

Greeny had heard enough. He stood and moved from the shadows under the bushes into the moonlit centre of the stony path,

- It ay abaht 'avin' a loff.

He was also becoming a right boring bastard, Dean decided, as he retrieved the packet of his mother's tights from the discarded bag. But like the others, he stopped to listen to Greeny,

- Dressing 'im up so's we can scare 'em was yower saft idea, not mine - he nodded at Dean - Yer'm like a little fuckin' kid. And I doh know what yow'm on abaht, gettin' his dick out. Fuckin' bumboy.

Bully looked down. Greeny spat onto a pile of trodden-flat horseshit on the path and continued,

- We'm 'ere to give 'em a lampin'. A right fuckin' lampin', specially that fucking tart. Knock 'er fuckin' teeth out, she likes smilin' so much.

Dean nearly said something about how they might as well have a laugh while they were at it – you boring fucker - but just in time he saw how Greeny was glaring at them, his face taut and pale, and decided against it. What had happened in the woods the other night after Colin Bull left? Why did Greeny hate the new girl so much? His version of Friday night's events was so far-fetched as to be beyond belief. He claimed to have fucked the two girls and to have nearly gotten off with a woman CID sergeant in the police interview room before getting his face bashed in by a copper they all knew, PC Cooper.

Campbell finally broke his silence,

- We can do better than a lampin'.

His rich voice, the voice of a long-gone father from the islands, resounded in the stillness of the night,

- Mash 'er face up proper. She woh be smilin' then.

From a breast pocket of his Italian combat jacket, Campbell produced a white plastic bottle that had once contained light oil.

- Burn 'er face off. Got it from a battery.

Dean grinned, unseen in the dark. Good old half-chuck!

As the evening continued to cool after the long, hot day, a light mist rose from the still-warm brook, spilling onto the path where the four lay in wait.

***

- No milk, I'm afraid. So what's troublin' yer then?

Michael Betts passed Cooper a steaming cup of tea and settled down in the sofa opposite the lumpy armchair where the copper sat. Everything in the small cabin looked spotlessly clean, scrubbed even, but still Cooper felt a brief shudder of revulsion as he wondered where the water came from to make tea and wash cups.

- What's troublin' me?

Cooper hadn't planned a line of questioning or any strategy except to not leave Betts alone until he had some answers. He knew that were he to think rationally about where that would lead him, he would be unlikely to follow through.

Betts appeared tranquil, confident, his arms stretched out either side of him along the top of the small sofa. He had taken off his work shirt to reveal a greyish vest and with his arms extended horizontally his deltoids and trapezius muscles bunched and peaked.

Don't think about it. Just say what's on your mind and go where it takes you.

- I'll tell yer what's troubling me. Two deaths. Michael Hickman and old Driscoll the farmer.

Cooper had hoped to shock some kind of reaction out of Betts by mentioning the old man's death, which even he had only heard about that morning. But the recluse didn't blink,

- Right. One of them's a little bar-steward riding a motorbike in the woods at night. Down a rocky path. Accident waiting to 'appen. So that's no mystery. The other's an old bloke. What did Driscoll die of then?

Cooper studied Betts' face but saw no hint of feigned ignorance

- Found hanging from one of his trees. There was a kicked-over stepladder. A mate at the station called me this morning to tell me.

Betts rolled his eyes and nodded,

- There you are then. Suicide.

- Not necessarily. Where were you last night then, bouncin' at some pub, I imagine?

The deltoids rippled as Betts raised one hand and ran his finger through his greasy brown hair,

- Saracen's 'Ead, Dudley. Rough as fuck! One chap got a right kickin' before we could get over there to split it up. Ambulance job. I 'ad to make a statement to one of your colleagues as a matter of fact.

- I'm sure you did. I woh even bother to check that out. You doh get out much, though do yer? I mean, 'ow often do you do the bouncin'?

- I do the minimum to be honest. I'm ninety-nine percent what they call self-sufficient but yer needs a bit o' money for some odds and ends so I do the odd bit o' door work.

Cooper leaned forward in his chair,

- But yer know what gets me, Michael? Whenever you do go an' do some door work, whenever you do have an alibi, seems like there's always some kind of unexplained tragedy.

- I doh call crashin' yer motorbike the way 'e did unexplained. Like I say, accident waitin' to happen, more like. An' if yer think it wor an accident, I'd be talkin' to the other little bastard what was with 'im when he crashed. He's yer suspect, not me. Same goes for Driscoll. If it wor suicide, there's better suspects than me about, I reckon. 'E´d have made 'is enemies.

- Right. And next you'll be telling me it's not suspicious that your family's around again, just when all this happens?

Cooper was still watching Betts carefully. Had his eyes widened slightly then? Had the muscles on his neck just got that little bit more defined?

Go on. Push it. Start something.

- What's Rosie Betts to you then? Niece? Don't tell me daughter? She's been pretty friendly with Simon Green, from what I've heard. He's one of Hickman's mates, with him the night he died. And she had some kind of contact with Driscoll. He knew 'er.

Cooper felt sick. He was going to do it. He leaned further forward in his chair,

- You think I'm fuckin' stupid doh yer? There's some fucker, some fucker with a muscular body, a lot like yours, running around dressed as a fuckin' goat or a devil or fuck knows what...

It wasn't working. He was swearing a lot but the rage wasn't coming, not like it used to. He just felt sick and weak with fear but had to go on. He wanted to stand up, to tower over Betts before launching his attack but was worried he would bang his head on the low ceiling,

- ...and I know you're involved. Like you were involved in the fire, back then. It was your idea to build the fuckin' pile of shit and to make it into a camp. You made sure you weren't around on the night but it was your fuckin' idea! A bonfire in summer!

He could have said more. About the bronze figurine. About his dreams. But he paused.

Betts blinked back at him impassively from the other sofa, his arms still extended along the back of it and Cooper knew that they would not be fighting today. Either his courage had failed him or pragmatism had kicked in just in time. He would not be trying to beat the truth from the man in front of him because he evidently couldn't do it. He knew about fighting, had grown up winning fights and had continued to win fights as an adult but he knew he couldn't win this one. In watershed confrontations as a boy he had sometimes forced himself to start fights that he did not expect to win, driven by rage or the fear of humiliation but he felt no rage now despite his attempt to work himself into a fury. And he was not young any more. Perhaps that was the problem.

Betts was still watching him,

- You talk about my family and you're on the right track. We're an old family. Group of families really, and we 'ave our traditions. But it's not like we all stick together, not like you imagine. There's some that's abandonin', forgettin' it all, maybe never even believed in it. That's why some special measures 'ave 'ad to be taken in recent years. Some rules broken for the good of all. Go and see my cousin again, Amalia Betts, if you really want to know. You'll still find 'er at the fair on Jubilee. Say I said to tell you everything - if you agree to the price.

- What price you talkin' about Bettsy? I can't pay much you know.

- Just tell 'er what I said.

***

The heavy old Vauxhall swayed on its soft suspension as it slowed and then turned left from Clifton Street onto Turls Hill Road, heading towards Whites Lane. Its headlights lit up other cars parked outside the houses near the allotment gates but encountered no traffic. After passing the allotment entrance its lights went off and soon after that it quietly pulled onto a stretch of gravelly track that lead to some lock-up garages and halted, out of sight from the road. Inside three large men sat and waited.

***

Cooper was flying. Cartwheeling and spiralling through the evening sky, gravity could not hold him and he felt young again. A dark blue heaven soared above him as the fields, woods and allotments of Hurst Hill and Woodsetton spun below. For a moment he was overcome by dizziness, then nausea and the beginnings of panic before a damp cloth passed across his brow and some soothing words, indistinct and foreign, steadied him enough for him to focus again on the landscape slowly revolving under him.

Far below he saw the Tipton road bisecting the green of Woodsetton's heathy wasteland and Driscoll's fields. On one side of the road he could make out the shimmering surface of Parkes' Hall pool and the stream that fed it, and on the other, the Turls

Hill brook and the still, deep waters of Driscoll's pond, normally hidden from view by its screen of trees but visible now from above like a dark gash in the midst of the fallow fields. More than just see the places, though, he knew and felt their essence and history as only a local could: the sombre legend of the big pool; of hopeless dredging and dragging for the bodies of dead infants. He felt too the effervescent excitement that the smaller, secret pond, inert and barren in winter, could inspire in a boy, or a grown-up boy like him, in a summer like this: hidden from view and perpetually topped up by its own clear, bubbling spring, a forbidden oasis for daring fisher-boys and secret swimmers.

He saw a copse of trees, too, in the middle of Driscoll's land, the abandoned garden of some vanished house, where feral plum, pear and quince trees offered a first taste of summer to the suburban scrumpers and roughnecks of Coseley. Now the lane and then the woods themselves came into view. Some of the horse chestnut, oak and beech trees bordering the lane were leafy old giants, rising nearly to the heights of his drifting vantage point. The varying greens of the treetops, gilded by evening sunlight, inspired in him a longing for the comrades and adventures of his adolescence. There was the small orchard, near the top of the lane, where his little group had broken up the boredom of an interminable summer afternoon with a monumental apple-throwing fight, three against two, the yellow apples so overripe that they splattered explosively on impact. He found himself biting into one, juice dribbling. It was momentarily delicious then he was spinning again, too fast, wanting to vomit.

The cloth on his brow calmed him again then he heard the gentle voice, or rather it seemed to appear in his head, with a question that was really a statement.

It was true. It hadn't all been fun. And it wasn't always summer. There had also been mud and ice, cold and boredom, a lot of cruelty and the odd fight. But they were rough lads! Hard, Black

Country chaps and wenches. It was all part of growing up.

The voice insisted, patiently.

Harder for some than for others? Well, every fight had a loser but there was usually a handshake...

The voice once more with a question.

Him? I had nothing to do with that. That was going too far.

And then he was there; a colder, greyer day, early spring perhaps. He was not flying now but still high above, standing on the bridge over Coseley canal tunnel, looking down to the coal black towpath and canal bounded on each side by a steeply-sloping wasteland of bramble and nettle. In the middle distance, where the corridor of land widened and flattened out, there were canal-side meadows of long grass clipped by chained- up carthorses but here under the bridge the strip of land narrowed to a man-made, overgrown gorge. In the middle of winter, the canal itself would freeze over and kids would cheerfully lob bricks from the crumbling wall onto the thick layer of ice below. Now exercise books and papers floated on the yellow-tinged canal water and a school bag, emptied of its contents lay amongst the nettles.

They said he was a bummer, a shirtlifter, but they knew he wasn't. It was just an excuse.

The boy lay face-down, covering the sides of his head with his hands. His pants, blue y-fronts with white trim, hung from the branches of a leafless bush. His grey school trousers lay on the black towpath, half inside-out, one leg trodden into a black-rimmed puddle, the other dangling in the cut. Two of them were kicking him and the other was struggling to get in a blow with an unwieldy tree branch. The kickers laughed at the kid with the branch and pushed him away.

The towpath was a shortcut. Boys and girls on their way to school looked quickly away then dawdled or turned back to find another route not wanting to admit the horror into their worlds.

I heard about it but I wasn't there. I was seeing a girl. That was them three: Braiden, Scanlon and Kennedy.

Cooper started out of sleep. The euphoric sensation of floating and observing was gone now and he felt a kind of anticlimactic stillness. He was lying on a soft surface in a darkened room which, in his confusion, he assumed was his bed. The warmth of the room comforted him after the chilly scene of the towpath beating, widening the gap between past and present, dream and reality. He sat up and placed his feet on the floor. It was a sofa not a bed. And not his sofa, not his flat. The drawn curtains let in a little weak light, as if it were dawn or dusk outside but from the warm stuffiness of the air he knew it must be evening. He sat with his face in his hands, elbows on knees, and closed his eyes as he gauged whether he had the strength and will to move. He felt hungover but without the headache. When his eyes were closed, he could not stop seeing the pale nakedness and helplessly flailing legs of the boy on the towpath, the harsh contrast of warm pink and white against coal black.

Had they been that bad, his lot? He had never seen the beating and shaming that he had just, somehow, dreamt about, had only heard about it, heard it bragged about, in fact, as a particularly inventive and extreme attack on a younger kid who had been unlucky enough to attract the attention of his three mates. What had the kid done to provoke it, anyway? He could nearly remember. At the time he had been more interested in the girl he was seeing, a posh girl for once, the daughter of a man who owned a factory in Tipton. And there had been other things going on too, exciting events that made him feel alive and gave him a reason to live: other scraps, some of them against opposition that could fight back; chances to get hold of some booze, forays into enemy territory of Sedgley or Tipton or trips up town, other, more brazen girls to roughly court and impress.

Back then he won all his fights, no matter how drunk or out-numbered, didn't get out of breath after just a few punches. And failure in sex never occurred to him; the only question was how long it would last.

On opening his eyes again, he realised that there was a woman sitting on an armchair near the sofa, her legs drawn up under her. Her face was in shadow but he knew who she was and, suddenly, where he was.

Go and see my sister again if you really want to know.

Amalia Betts. When she spoke, he knew from her voice that she was smiling,

- So now you know a bit more about what they'd done, how bad it was. That should be enough, right? Now you can walk away and let sleeping dogs lie.

She waited. He saw that there was a mug on a small table next to the sofa where he sat. As he became more alert he was able to make out the outlines of bulky shapes in the darkness around him: other armchairs, large, solid cupboards, a wardrobe with dust-coated mirrors on the doors. In one very dark corner there appeared to be another armchair. The chair seemed to be pressed down under a mass of impenetrable darkness and weight. He could not see what it was. Her voice came again, from the side of most light,

 - You don't need to know everything, do you?

His face still in his hands, he looked at her between the gaps in his fingers. He would not look into the dark corner, not yet, but he still had some courage. He couldn't fight so well any more, maybe not even fuck, but he had some courage left,

- Tell me everything.

- If you drink some more of this, and try to relax, let me guide you, then I won't need to tell you. You'll remember. You'll remember it so well, it'll be like living it again.

Her voice changed,

- But if you decide to do that, you won't be walking away from here. We couldn't let you.

In the twilight of the caravan, the liquid in the mug was as black as night. It tasted strangely metallic in his dry mouth but also of mud, flowers and leaves, like the woods in summer.

***

It was very dark and for a summer night almost chilly now that the mist from the brook had swelled and thickened around the four boys' hiding places behind the conker tree and in the bushes. Dean, smaller and skinnier, felt the cold most,

- Oo says they'm comin' this way anyway? Could come dahn the Gorge. Dahn the Sedgley rood'd mek more sense if they'm gooin' to Jubilee.

Greeny spat in his direction before responding,

- Lisa Stanley said. They'm comin' dahn the lane. It's gonna be romantic. He probably thinks 'es gonna get 'is end away.'

Dean snorted,

- 'E wouldn't know what to do if she dropped 'er fuckin' drawers in the middle of Driscoll's fields, little fuckin' puff.

- No-one's gonna *want* to fuck the slag after she gets squirted in the face wi' this stuff' - said Greeny.

He had taken the plastic bottle from Campbell to 'have a look' and never given it back.

With the falling of darkness Campbell had stopped talking altogether except to ask for fags now and then. A glowing fag end near the base of a bush suggested he was sitting or squatting. A resounding fart came from the side of the track where Colin Bull sat on one of Driscoll's fences,

- Oof, drop that in yer knickers.

Dean had been glancing up the lane towards Sedgley now and then although at this time of night the old track was only visible as a halo of vegetation around a tunnel of black. But then,

- They'm comin'. It's them. Bully, get yer tights on yer 'ead.

Greeny sighed,

- Just remember, if they leg it the wrong way and we doh catch 'em. It's yow two soft fuckers that's goin' after 'em.

Dean was excited now,

- Doh worry. They ay gonna run past 'im dressed like that and if they run away from him the three of us is waitin'.

Dean and Greeny climbed over gates into a field, Campbell hid behind a large tree so that the approaching couple would walk past without seeing him. Bully took up a position behind another tree further down the lane just before the turn off where a secondary track veered into the woods. Rosie and George would go past the others without knowing it, then Bully would emerge from behind the big tree in his costume and drive them back to his waiting mates. Then the fun would begin.

***

Cooper was kissing Amalia Betts. They were young. She drew her face away,

- I've got to go now.

The summer daylight was finally fading, Venus had risen, and the trees around them were now picture-book silhouettes against a blue-black night, but the pupils of her dark eyes still flashed with the light of the long summer day. He had her pressed against a tree and, as their bodies pushed together, they still pulsed with a residual heat like the sun-warmed limestone walls of the nearby quarries.

He heard shouts from the other side of the horse meadow, where Braiden and the other two were messing about drunkenly near the camp. He could hear drunken shouts of 'bastard' and other indistinct cries which then always dissolved into rough laughing and whooping.

A thought from another time and place intruded,

What's in the dark corner?

then was willed away and he was back with Amalia. Young Amalia.

- They like me scrumpy, don't they? Probably think *they're* getting a turn with me next! Daft sods!

He nuzzled her neck with his head then tried to kiss her collarbone and to push aside the neck of her white blouse with his nose. She squirmed and laughed. He could smell her and something else. Some plant. Something flowering in the cool green around them. Too addled by drink to mock himself, the local hard man, for thinking of flowers, he tried to remember as he moved up from the collar bone to kiss and bite her neck. He remembered.

Honeysuckle.

Now their heads were level, as she was as tall as him. She seemed about to throw her head back and succumb again and he pressed his body against hers. He was hard as a rock again, somehow, after all they had done. While her arms and legs were surprisingly firm, firmer than his own, she was still soft in places and her body yielded in a way that made the blood run fiercer and his groin ache. But she laughed again and pushed him away,

- In serious. I've got to go. An' don't tell me cousins 'bout this.

He swayed backwards and staggered to stay upright, still only one thought in his mind. Even when he was sober, she was too big and strong to push around much but he could try. He barged his body into hers again, trapping her against the tree,

- Stay a bit more.

- I'm going.

She said 'going' properly, slipping out of dialect and it made her more sexy. The ache became a pain.

- You remember what you're supposed to do, if you want us to be together?

She was still talking posh. He rubbed his groin against the side of her hip. He tried to kiss her neck again but she had raised her elbow to his chest to form a barrier between them and he couldn't get at her. She spread both hands to frame his face and raised it to look into the eyes of the grown boy before her. He was groggy and malleable. She had him.

- Later. - she whispered - Do what you have to tonight and I'll see you later.

***

George saw it first.

A tall, broad figure was emerging from behind a large tree. It had the general shape of a man yet the body was shrouded in white like a ghost, the feet were invisible in the darkness and above the white body floated a monstrous head, bald and shiny, the weak moonlight exaggerating the squashed and distorted features of the face. Its rasping breath came fast and loud as it lurched towards them.

George backed away. His mouth moved but he could not speak. The absurd apparition was not a ghost. Ghosts came in dreams or stories so this was not a ghost. He stood transfixed as his mind raced to make sense of what he saw and a terrible, inexorable logic played out against his will: this was an enemy who had been waiting for them and had gone to a lot of trouble. He wouldn't be alone.

With this realisation, came a wave of nausea: he felt the muscles of his thighs dissolve and his knees nearly buckle under him but at the same time he knew that if only he could start running, he would fly and never be caught.

George looked around wildly, scanning the bushes for other enemies, for an escape route between them. Then he saw something incredible.

Rosie was smiling, almost laughing. She was looking all around too, while glancing back at the advancing figure from behind the tree now and then but she seemed more excited than scared and to his complete amazement she then squeezed his hand and mouthed, 'Don't worry', before calling out,

- Which one's this then, Campbell? Bully? Too tall to be Dean! Too thin to be Greeny! Where's the rest of yer?

The figure in the sheet stopped his theatrical heavy breathing and stood still, hesitating a moment before pulling the pair of tights from his head. It was Colin Bull, grinning lopsidedly but pale and ill-at-ease.

The galvanised steel gate to their right rattled and clanged as Steven Campbell clambered then vaulted to land on the rough track before them. Grim-faced and resolute, he puffed out his large chest and stood with arms folded, long legs wide apart.

Dean Wilson emerged from a shadowy recess between bushes and fence on the other side of the path to Campbell. Cockily he sauntered, towards them,

- Alright George? Come for a romp in the woods with the missus? 'Opin' to get yer end away was yer?

His tone was confidential, the expression on his face open and friendly. This was how the little coward always acted when setting up a victim for his harder friends, George knew. He felt a dangerous rage energise his body. The red-head kept on coming, now glancing from George to Rosie and back and grinning as his gaze lingered over the front of her body,

- Spect yer won't mind us 'avin' a bit of a go fust, will yer...?

As fear turned to incandescent fury, George's body had ceased to exist, he was now a creature of speed and instinct with no physical mass to slow him down. His fist flashed out, a right cross, just like Ray Robinson on TV, a punch so perfect that he felt no impact or even movement himself. Dean's head spun sideways, his body stiffening for an instant before falling limply to the floor.

Colin Bull blinked in surprise but didn't move. Campbell's eyes widened and he unfolded his arms and started towards Rosie and George but then paused as Rosie leaned forward and shrieked with laughter, hands on knees.

Behind George and Rosie a deep and world-weary voice,

- Some fucker grab 'em, then. We've 'ad enough pissin' abaht tonight.

George turned to see Greeny in black trousers and t-shirt, holding a small plastic bottle in one meaty hand.

Colin Bull skipped over Dean's unconscious body so that he was suddenly right in front of George. George threw another punch but he had lost the focus of his sudden anger and Bully swayed backwards out of range before surging forward to grab hold of George's forearm and spin him around so that he could grab him from behind. Campbell grabbed Rosie from behind too, tying up both her arms with one of his and wrapping his other arm around her waist. She was still laughing and did not resist. Bully and Campbell dragged their captives around to face Greeny.

Greeny approached George, swaggering, legs relaxed. He spat near Dean's fallen body,

- ´E's right you know. We am gonna 'ave some fun with yer missis. Fuckin' bitch. But it's not what yer think.

- Fuckin' right mon – said Campbell.

Rosie had been looking down at her feet, still apparently chuckling to herself but now the mottle-faced boy yanked her head back by her hair, exposing her face to the moonlight. She stopped laughing.

- I've got me lickle bottle of battery acid...

Greeny held up the container to the light,

- ...and I've got me fuckin' slag what needs to learn a lesson...

- Fuckin' 'ell Greeny.

Bully had spoken. Greeny glared at him narrow-eyed,

- Doh you be fuckin' shittin' aht on me now, yer big puff...

Bully had let go of George but George just stood there, not trying to run away. Both of them were looking behind Greeny.

Bully spoke again,

- There's three blokes.

Greeny didn't want to listen to Bully now,

- Yer what? – he said, without taking his eyes of Rosie.

- E's right, mon. Three blokes.

On hearing it from Campbell, Greeny turned around,

- What the fuckin' 'ell?

***

Cooper was woken by a painful throbbing. His bladder, his balls and hard dick. He was in total blackness except for a greyish spot that looked distant but which he knew was close. He crawled blindly through the tunnel of crates, planks and broken furniture, oblivious to splinters bumps and grazes until he was outside the pile of wood in the lesser darkness of the woods. It was a starry, nearly cloudless night with just a sliver of moon. The only sounds were occasional snores and snuffles from the three sleeping back inside and the distant creaking of the taller trees in the breeze.

He flipped out his sore, swollen penis and began to piss, making a golden, strong-smelling arc that soon fell to spatter against the wood of the bonfire camp. Relieved by the release of some pressure, although his balls still ached, he took in a deep breath of the night air, knowing he would love it.

Honeysuckle. Burnt hawthorn. Earth and squashed grass.

He was still drunk, was groggy but wanted to be more so.

Look at the thing in the dark corner.

The reality of his youthful mission in the woods had wavered then re-established itself with a shimmer. What thing? What corner? He was in the woods.

He had to do something. He knew it was important and that he had been reminded many times but he couldn't...

He saw them and remembered: two metal oil cans of a gallon each, left against the side of the wooden structure. He squatted, opened one and sniffed to check. He had heard that the motorbike boys got a buzz from sniffing petrol so he sank to his knees, put his mouth near the open can and inhaled deeply again and again. No buzz came for a while but when he closed his eyes, he felt the world change and had to sit down. He fell back and lay on the cool horse-cropped grass of the meadow, looking up at the sky. He closed his eyes again and the rhythmic glug of the petrol emptying out of the overturned can filled his consciousness. The insistent voice came back, reminding him of another existence where he was an old man, a copper, of all things,

You think it's too dark but look at him properly and you'll see. Him in the corner seat. The old one.

Once more the old dream plays out. From treetop height, he looks down on the patch of grassy land lit up by tall flames rising from the rough wooden structure. The wood of the camp itself is barely burning yet. Bluish flames dance on the splintery surfaces, fuelled by petrol and air, heating them until the scorched timbers burst into yellow and orange tongues of fire. A plastic sheet covering part of the roof curls up and bubbles in the sudden heat, adding toxic purples and obscene baby blues and lilacs to the colours of the bonfire. A lone tyre, ballast to hold down the plastic sheet in case of wind, lies inert as the flames begin to lick around it. Its time will come too, to blossom into flame and roar.

A shout from inside, the voice too high; a shriek, all bravado gone. The sounds of confused scrambling and bickering. He has taken their torch. It's dark in there except for the smoke-filtered glow of nearby flames, all around.

It takes minutes not seconds because of the dark and the smoke but at last they come crashing out, one by one, coughing and swearing, their smoke-stung eyes near blinded by tears. The hulking man-beast waits with his club in the shadows at the edge of the meadow.

This time you'll see his face, see who did it. That's the deal.

The killer walks stiffly into the light of the clearing. There is only one crawl-way out of the pile of burning wood and he positions himself to face it, ignoring the heat.

Looking down at the first pale and squinting face to emerge before him he feels the righteous power of the moment. He raises his heavy club high above his head then brings it smashing down.

It's me. I'm doing it, not watching.

There is something on his face, protecting it from the heat and framing his vision but other than that he is naked. He feels the exalted strength in the bulging muscles of his thighs, shoulders and forearms as he grabs the unconscious youth and heaves him out of the narrow exit.

Another one emerges, spluttering and gasping.

They are like worms to me.

The club swings down again.

Or insects. I am a God.

He twists his torso to haul the second, now limp, body to one side and clear the way for more slaughter. The final boy, slighter and more agile than the others, sees what is happening and tries to escape by clambering to one side over crates and planks still hardly touched by flame but he leans forward and swings the club in a wide arc, knocking the boy's feet from under him then pulls him backwards, wide-eyed and clawing, from the pile onto the ground. Two heavy blows finish him off.

The thing in the corner is moving. In that other life.

He throws the club into the hottest part of the fire and watches for long minutes until the flames take hold on the dense wood.

The fire is raging on three sides of the camp now but he lifts the bodies one-by-one up onto a section of the top where some damp plywood is steaming but not yet alight and from there swings them as close as he can to the centre where they had once slept. He feels every muscle in his body but not the trickling sweat that shines in the firelight.

He's coming.

You still can't look, can you?

He feels safe near the bonfire and strong even when he throws the mask in the fire and puts his clothes on. He doesn't have to enter the shadows yet.

He has left some petrol in one of the cans and now he pours it on his leg. With a long stick, since the fire is now too hot to approach, he drags an ember toward him. It glows orange under a cracked skin of grey ash. He cannot leave unscathed. He must burn himself. Only then can he go for help.

Then the heat of the fire and the scents of the woods at night are gone. He is not young, not a creature of passion, but a middle-aged man, lying on a sofa, in a caravan, feeling sick and looking up at a giant that has risen from the shadows. The body is huge and the face hidden in shadows but the voice is not threatening,

- So now you know, eh, Cooper? Is that what you wanted? Or do you want more, the whole story, from the start?

When there was no answer the dark figure spoke again,

- Might as well be hung for a horse as for a sheep, eh?

***

Dean Wilson couldn't understand where his blankets had gone. He would give the old girl a right bollocking if she had pulled them away as some sort of joke. And there were lumps and even spiky bits of something in his bed. If it was his sister Gail, or one of her daft boyfriends pissing about, he'd think of some way to... But no. None of that was right. He was outside. A warm summer night in the woods. Not exactly the woods. The scrubland between the woods and some fields, near where the brook comes out of the sewage treatment plant. Someone had somehow trampled down the thick vegetation of nettles, bramble, mugwort and cow parsley to make a circular space between the path and the brook and there was a small bonfire of twisted hawthorn and other branches blazing away in the middle of the clearing.

And there were bodies lying on the floor.

The big body closest to him was broad-shouldered and heavy-hipped just like Greeny. It even had Greeny's clothes and his blond hair. But Greeny wouldn't sob and sniffle like that. The other bodies were further away and were partially blocked from view by the closer one. Dean sat up to see more but then had to close his eyes and wait for a wave of dizziness to pass. Who had hit him? He lay down again.

The body like Greeny's spoke,

- Am they comin' back?

It was definitely not Greeny's voice. There was no threat there. It was a small voice, tired and laden with fear.

- 'Oo yer talkin' abaht?

- The three blokes. Am they comin' back?

Since this could not be Greeny, he could answer any way he liked,

- What three blokes? What yer on abaht?

- Three big blokes. Brick shithouses. Fuckin' lamped us. Did what they liked with us...

The voice seemed to run out of breath and faded. There were some gasping noises then it started up again.

- ...specially them two. In front o' the wench too. Made sure she saw it. Loffin' she was.

- What was they? Parkfielders? Gippos or summat?

- You was out of it. Knocked out by a wanker! - for a moment it did sound like Greeny - I was out of it for a bit, after they got me in the neck. When I woke up I could still see, just couldn't move. Saw what they was doin' to 'em. Saw that wench, pissin' 'erself loffin', 'angin' all over her little boyfriend.

Dean managed to rise to one elbow. When no dizziness came, he rose further to a sitting position. About six feet beyond Greeny lay Campbell, face down on the trampled undergrowth. His jeans were stained with some dark and sticky-looking liquid, its colour indeterminate in the flickering orange glare of the bonfire. Was his face in a clump of nettles?

A few feet beyond Campbell, a long body that could only be Colin Bull's lay stretched out in a similar manner. His clothes too were stained with blood. The remnants of a shredded white t-shirt lay along Bully's spine like a dirty white rope.

As he shakily stood up and prepared to run away, Dean's mind raced to work out what had happened. None of it made sense. Rivals from other areas? It would take a lot more than three of them to do this to Greeny and the other two. Gippos? Some were hard enough alright, but this?

He paused for a second before starting his run. Those two looked beyond help and anyway would be no good as future allies after this got out. He'd have to steer clear of them if they even dared to show their faces. Greeny was different. Greeny was not himself at the moment but maybe would be feared again one day. And in that case, you didn't want him to remember you as the one who legged it and left him in the woods.

Greeny still lay on his side, facing away from Dean and towards the two injured boys. Dean squatted down next to him,

- Come on Si - he rested his hand on a rounded shoulder for balance - which way did they go? Towards the lane or towards the allotments? We'll leg it the other way.

- Saft fuckin' piece of shit!

The language at least was encouraging. That's how Greeny was supposed to speak, even if there was a worrying wobble to his voice and the last word had cracked into a near sob,

- We'll go toward the allotments, I reckon - continued Dean - there's just one fence…

- Stupid piece of shit… - he ran out of breath, gasped and continued - I told yer, they got me neck. I ay runnin' nowhere. Or walkin,' ever again.

Dean stood up, recalculating. If Greeny was going to be paralysed, he didn't have to worry about leaving him. But he didn't want to run straight into the three blokes.

- Which way did they go?

Now Greeny was laughing, chuckling to himself good-naturedly, indulgently, as if an old-friend was starting off on some old anecdote, too many times repeated,

- Ah, yer stupid... fuckin'... mother... fucker...

The intakes of breath between words had now taken on a liquid quality, become gurgles.

Exasperated, Dean side-stepped over Greeny and then pushed him onto his back with his foot, so as to be able to see his face in the glare of the flames.

As a small child, Dean had seen the aftermath of a terrible road accident in which a cyclist had been scraped to death by the underside of the 126 bus outside Dudley Green Hospital. He was reminded now of the horrid white meat, marbled by blood, that he had seen that day as the firelight played on the dissolved tissue around what remained of Greeny's eyes. The flesh had bubbled and puckered so much that it had bled from deep cracks. That blood was now largely congealed, forming dark striations over the white skin of his once-handsome face. But what shook Dean the most were the bleached-out eyes, now colourless blobs of unprotected jelly where the eyelids had dissolved away.

The battery acid.

He would go before they got him. He could not risk either of the two paths. He would crash through the nettles until he came to the brook then wade it or jump it and go through the horse fields then somebody's back garden and onto the road with its streetlights and cars. Maybe he could get to Sedgley police station.

He heard a familiar sound behind him and spun around.

Her blond wavy hair was more tousled than usual and she was grinning lopsidedly, not unfriendly but mischievous and complicit as if a teacher had just told the two of them off. Even in his state of near panic, he took in that she was wearing only a long t-shirt and also the shape of her body under the thin white cotton. She stopped smiling and looked him levelly in the eye. Her mouth was slightly open, her lips wet, her brown eyes black in the night.

- Pardon me!

Rosie giggled. She had burped.

From far away he heard a car engine racing at a missed gear change but, and this was impossible, it seemed to come from Whites Lane rather than the nearest road, which lay in the other direction.

- Want some?

She held up a stone flagon, of the type used for scrumpy cider, dangling it carelessly, one finger in the hole at the neck,

- Or are yer gonna wait for me cousins to come back?

He took a step back but she moved with him, smiling broadly.

- Yer should wait for 'em. 'Ave some fun. A bit of rumpy-pumpy. We was all at it before. Me an' George. Your mates.

The car engine was screaming now, getting louder as it got closer. But there was no road there.

- 'Course your mates couldn't get it up in the circumstances and all but that's alright. I 'ad a play with 'em anyway.

A hundred yards away, the headlights of a large car danced and jerked as the wheelspinning vehicle careened and bounced through the vegetation, mowing down nettles and cresting clumps of bramble as it surged forward.

- 'Ow 'bout you, Dean? Do you think you'll get it up for us?

She moved forward and snatched at his groin, shrieking with laughter as she cupped his fear-shrunken genitals before he lurched backwards, tripped and fell on the uneven ground. He twisted around and struggled to rise to begin to sprint for his life but she straddled him from behind, grabbed his hair, and swung the heavy stone flagon over and down, smashing it against his skull again and again until he stopped moving.

***

- Dean. Is that you?

It was Greeny's voice. Dean groaned.

- Dean? Campbell?

- Let me sleep, will yer?

- What's gooin' on?

Dean willed himself back toward a welcoming and final sleep.

- Dean!

- I'm gonna sleep!

But now sleep would not come. An acrid smell irritated his nose and eyes. And Greeny's insistent questioning had jerked him back to wakefulness too many times,

- Where am we? What's burnin'?

He opened his eyes and saw that he was in the driving seat of a car. It was dark and hot. Very hot. Outside, a faint orange glow under-lit plumes of charcoal-grey smoke that were rising from somewhere down near the floor, spiralling up past the closed windows, eddying around the chromed wing mirrors of the big saloon car.

- Where's the fire, Dean? What's gooin' on?

Dean tried to move but found that his wrists were bound to
gether tightly, not by rope but by a strip of clothing, part of a t
shirt. One of his arms was inside the hoop of the big, old-fash
ioned steering wheel, the other outside. He wriggled his body
but found that he was held by a seatbelt, pulled tight across hi
chest and, with his hands trapped as they were, there was no
way to release it.

- It's rubber ay it? Am we in a motor?

Dean tried drawing his arms back to pull his hands from thei
bonds but his seat had been shoved so close to the wheel tha
there was not enough space to pull with any force at all. He the
tried twisting his hips toward the gear stick, hoping to get on
or both legs free enough and high enough to kick at the wind
screen. By squashing his upper body down as close to the door a
he could, he got his left leg up to where it could just make con
tact with the windscreen when fully extended but then foun
he could get no power into his kicks from that angle. The rubbe
sole of his Adidas trainer bounced uselessly off the hardene
glass and then he relaxed, defeated.

The blinded and maimed leader continued,

- They cor leave us 'ere. They ay gonna go dahn for murder. It
just to put the shits up us.

Exhausted and devoid of hope, Dean tried to dream of hom
again. The dry, sickening heat inside the car reminded him o
the blast of hot air that came out of his mother's oven when sh
opened it to slide out the roast chicken and pour its juices ove
it with the big old spoon that served as a ladle in their kitche
Then, as he basted in his own sweat, he thought of the joints o
pork she sometimes cooked, tied up with bits of white strin
that always turned brown with the juice from the meat. H
could smell it now, juicy roasting pork, fizzling and crackling i

its own fat.

The screams from the back of the car surprised him, but only momentarily. Of course that would be the other two. Of course they hadn't been allowed to escape. It would be madness to leave witnesses. The car had been parked on top of the fire he had seen earlier, probably so that the petrol tank in the back was right over the hottest part. The fire must be worse back there and they must be roasting. Hence the screaming and the smell of crackling. At some point there would be an explosion and the car would become a fireball. Four less joyriders in the world.

Greeny had not finished,

- That's it! That's what they want! Screaming! Beggin' for mercy! Let's say we'm sorry and they'll stop it! Dean, break a window and tell 'em!

Dean wanted to see the men who were killing him. He pushed against the dashboard and central console with his feet, wriggled his back and flexed his elbows until his face was at window height again.

Through the smoke and flames he saw something like a man. The legs were invisible from Dean's point of view, the torso was muscled and lean. The giant figure stood hands on hips and threw back his head as he laughed at the trapped boy before him.

Inside the car, Dean and Greeny now heard a high-pitched whistling note like a kettle on the boil. The hot petrol tank had ruptured due to the build-up of pressure inside and was now venting hot vapour from a split in its welded seams. The vapour ignited and with a loud pop the backrest of the rear seat was blown forward by the exploding petrol tank and the passenger compartment filled with billowing clouds of burning fuel and plastic, instantly consuming all the available oxygen. Drops of molten plastic from the seats spattered the boys' skin and burned deep into their flesh as they inhaled the choking mixture of fumes and carbon dioxide.

**

PART FOUR

Thursday 29th July 1982.

The table in the interview room in Sedgley police station has a matt black finish but Wenton had realised that if you looked closely, and at the right angle, the harsh neon lighting illuminated layers of otherwise invisible graffiti that generations of detainees had biro-etched into the surface while left alone to fret and stew. There were three types of scrawling, he noticed: names of local roughnecks and goodtime girls, *Parkesy, Brett, Shazza, Trace, Lisa D.;* tribes, *Gornal Skins, Rude Boys, Pensnett Modettes;* and small pictograms including swastikas, 'A' for Anarchy symbols, schematic penises, and the stylized NF logo of the National Front. As Wenton studied the scribblings, he wondered whether, now that he too was an outlaw, he should make his own mark on the surface. But if he signed up to the devil's deal now, like all those chaps and wenches whose signatures lay scratched out before him, what teen gang would have him? What Shazza or Trace would want him, with his balding scalp and elbow-patched jacket? And even if one did want him, would he be any good to her now, after years of wanking over impossible fantasies?

Don't sign up. Deny it all.

Soon things would be out of his hands, thankfully, and the sleepless nights and uncertainty of the last few weeks would be over. For the moment, he felt sick. He had never been arrested before, had not even been arrested now, technically, just asked to come in to make a statement. But the statement they required was about a crime that he had committed and he knew that if he had declined to turn up for interview today, the bored young copper who had come to his home would have returned another day to arrest him. Now he was waiting to hear exactly what form the charge would take and to get some idea of what it would mean for his career and for his mother. He fixed his gaze on the pitted wood of the old table before him, avoiding the neon glare reflecting from the pale blue wall tiles.

Initially, in the days immediately after his offence, there had been hope. He had soon learned that PC Cooper's visit to the school was not about his flashing at all but about the death of Michael Hickman. And, he had reasoned at the time, with a death to look into, perhaps the police wouldn't even be interested in a bit of harmless flashing. He could probably relax. Maybe. And nobody had seen him even leave the house that night anyway. It would be their word against his. Two little tarts against the teacher. And as he had waited and then waited more for the knock on the door that didn't come, he had begun to feel that he had got away with it. He would not have to explain to his mother why he had lost his job. And he would never do it again. Not so close to home.

But then at night the doubts would come. Lisa Stanley had been unable to hold his gaze that Monday morning. She knew something. Of course, she wasn't one of the girls he had flashed at but she knew them; she was younger than them but she was popular, envied, even by older girls so they might have told her. Even if they hadn't told her directly, bombshell news like that could easily spread around the playground in only one morning. And even if Lisa knew nothing, that same copper would be going to every class in the school and asking the same question, including those older girls' classes. It was a matter of time.

And then there were the other teachers. Mr Hurley, the broad-shouldered and moustachioed PE teacher who had always ignored him as far as possible would now make eye-contact in the staffroom, smiling mockingly over his mug of tea, an amused twinkle in his eye. What had he heard? Anita, the young English teacher, always shy but friendly, now seemed to be around a lot less. She had said something about trying to prepare her classes more at home, which could be true, but why start doing that exactly now, at the end of term? When their paths did cross, she would make flustered excuses and leave, or so it seemed to him. And Mr. Langley, the floppy-haired Art teacher, with whom he had sometimes chatted about politics or the Peak District was suddenly colder and more distant. Or was he? Had they really been friendlier before? These were the questions that occupied Wenton's waking nights.

Then one playground incident had confirmed it all for him. He had almost missed it. If he hadn't turned around he would never have seen it. But the soft plastic football had bounced off his back during his break duty and he had turned around, startled, to see what was happening and there he was, Dean Wilson's younger brother, Wayne. He was playing to a crowd of third-year girls who were sitting on a low playground wall, driving them into shrieks of laughter by walking behind Wenton with his little finger poking out of the fly of his trousers. Engrossed in the demands of his own performance, Wayne did not notice Wenton turn to watch him and continued his exaggeratedly lascivious walk, his free hand waving in the air for balance as he pouted and swayed and the little finger waggled worm-like before him. Wenton could not pretend he had not seen. The mime had been acted out right in front of him and was unequivocal in meaning. Wayne realised that he had been caught as the girls' laughter changed pitch from hearty shrieking to helpless snorting and whimpering. Instead of trying to make a getaway or disguise what he had been up to, the boy grinned brazenly at Wenton for a moment before zipping up his fly and quickly walking away. Wenton hated himself as he smiled weakly, picked up the still-rolling ball and threw it back to a group of fifth years, who had also stopped to watch.

So they knew. The kids knew what he had done and would snigger and whisper about it. And it was possible, probable even, that some of his colleagues had heard something about it. But that was it. Nothing else had happened. PC Cooper had never come knocking on his door. No kid had tried to blackmail him, neither for better grades (like they cared in that place!) nor for money. He had come to realise that despite his fears, him being a flasher was no more disturbing to the kids than the behaviour of some of their other teachers. It would no more have occurred to them to report him to the police than it would have to report Mr Snipes the P.E. teacher for beating up cheeky boys in the toilets, or Mr Blair the explosively violent R.E. teacher who slapped you around the back of the head for talking in class, or the legendary Miss Timmins, who taught swimming at Coseley baths by pushing you in the deep end. But then the knock had finally come and now he found himself here at Sedgley police station, studying the graffiti of his fellow transgressors.

The door opened and Detective Sergeant Halstead came in.

Wenton cringed inwardly. He had mentally rehearsed and prepared for this day many times but he had always imagined being questioned by burly, uniformed male constables. They would despise him and mock him, he knew, but at least they were men, crude, uneducated men who he could still feel superior to in some residual way. To be asked about his most shameful secret by a young, more or less attractive woman like Halstead was much worse. She looked competent and professional as she sat down and smiled at him coolly,

- So Mr. Wenton do you understand that you are here to be questioned about allegations of indecent exposure, committed outside the lock-up garages off Turls Hill Road on the night of Friday the sixteenth of July nineteen eighty-two, that you have attended the interview voluntarily and are not currently under arrest but that any statement you may make...?

Wenton listened, incredulous, to the practised patter. He had finally been caught and it was really happening, with some of the details of the tired police films and TV series he had seen over the years, including a sparsely-furnished interview room and a reading of his rights. The dramatic words, and the legal challenge that they implied, heard so many times in fiction, now arrived devoid of any thrill. It was depressing procedural detail that was all, a necessary stage in the process of convicting him of a risible crime that had already made him an outcast and a laughing stock and was about to end his career and cause heartache to his mother.

Halstead watched with detached interest as the man before her sighed deeply and massaged his temples then rubbed his eyes with the heel of his hands. Who knew what went on in the mind of a flasher? What did this flasher know that could help her in her search?

- I said, do you understand, Mr Wenton?

Wenton stared at the blue-inked graffiti on the table. He could not look up,

- Yes, I understand.

- Right, good. The allegation is that on the night of Friday the sixteenth of July between ten and eleven pm, you exposed yourself to Deborah Hackett and Rosalyn Braden, in the parking area of the lock-up garages off Turl's Hill Lane, Hurst Hill, Coseley. Do you admit that you were in the area of the lock up garages that evening?

- It's possible I went past them. I was very drunk that night and I don't remember. But I live near there so it's possible.

He had intended to say that he hadn't gone out that night, and let them prove what they could but this terse young woman and her manner had unsettled him. And there was something else. He wanted to hear her say it.

Halstead looked down unnecessarily at her notebook.

Wenton looked up, compelled. He studied her face. Heart-shaped, he thought. She can't be older than thirty. Her mouth was slightly open. Perfect lips, slightly reddened by subtle lipstick. Severe clothing enhanced the femininity and youth of her face.

Finally, she said it again,

- Do you admit that you exposed yourself to the two girls?

She flushed slightly but held his gaze. He looked down quickly at his hands resting on the table. Silvery-blue graffiti on the table glimmered into view: *Bilston Rude Galz sukz dikz. Shazza woz ere.*

- I needed to go to the toilet. I didn't know they were there.

- You said before you couldn't remember going near the garages. Now you remember that you needed to urinate?

One of his fists clenched then relaxed. He did not look up.

Bramford Skins. WBA rule.

Her voice came again, kinder. Pitying?

- Look there are two of them. They're both saying the same thing and they've got no reason to lie. Why don't you admit to the indecent exposure and we can try to turn it around for you?

He looked up at her. She held his gaze again and spoke slowly,

- I don't care about indecent exposure but I need to know about what's been going on up in those woods and according to these girls you were in Whites Lane that night.

He was still looking at her, wide-eyed and tense.

- If this interview was about convicting you of a crime, I couldn't even do it on my own. There would have to be another officer here taking notes. This is off the record.

Wenton was listening.

- It could still happen. I could call an officer in here now. We like to catch flashers before they move on to other types of offences but I think there's something more serious going on. So I need you to give me some information and maybe in return we can save your job.

Wenton's eyes opened wider,

- Did the girls report me or was it a parent? Does the school know?

She smiled frostily,

- Nobody reported it and the school doesn't know yet.

She let that sink in.

- I spoke to the girls based on something written in a colleague's notebook. He'd heard about the flashing from a girl called Lisa Stanley but he didn't follow it up. He was only interested in the dead boy and he thought you couldn't be involved in that. Now that colleague is the subject of a missing persons enquiry and I'm not so sure you couldn't be involved.

She paused again. Give him time to realise it's not about him and his dick.

- If I don't follow this up, it will blow over. By the time school starts again, those girls will have some other funny story to tell. Or we could end your career. You live with your mother, don't you?

- Yes.

- I bet it'd be hard to explain to her, wouldn't it? Why you left teaching so suddenly? You'd probably have to stop her reading the newspaper for a while too.

She leaned forward across the table. He never got this close to women. He was erotically aware of her full face, dark red lips and above all her confidence as she spoke slowly and deliberately,

- Nobody cares about you showing your penis to some girls. We've had five deaths up those woods in the last two weeks, another one nearby, and now an officer is missing. You were out on the night of the first death, pissed as a fart, skulking around, flashing. Technically you could be a murder suspect for that. Still could be. Then it would be in all the papers, what you were doing. Couldn't keep that quiet if we wanted to.

She paused again.

- But right now, I need to know everything you saw that night, even if means nothing to you. Tell me everything and you might not hear anything more about the flashing.

He had been staring but would not look her in the eye now. His eyes were flitting around the surface of the black interview table as if looking for an answer to his torments there.

Wanderers. Fuck the pigs. Clockwork Skins.

No answer came.

- Can you promise I won't get charged with the other thing?

She didn't answer. He continued,

- I saw a man. That Friday night in Whites Lane. I know his name.

***

The large, red-brick Edwardian house was set well back from the street like all the others in the row and to get to it Halstead had to walk a long gravel drive through a garden overgrown with shrubbery. The house was in a well-off neighbourhood in the village of Kinver but the out-of-control vegetation was more reminiscent of some manor house park gone wild than the privet-hedged gardens of suburbia: dark-spreading rhodo dendron and lush magnolia kept out the evening sun and four towering monkey puzzle trees had shed brittle evergreen branches onto the gravel driveway and on the long, damp grass of what had once been a lawn. Gravel crunched under her feet and unseen song birds whistled noisily in the bushes as she approached the door of the house, where the driveway widened out into a parking area. Halstead studied the array of vehicles parked there, looking for some clue as to what might await her inside the old house: a Mini Cooper or a replica of one, its wide wheels and scuffed bodywork suggestive of hard-fought races in country lanes; two new-looking Volvos, a saloon and an estate, all-weather cars that would hold their value and last a lifetime, their common sense stolidity generationally opposed to the juvenile delinquent Mini; a Japanese pick-up truck with oversize tyres and an array of forward-facing lamps bolted to a roll bar over the two-seater cabin. The smart Volvos seemed in keeping with this genteel neighbourhood, in which most of the large old houses were still intact, yet to be divided up into flats and bedsits, but the Mini and the truck, in combination with the dank, neglected garden added a jarring, ruffian note to the scene. Any parking space that would have been left over was occupied by a rusty builders' skip, half-full of rubble, broken plasterboard and wood. Halstead did not need the space, her own Mini, a discreet, un-customised one, was parked around the corner.

There was a wooden porch, not as old as the rest of the house although its white paint was flaking from the timber in places. She pressed the brass button on the outer door then, when no response came, stepped into the porch and pressed a newer-looking plastic bell inside. There was an array of masculine footwear strewn against one of the inner walls: large steel toe-capped wellies, paint-spattered work boots and Doctor Marten's shoes, a pair of brown dealer boots, twisted old Umbro and Dunlop trainers. Hanging from a peg on the other side of the porch was a rough and ready collection of outerwear: dusty donkey jackets, some with orange plastic across the backs, a creased and greasy leather box jacket, a brown sheepskin coat, green and black pilot jackets, a faded denim jacket, impossibly large, and hanging from a coat peg, a flat cap of the type worn by old men.

Through two large frosted-glass panels in the heavy front door of the house itself she could make out lumbering, optically blurred movement, back-lit by a flickering glare from some other room inside. The indistinct shape got closer: a tall and very broad man was approaching. He appeared to have dark hair and something about his gait told her that he was the right age.

That'll be him.

She felt her pulse throbbing in her chest.

***

The living room was large and gloomy, what little light there was came from the adjacent kitchen and from some French windows that gave out onto another garden as damp and overgrown as the one she had entered through. To Halstead, used to fitted carpets and wallpaper, there was something foreign, somehow exotic about the room: polished wooden floors and large rugs, big low-lying sofas, painted but un-papered walls, bare except for bookshelves, paintings and the odd hanging artefact or ornament from distant lands. On the floor between sofas and rugs there were two huge oriental vases and various statuettes of animals or mythical half-animals. She could hear, but not see, activity in the kitchen; it sounded like cooking or getting ready to cook, the clanking of pots and pans, the opening and closing of cupboards, and the voices of young men, deep and jocular, occasionally breaking into laughter.

Richie Betts, slouched against the back of the large leather sofa, arched his neck backwards and called to the kitchen,

- 'Ear that boys? The lady wants to know where I was on the

night of 16th of July. That's a week last Friday, to you.

He winked at Halstead, completely relaxed,

- They don't know what month it is, never mind the date!

A powerfully-built teenage boy in a stained t-shirt and jeans ripped at the knee loomed into the kitchen doorway and leaned against the door frame, drying a cup with a tea towel. He had dark copper hair and intense brown eyes.

- Ooh, let me see. You would've been here with us that night, dad. If I'm not mistaken. We had our girlfriends round too, if I remember right.

He had spoken slowly, affecting innocence but exaggeratedly so, like a pantomime villain caught in the act and fooling no-one. He ducked back into the kitchen.

Richie turned his gaze back to Halstead, drinking tea opposite him on an armchair. He grinned,

- Doesn't he talk nice? I grew up in your neck of the woods, Bilston, Coseley, Sedgley, those areas, and it was a bit rough and ready. Not much school, finding and selling scrap metal, tatting we called it, buying and selling stuff. But I knew I'd get out of it. And I always said if I had kids I'd give them a better start than I had. Private-schooled they are, all three. Rugby team, football team, athletics, they think the world of 'em at that place.

She didn't feel the need to speak as long as he was talking, filling in the gaps about who or what he was. He smiled, the gentleman host, but like the boy, his tone was mocking, exaggeratedly polite and formal,

- So that will be it as far as I'm concerned, I suppose. You've established that I've got a, what do they say? Sound alibi? Watertight alibi? And you'll want to be on your way, I expect.

- What about last Sunday night? The 25th?

She had snapped the question out abruptly, irritated that he was treating the questioning as a game. He paused and raised hi eyebrows, then continued with the air of a host gracious enoug to overlook some out-of-character rudeness,

- I could ask Ruben again but you'll find the answer will be muc the same. We don't get out much you know, apart from wor and for the boys' sports events, and those girlfriends practic ally live here. Lovely girls, from really nice families. They'd g through fire for my boys, too. Won't hear a word against them.

He sat up straight, putting both feet on the floor and slappe both meaty hands on his thighs,

- So that's that sorted, right? I expect you'll want to be off fo: lowing other leads. Better ones. And to wrap up whatever mys terious crime you're investigating, I'll warrant.

He stood up, looking down at Halstead expectantly, a pleasar smile on his face.

Halstead smiled too but did not stand,

- How often do you go to Whites Lane, Mr. Betts?

The big man sat down again, leaning back, still expansively a ease. She knew that he was nearly fifty years old but the ha: that brushed the collar of his black polo shirt was as shiny an black as that of a much younger man, and,

That chest.

He grinned, his lean face and neck a network of sinew,

- Am I under arrest? Are you taking down my particulars as w speak?

His questions focused her attention back on the work at han to her relief.

- At the moment we're just talking. You're helping with enqui ies in a missing persons investigation. But you should probabl cooperate unless you do want to be charged.

His face became serious for a moment,

- Don't think there's much you could charge me with, and hope for it to stick. But then I'm a respectable citizen, happy to help with enquiries. Whites Lane? I know it well from my youth if it hasn't changed. The woods. Bluebells in spring? The old quarries, I remember when they blocked up the mine shaft at the bottom of the big one. Before that you could get to the caverns under Dudley Castle if you had the nerve. Come out in the bears' enclosure, or that was what they said. Don't go there now, haven't for years.

- You don't visit your brother?

- You know Michael?

Richie Betts seemed genuinely amused,

- 'E's a funny bugger! Doolally they'd say around there. Touched. Invented his own religion and all. Writes poems. And stories 'bout warriors and gladiators and whatnot.

- Do you ever visit him?

- No. If you'd ever met him, you'd know why not. You know he was locked up, right? Picked up for fighting but they made the mistake of listening to his fairy tales so then it was straight to the loony bin. Told 'em he was descended from Genghis Khan! I try to help him out, fix him up with work and the like. On the doors or building work. But I meet him in Sedgley. The Red Lion or the Beacon Hotel. Don't fancy traipsing through the mud to get to whatever shed 'e's living in now. He could live here with us, you know, if he wanted. Could camp in the garden if he liked.

- So he must be a hard man if he works the doors. Likes a scrap?

Richie Betts shook his head,

- No, no, they don't like it, the establishments we work with. Not like the old days! They won't have troublemakers.

t struck Halstead that Betts was good looking when he smiled like that. Very good looking. How had she not noticed before? He was still talking,

- That's why they like him, keep using him despite him being a bit scruffy. Even the biggest nutters out there want to be mates when our Michael looks 'em in the eye. He's their nuclear deterrent. He'll get work as far away as Birmingham, all over the shop. He would've been up Brum that Sunday night in fact, if I'm right. Roadie. Security really. A big concert at Bingley Hall.

How can a man so bulky be so lean?

Halstead thought of the strong men she knew: beer-bellied coppers, the butcher in the Coop supermarket, some beefy draymen she had seen hauling aluminium barrels outside a pub. None were lean. None were handsome.

Concentrate.

- What about your sons? You have three, don't you?

- What about them?

- Do they know Whites Lane?

His face contorted into an expression of puzzlement so extreme as to be a caricature,

- Why would they go to that bit of wasteland? If they wanted a bit of fresh air, and if they had the time between the sports and the girlfriends, there's bigger and better places to go to around here: Kinver Edge, Malvern just down the road.

He called into the kitchen again,

- You hear that Ruben? You ever been to Hurst Hill, Coseley? That dump where uncle Michael made a play-camp?

The boy appeared in the door again,

- Can't say I know it dad.

He had replied in a cockney accent. He slipped back into the kitchen.

Typical teenager, you see? Not interested in visiting relatives. Nor following traditions unless I make 'em. They're all big boys now, bigger than me, one of them. And the local girls seem to find them inexplicably attractive. Mind you that's always been the way in our family.

Halstead found herself thinking of other big men she had seen, not in real life but on television. She had seen men who were both big and lean on television, they did exist somewhere: Marlon Brando, of course, had been like that when young; and a heavyweight boxer she had once seen chasing ineffectually after Muhammad Ali in a televised boxing match. But in the flesh? Never.

I see you're admiring my collection.

She realised that as her mind wandered, she had been looking at the objects that were hung on the walls or resting on the top shelf of a row of bookshelves that covered one long wall. Japanese artefacts: a Kendo mask and staff, a short, square-tipped sword; but also old books, artwork and maps. Why couldn't she focus? This was not like her. She had to draw him out, challenge him. She must not let her voice betray the nervousness she felt,

Your family seem to be around a lot when there's funny goings on in the woods, Mr Betts. Now a colleague has gone missing and I need to know what you know about it.

She felt her face flush as she spoke.

Missing, eh?

He rose and moved behind the sofa to the bookcase. For a moment, she had a view of his back square-on to her, impossibly wide and v-shaped it tapered down to relatively narrow yet powerful hips, in black jeans, which soon widened again into large, rounded thighs. She shuddered and caught her breath. It was happening again, like in the police station with that boy! But much more powerful this time. An inexplicable, mounting desire that would have to be satisfied at whatever cost. Then an old memory began to surface, unasked and unwanted,

There was a stallion.

Richie Betts was talking again,

- A thing happened twenty-odd years ago. An accident with a bonfire. You must have heard about that and got the wrong end of the stick. They wanted to blame me and me brother but we were miles away and we could prove it. Since then nothing. A kid died in a motorbike accident, I heard about that from me brother. And from what I see in the paper, now four local wasters have got killed joy-riding, trying to burn out the car they pinched. Accident waiting to happen and no great loss to mankind anyway. Foul play is not suspected according to the paper. But even if it was, Michael was working in Birmingham, me and my lads was here, with their girlfriends. Like I say, all from important families, those girls.

He half-turned and looked her in the eye.

- Whatever happens the women always stick by us. Putty in our hands. Funny, isn't it? Couldn't tell you why or how but it's always been like that for us.

He touched the kendo mask, still looking away.

- I don't live in the past like my brother. I respect it. Respect the old ways and our people's traditions but I think you should travel, too. Travel and learn from other cultures.

There was a stallion in the fields one foggy winter morning. I was twelve.

He picked up the Japanese mask and walked around the sofa, towards her.

- This thing gave me one of my best ideas, can you imagine? - A lopsided grin.

She remembered the bulging muscles of the stallion's hindquarters as he reared up and a foot-long penis unsheathed and be

ame rigid. A thick, mottled stick ribbed with veins, ready to
lunge into the mare. She wanted that.

His black shoes came into view as she continued to stare at the
floor.

want it.

I was a masked wrestler! In Asia. They called it wrestling but
they were real fights in those days, underground, not many rules
to speak of. Mainly in Japan, also Thailand, Cambodia. 'Course
a lot of the betting money was Chinese, you know how they
love a gamble, and that's how I made me money, winning fights,
throwing fights, whatever paid most on the night.

*ong, thick and stiff. Still spurting jets of pearly-white sperm when it
lipped out.*

She was watching his pacing body, only dimly aware of what he
said,

But the beauty of using the mask is, if you've got to be somewhere else, or you're sick or don't feel like it, and if you've got a
mate, or relative, about the same size as you, he can substitute
or you, can't he? Put on your mask, do the dirty deed and nobody's the wiser. You could be miles away, in another country
even, while somebody else fights your battles for you.

He was behind her now. He caressed the back of her head, loosening her hair then began to push down on her shoulders toward
the big leather sofa.

But the movement was too abrupt. The spell broke.

Get your fucking hands off me.

He backed off spreading his arms in a gesture of incomprehen-
sion, a much-practised apologetic smile already forming on his
face. As she brushed past, he saw that she would not stop and
moved to grab at her arm, then thought better of it.

The door slammed and she was gone.

A floppy -haired young man looked in from the kitchen, grinning, gap-toothed but handsome,

- Getting old, Dad. Past it. Should have let young Ruben have a go.

Richie Betts gave a wry smile, then,

- Doesn't matter. They've got nothin'.

***

Sunday 1st August 1982.

It was a sunny morning, already hot. The fair was packing up to leave. The rides had shut down days ago and had been packed and loaded onto the creaking, paint-faded lorries that carried them around the country. Some of the caravans and mobile homes had gone on already to the next site, leaving behind muddy footpaths that led nowhere except to imprints of shade-bleached grass where they had rested. But most lay parked in the same places.

George knocked on the painted aluminium door of Amalia Betts' caravan. Just a couple of seconds later it opened,

- She's gone you know. Overseas. With relatives.

Just like that she said it. As soon as she opened the door.

- I know. She told me she had to go on to the next place.

Amalia Betts' expression softened a little.

- She's in Ireland by now. France after that.

- It was you I wanted to talk to.

Amalia raised her eyebrows,

- Come in.

But she did not invite him into the kitchen or living room. She led him into the business end of the caravan, the room near the door, where she did her readings. It was nearly dark in there. The windows seemed to have been boarded up from inside with plywood or similar and let in only a little light, through gaps at the side. Dust motes floated in these bright beams. They sat at the same table as their first meeting, facing each other as they had then.

Can I get you a drink?

She smiled mischievously.

- No thanks. I wanted to ask you about my mother.

Her body seemed to stiffen. It wouldn't have been noticeable to a casual observer. But George had been waiting to see her reaction.

- I can't tell you much about that.

- Rosie said you knew her.

- Yes? What else did she tell you?

- Only that. That you knew her. She wouldn't say anything else.

- I see. Well what would you like to know?

He had many questions: where did she come from? Did she love my dad? Why? It would sound funny, he knew, but why? Where is she now? But there was one above all others that surged into his consciousness and seemed to erupt into the small room,

- Why did she leave me?

Amalia sighed.

- Those were other times and she was very young. Like your dad must have told you, her people were strict, they lived by the old rules, and – she sighed again - they made her give you up. He told you that much didn't he?

She looked at him, waiting for his affirmation. Were her eyes slightly watery?

- Yes. But that was it. That was all he told me.

- And he should have told you that she did love you and didn't want to give you up. Did he?

- Well, yes.

George wouldn't normally dare to lie to this woman who dealt in lies and lived from them but it seemed necessary now.

There was silence for a while.

The travelling woman had composed herself and began to talk,

- She gave you a great gift, you know. Even if she couldn't keep you.

- What's that?

George would later look back on this part of the conversation with amusement and no little shame at his childish avarice: anything seemed possible in that caravan after the events of the last few days and so for a moment he thought she was going to reveal some treasure or inheritance.

- You must have noticed that you've been getting stronger? A bit better at sports and things like that?

- A bit. Yes.

In the football match on the school playing fields. At the pool. Flattening Dean Wilson.

- Good. That's good. Well, it's going to continue. You'll keep getting stronger, better at physical things as you grow into a man now.

George was lost for an answer. It didn't seem like that great a gift. Amalia Betts continued,

- Your mother was from a family who are all very strong like that. I say family but it's not just us, the Bettses, there are some other old families too, a kind of big clan if you like. We normally marry our own, within that big group, and keep our traditions, but an exception was made in your father's case. To give you a chance.

- So I'm from a strong family, then?

He could almost have added 'so what?', still thinking about the inheritance that she might have offered but didn't. But he had another question,

What do you mean to give us a chance?

She sighed,

- Most of the clans are forgetting the traditions, nowadays. Or just don't believe in them. Our lot remember, but not all of us, and we won't be around forever. Some of us thought that if we broke the tradition, mixed our blood with yours, you'd be able to look after yourself a bit better.

George remembered the carnage he had seen. The three men Rosie had called cousins,

- You mean I'm going to be like...

- Yes. I mean, you might not grow as big and powerful as some of our men. You wouldn't want to be like them, they can be a bit of a nightmare. But I don't think you'll be needing our protection much either. 'Specially now that lot are out of the way. You might even find you're popular with the girls, like our boys are. I hear there's some pretty ones at school.

He preferred her like this. Cheeky again, not sad like before.

There was nothing else to say. George gave a weak smile and stood up.

She followed him to the door and he was about to mutter some inadequate farewell, a 'bye' or a 'see ya' when she put her hand on his shoulder. He turned and she embraced him. For a moment, his whole body stiffened. He wasn't used to this. She released him quickly then seemed to think again, or perhaps stopped thinking, and hugged him again, this time resting her forehead on his shoulder, near the neck. She held him for minutes, it seemed, then let him go.

***

The Listener and the Teller.

The listener tried to move his body but couldn't. How many times had he sipped the potion, the toxic, vegetal potion, while listening to the teller of tales? It had freed his mind to believe, to travel to other places and other times and see long-gone scenes as if they were playing out in front of him but it had shackled his body to the limestone floor of the dark cave where he lay.

He squinted to see the teller, finally silent, who was seated in near darkness in another corner of the small, candle-lit cave. He would try to speak now after so much listening,

- Do you expect me to believe all of that? Cavemen... or something? Witches and devils? Hundreds of years protecting one family?

- Thousands. More than two thousand. The agreement was that you drank what you drank and I tell what I know. Nothing about you having to believe it.

The listener grunted then groaned with pain as harsh spasms raged inside him.

The teller knew what the spasms would lead to, as did the listener if he could remember their bargain: after knowledge comes oblivion. Out of pity and a sense of duty the teller kept talking, he would keep his side to the end,

- My own brother doesn't believe half of it, even the stories we heard together as boys from our grandad. He thinks we're just a kind of gypsy or some other kind of travelling people. He thinks I make too much of it all. Him and his boys call me Cro-Magnon man.

The listener groaned again and somehow found the strength to curl up as pain racked his body.

- But what they don't understand is that I travelled all of Europe collecting this history, putting it all together with what our grandad told us, talking to the old 'uns of each of the seven families. Then I wrote

it down as a proper history of our people, going back to Spain before the Romans. That's valuable that is, scholarship and keeping up the old traditions, more valuable than getting rich and driving big cars, which is all that lot think about.

The listener was trying to vomit but it would not come. After a while that stopped and he spoke,

- Take me outside. I want to be in the woods.

Printed in Great Britain
by Amazon